More praise

"From its opening pages, it is clear *From Bruised Fell*, though a work of art, will not be a comfortable read . . . (it is) a haunting and cautionary tale and because it's Finlay-Young's first novel, promises much compelling reading for the future."
—*Edmonton Journal*

"Finlay–Young . . . takes the risk of entrusting the story to a ten–year–old narrator, a risk that pays off. *From Bruised Fell* succeeds because of Missy's voice and her wrenching account of a child's fears and desire for 'normalcy.'"
—*Canadian Literature: A Quarterly of Criticism and Review*

"[B]eautifully written, minutely observed, and a distillation of the uncanny insight of childhood."
—*The Courier* (Vancouver)

"[A] stunning debut . . . "
—*The Coast* (Halifax)

"*From Bruised Fell* questions the very nature of families, how and why women mother, and whether some women should become mothers at all."
—*Eye Weekly*

"[A] powerful, horrifying indictment of the harm parents can inflict on their children, often with the best of intentions."
—*Ottawa Citizen*

"Filled with grief and betrayal this is a powerful book that will take you back to your childhood years—no matter how happy—and those raw, unspoken emotions we used to know so well."

—*The Daily News* (Halifax)

"This is an extremely intense and emotional book. It is beautifully written with sharp and shining details. The style is spare and haunting."

—*The Constant Reader*

"The author's control over her imagery . . . is impressive and her characterization uncannily convincing. Finlay-Young has important things to say about the conundrum of family and the mysterious chambers of the human heart."

—*Quill & Quire*

"The novel's elegiac tone is powerful, sure-footed and original. The sensuality of a world seen from a child's perspective is convincingly rendered."

—Sarah Sheard, author of *The Hypnotist*

PENGUIN CANADA

FROM BRUISED FELL

Jane Finlay-Young emigrated to Canada from England's Lake District in 1963. She now lives in Toronto with her husband and son. She is at work on her next novel.

from *Bruised* *Fell*

Jane Finlay-Young

PENGUIN
CANADA

PENGUIN CANADA

Published by the Penguin Group

Penguin Books, a division of Pearson Canada, 10 Alcorn Avenue, Toronto, Ontario,
Canada M4V 3B2

Penguin Books Ltd, 80 Strand, London WC2R 0RL, England

Penguin Putnam Inc., 375 Hudson Street, New York, New York 10014, U.S.A.

Penguin Books Australia Ltd, 250 Camberwell Road, Camberwell, Victoria 3124, Australia

Penguin Books India (P) Ltd, 11, Community Centre, Panchsheel Park,
New Delhi – 110 017, India

Penguin Books (NZ) Ltd, cnr Rosedale and Airborne Roads, Albany, Auckland 1310,
New Zealand

Penguin Books (South Africa) (Pty) Ltd, 24 Sturdee Avenue, Rosebank 2196, South Africa

Penguin Books Ltd, Registered Offices: 80 Strand, London WC2R 0RL, England

First published in Penguin Books by Penguin Books Canada Limited, 2000
Published in this edition, 2003

1 3 5 7 9 10 8 6 4 2

*Publisher's note: This book is a work of fiction. Names, characters, places and incidents
either are the product of the author's imagination or are used fictitiously, and any
resemblance to actual persons living or dead, events, or locales is entirely coincidental.*

Manufactured in Canada.

National Library of Canada Cataloguing in Publication

Finlay-Young, Jane, 1958–
From bruised fell / Jane Finlay-Young.

ISBN 0-14-301546-X

I. Title.

PS8561.I5515F76   2003   C813'.6   C2003-900829-0
PR9199.4.F53F76 2003

Visit Penguin Books' website at **www.penguin.ca**

To my father, Brian; thank you for your constancy,
your gentleness and your wisdom.

And my aunt Pat, for sharing yourself
so deeply and helping me understand so much.

And in memory of my mother, Joan,
though I hardly knew you. You have inspired this book.

acknowledgements

I AM MOST GRATEFUL to Matt Cohen: without his most generous support and advice I may never have seen my words in print; Anne McDermid, my agent, and Bethany, her assistant, for taking me on and finding me a home at Penguin; Meg Masters and Cynthia Good at Penguin who first read my manuscript and believed in it enough to produce this book; Barbara Berson, also at Penguin, and Meg (again) for the gentle editing; Cheryl Cohen, for her respectful and sensitive final edit; Christine Slater, for her astute feedback and enthusiasm especially in the beginning when so much felt unformed; Sarah Sheard, who read the manuscript in its infancy and gave me the feedback and encouragement to last me through many drafts; my writing group: Heather, Marina, Martha, Michele, for their weekly involvement, their wisdom and friendship; Janice Greene, my writing-buddy, for her enthusiasm, encouragement and early-morning coffees; Jill Ker Conway whose life is an inspiration to many, and whose interest in my work is a great compliment; Brenda McGilvray, for the printing-off, the interest in this book, and the sometimes unsolicited opinions; Lynn Riley for her generous spirit (Fred too!) and advice on things medical; the Toronto Arts Council for financial support; the Writers' Union of Canada for their mentoring program, which enabled me to work with Matt Cohen; Jean, my step-mum, for her always open arms, her nest-building and making my father so very happy; my siblings, Helen, Katie, Rob, Dawn and Austen, and my friends (you know who you are) for their patience and understanding of my often hermit-like behaviour; Yasha, my son, for his gentle presence and generous heart; Jim Williams, my husband, for his constant support and dedication, his belief in the work when I (regularly) lost heart, his reading and rereading, his attention to the many details of our lives that made more time for me to write, and, finally, for the fun we have together.

from
Bruised Fell

1965 to 1967

one

Mummy sits still behind the floaty smoke of her cigarillo. There's a shadow across her face like a cloud. It's from the veil of her bride's hat, though it looks like something else. It looks like she's wrapped up, like she's dead under there and not breathing.

I thought brides got married, I whisper.

Her eyes roll under their skins.

Yes, she says, moving her lips a little, and some are married to God.

She lifts the veil to take another puff. She doesn't look like a bride. Her hands are shaking and her eyelids are purple. There's a scowl on her face, not a smile.

Churchill's dead, she says, holding one hand to her mouth to catch the words.

I never met him, I say.

There's only silence.

At least I don't remember, I say.

She laughs, a little laugh like a snort or a kick, and pulls the veil back down.

Churchill is on the television. Dead in a box. Sliding along on a boat, on the river. The bells of London chime all at once as he drifts by. Cranes along the river start to bend together, bowing like giant insects, like grasshoppers curious about something they think might be food.

Why are they doing that? I ask, my voice sounding like a speck of dust floating in the room. Mummy has her head back on her chair and is letting the smoke out slowly through her nose.

They say he's a great man, she says, squeezing her eyes tight shut and rubbing her forehead, but only God can judge that.

Black dresses and skirts and suits. Black cars. It's all black. Mummy thinks black is a bad colour for death. She says in death you're closer to God and God is more the colour of white or gold.

Sit still, she says, when the couch pinches at the backs of my knees and makes me shift about. Show some respect. Her eyes open and look me up and down. And stop staring, she adds, stop looking at me like that.

Her fingers pick at a hole in the armchair. Pick, pick, pick. Then she pinches herself on the neck and pulls at the soft skin there. She can't sit still herself, but I don't say so.

When she starts another cigarillo she has to bend over to find them, she has to take her eyes away from me and I sneak out quickly, towards the back door.

Stay out till tea time, she shouts after me before the door closes, I need my peace and quiet.

Outside, there's a wind against my face. A bit of sun peeks between the clouds but it isn't warm. The tall grasses around the house bend in the wind, showing a shivery white belly. They are taller than me; it makes them good for hiding, good for spying, though there's not much to spy on here, being so far out of town.

I spy, with my little eye, someone's pink hands in the grasses. Someone's goosebumpy arms. Someone's wet shoes. It's me! It could be Ruby, I suppose, but she's inside, having her afternoon nap.

The farmer down the lane puts out his milk cans to be picked up. I spy on him lifting the cans from his lorry onto the wood platform. He grunts when he lifts them and sounds like a pig. I call him Piggy, but just in my head. Piggy puts the cans out there every day and when he's done he sits down and has a cigarette. From where I'm hiding I can smell it. It's different from cigarillos, it's softer.

When the curtains are open I can spy on Mummy. On a day like today that's no fun because she will sit and not move. Except for that one hand that picks and the other that smokes. The days when she moves are good spying days, especially when she listens to music. Mahler is her favourite. She dances with the cigarillo, letting the ashes float to the ground like eyelashes, letting the brown stick shrink towards her fingers as she circles and circles about the room with her flowery dress swimming around her. She stops when the cigarillo burns her. That's what I wait for. I watch her lips when she shakes her hand and I know that she's swearing. Damn, maybe, or hell. She throws her hat to the floor, the one with the flower that's always falling off. That's when spying is fun: when you see things you're not supposed to see.

THE NIGHT CHURCHILL died I saw something I wasn't supposed to. Mummy stood on Piggy's wooden platform in her nightie. The hills rose up behind her like huge heads. And the small specks of stars in the sky were like eyes spying through a big, black mouth. No one was around but me watching from my bedroom window. She screamed and screamed. Why don't you take me? Why don't you take me? The moonlight greyed her hair and her curls caught the shadows so her whole head was black and white and her wide mouth moved up and down, up and down, like a doll that had come alive at midnight.

The next morning we listened to the grandfather clock strike eight o'clock and ate eggs on toast. Ruby spat hers out and rubbed the yellowy bits around her plate. My egg had a swirl of red that I dug out with a spoon.

It would have been a chick, Mummy said, if it had had a chance. The strap of her nightie slipped from her shoulder as she brought the tiny egg spoon to her mouth. I left the red bit out and smeared the rest of the yellow yolk across my toast.

Eggs are godly things, she said. They are round and whole. They are white and gold, the godly colours. She held her almost-eaten egg in her hand as she talked.

Perhaps your chick has been called away by God, she said. And then she let her egg go. It fell to the table and split in half, its shell cracked and crumbled.

CHURCHILL IS BURIED. Mummy pulls back the curtains and pushes the window open. It's all over, she calls out. My head pokes up from the grasses but she doesn't see me. Her eyes stretch over me, far out to the hills and maybe farther past them, to the sea. She stands a long time without blinking. Put on your flower dress and dance, I shout out to her, waving my arms in the air. Her blue eyes flash a little in the sunlight, they wander around the grasses until they find me. It's all over, she says to me again. It's almost a whisper.

Will you dance? I ask. The clouds and sun have patched themselves across the hills. She shakes her head and her hair falls forward.

Daddy will be home soon, I must change for tea.

She pulls her head back inside, leaving the window

open, leaving the curtains to snap about in the wind. I chop at the grasses with an old stick and listen for Daddy's bicycle on the path.

*W*ELSH RAREBIT FOR TEA, my favourite. Daddy pretends the rarebit is hopping around his plate; he pretends it's hard to stab with his fork. Ruby and I laugh. When Ruby laughs she squeezes her eyes tight shut and rocks back and forth. It comes out strange, like she's being pressed under something heavy.

Listen to this, Daddy says after tea. He pulls out a new record. They're all the rage, this lot.

We dance to the Beatles. In my sock feet I can slide and twirl. I swing Ruby by the hands, spinning her so her hair flies out behind her. I can do it using just one hand, she's so light. I'm so dizzy my head feels like little bubbles in a cup of fizzy drink. That's okay until everything starts to join together into one big blur. And even when I've stopped and put Ruby safely down everything around me keeps going. The whole world feels like it's running away and I don't know how to reach out and stop it.

Mummy doesn't dance even when we try to pull her up.

I'm pregnant, she says. Daddy hits his head with his hand and falls back on the couch, laughing. The couch with the two of them on it seems to tip and toss.

Wonderful! He rubs her tummy but she pushes his hand away.

You're making me sick, she says.

Perhaps she's feeling the world spinning too. Her head is turned so she's looking out the window at the hills. The hills are turning on their sides, pretending they're not hills at all.

I'll call Margaret, Daddy says standing slowly, she'll be delighted.

Tell her she can have this one, Mummy shouts out as Daddy dials the phone. She stares out the window, looking for something.

What? Daddy shouts back, dropping the phone down on its hook. Mummy raises a hand against him as he walks towards her.

Forget it, she says, just forget it.

Ruby keeps dancing. She dances even when the music stops, spinning and spinning till she falls to the floor. Her eyes keep going under her eyelids, darting like fish. With her eyes closed she looks like Mummy under that veil. There's a smile somewhere on her face but I can't tell where.

I TALK TO Auntie Margaret on the phone. Hello poppet, she says.

I like her voice, the way she talks so that every word jumps about. Shall I come down for a visit soon? she asks, pretending it's my decision.

Oh, yes, I say, yes please.

She makes us laugh. She'll play with us outside in the grasses. She'll run with us through the trees in the woods. She'll say something she's not supposed to, or she'll fall, or she'll spill. It's always interesting. It's always a surprise, especially to her. You'd never know she was the older sister, like me, and Mummy is the younger. Oh dear, she'll say, oh dear, oh dear. But it's not a worried "oh dear," it's something happy. She'll throw her head back and look at the sky when she says it and she'll smile a sort of secret smile. And Mummy will just watch her and shake her head and scowl.

Gillian, Auntie Margaret would say, and bite her lip to keep the smile off her face, life was not meant to be too serious. And she'd give me a wink.

Once, when we were playing in the closet, she told me Mummy sometimes finds things difficult. It's not your fault, Missy, can you remember that? I nodded. I couldn't see her face but I could feel her hand find mine and give it a squeeze. And I could hear her breathing and the wet sound of her tongue moving in her mouth.

two

ANOTHER CHILD and no more time for me, Mummy tells her friend as they sit around the kitchen table smoking and getting organized to go collecting for Oxfam.

Ruby and I have been put outside to get fresh air. We are sitting on the back steps, tying dead grasses together to make necklaces. I do most of it for Ruby because her fingers are clumsy. I don't close the door all the way so I can hear what they say. Her friend is a gossip; I've heard Daddy say that. Gillian, he says, don't tell that woman so much, she'll talk your secrets all about town. But Mummy tells her everything. That's why I listen in.

Something, Mummy whispers to her friend, will have to be done. I've too much to do to be bothered with three.

From where I sit I spy smoke coming through their noses. It gathers in clouds around their faces just like the clouds beginning to join together above Ruby and me.

IT RAINS WHILE we're out going door to door for Oxfam. Mummy carries her satchel of pamphlets and says the same thing at every door. Think about the poor in Africa, she says, the starving children. She's wearing her grey hat, the one she has for church.

Mummy's friend decided not to come. She says her friend is lazy and just wants to sit around. She says she's not serious enough to do God's work. So we do God's work together. I hold the little box of money in one hand and Ruby in the other. After lunch my arm aches and I say so.

Buck up, now, Mummy says. This is important work. Stop thinking such selfish thoughts.

And then the air goes white with rain. It rains so hard that we can hardly see across the street. We find a place to hide under a piece of roof.

The floods, Mummy whispers, grabbing my hand and Ruby's and pulling us into a wall of water. We'll shelter in the church, she shouts, the rain banging at the pavement so we can hardly hear.

It's empty and quiet in the church, the only sound is the rain dripping off our coats and onto the stone floor. There's the rain outside, too, but it's far off. A dull light comes in through the stained glass. Jesus with his hands out to us. Mary with her baby. People on their knees to Jesus. Mummy is on her knees, too, looking up at him. Jesus with his hands out like he wants to take something from you. Coloured light is sprinkled over her face. Her lips move. Her body rocks back and forth. Jesus keeps asking. His fingers wiggle, they're saying, "Hurry up, give it to me." And Mary holds the baby in a strange way as if she's thinking she might drop it. Maybe Jesus wants the baby, maybe he thinks Mary is too careless.

Sometimes, I hear Mummy whisper to God, sometimes I don't know what it is you want from me.

AFTER THE RAIN we stand outside the church and Mummy lights a cigarillo. She blows the smoke out through her nose. There's a wind that frills at the bottom of our dresses and shivers up our legs. It sucks the smoke straight up so we don't have to smell it. Mummy kicks at a few pebbles by her feet and we watch them bounce down the wet stone steps till they hit the bottom.

God pulled us in there for a reason, she says, squashing the half-finished cigarillo under her shoe and kicking it off the steps too.

Suddenly her arms are in the air and she looks like she's falling off the stairs. But she stays on her feet as she bounces down them and floats across the empty road. The wind, she shouts. She has her mouth wide open and all I see is the dark hole it leaves on her face. Her hair is dancing above her head, tossing about like angels or snakes. Sorry girls, she shouts and laughs. I'm taken by the wind. Sorry, sorry, the wind wants me more. She's laughing and waving, up on her tiptoes, her finger-tips wiggling, her voice scratchy and light as it sails up into the sky where the smoke went before it disappeared for good.

Ruby falls. She sounds heavier than her little body should sound. Deep, like an empty cave, and hollow. She falls on her bare knees, on the wet stone. And then her face hits the ground. Mummy, Mummy, Mummy, Mummy, Mummy, I hear her calling over and over into the ground without a breath or a break. She thinks no one can hear. Then, once she's gone quiet, one hand reaches out and finds a stone, a smooth black one. She clenches it in her fist and pulls it in underneath her. When I get her up there are tears on her face, a scratch on her nose and blood running down from her knees.

You're shaking like a little dog, I say. But she's not listening, she's staring straight ahead, down the long tunnel of houses, after Mummy.

By then Mummy is a long way down the road, no bigger than a freckle. We can still hear her splashing as she runs through the puddles. We can hear her laughing, it bounces off the houses and into the empty sky.

We have to wait, I tell Ruby.

There's nothing else to do.

Ruby stands perfectly still until we see her. She grows bigger and bigger. First her face, then the pieces of it, then the lines around her eyes and the mud splashes on her legs. Ruby laughs and lifts her arms. She gets up on her tiptoes and reaches.

Next time, Mummy says, it may be different. She bats Ruby's arms down and we follow her home, running to keep up.

JESUS HAD BEEN speaking to Mummy in the church.

Jesus is trouble, Daddy said last night when they were having a bedtime sherry. Then I heard the door slam. From my bedroom window I could see her running in the moonlight, past Piggy's platform and down the lane towards the sea.

Gillian, Daddy called from the front door, Gillian. He called her name over and over as she started to shrink away. But he didn't follow her and after a while she got swallowed up in the dark.

THINGS ARE ALWAYS changing, Mummy said after Churchill's funeral. You can never second-guess God. And now she's saying this again, in the hospital where the little baby died. It was only three inches long and didn't look human. She showed us the size with her shaking fingers.

What did it look like? I ask. Mummy closes her eyes to remember.

Like a monster, she says, opening her eyes to look out the window. Like the devil himself. In the corner of her mouth there is a smile.

The room is spinning. Daddy sits in a chair with his head dropped into his hands and Ruby is so still that I almost forgot she was there. All that moves is one of her fists, rolling that black stone over and over like it's tumbling down a steep hill and can't stop.

I spy, with my little eye, I say, fingers and toes and a baby that goes. The words pop out loudly instead of staying in. Mummy's smile jumps off her face.

Shut up, she says, keep those stupid rhymes to yourself.

And then she gives me a push that bumps me against Ruby. But it's Ruby that falls to the floor, not me.

three

MUMMY'S SKIRT JUMPS and snaps as she reaches up to hang the clothes. She pegs them to the line: jabs the peg at the shirt, the towel, the pants. Sometimes she has two pegs in her mouth at a time. They look like a mouthful of awful teeth. Sometimes she stops and looks far out, towards the sea. Perhaps she's hoping for sun, hoping the wind isn't bringing more storms.

The wind is screaming in my ears. I hold both hands to my head but it gets in anyway. It sneaks down my sleeves and collar. It scratches at my eyes. I catch a bright patch of sky between my eyelid squints: it floats over the ocean.

Look, I say, the sun. But she's too busy fighting with the clothes to notice.

INSIDE, RUBY KICKS her short legs pink. Kicks and kicks and calls in that squeaking way, high and sharp throughout the house. Mummy's cigarillo is only half done, the ash hanging on. Even Ruby's screams can't knock it off. There's a half cup of cold tea on the kitchen table and toast rinds and a greasy butter knife. There's a little mirror and a tube of lipstick. A pen and a closed book. Mummy hates to clean. Cleaning is a plot, she says, it kills off women's minds.

The wind is banging at the windows. Ruby won't stop her kicking and screaming. She will carry on till Mummy goes to her. Every day they have this battle, and every day Ruby gets her way.

She calls the same sounds out, over and over, as I stand by her bedroom door. I touch the wood and feel it shake. SHHHHH, Ruby, I say, seeing her through the keyhole. Her eyes are squeezed shut and her mouth is so wide open that there is no room left on her face to speak into. I don't like going in there alone. She won't look at me because all she wants is Mummy. Nothing else will do.

Quiet! Mummy shouts, heaving the door open. Her voice is shaking. Her cigarillo see-saws between her fingers. She stares Ruby down. Ruby cries louder with her eyes so wide open they bulge. Outside the trees are groaning in the wind, but Ruby and Mummy don't notice. Ruby's face is as red as her screams.

Stop, Mummy says. Leave me alone. Let me have some peace.

An ash or two flutters to the floor as Mummy turns and leaves the room, without her.

This has never happened before. Ruby's mouth shuts and the noise stops. The sun that was there before is gone. Ruby screamed it away, and now the clouds are back, turning in the sky like someone is stirring them.

I SHALL LEAVE you one day, Mummy says, watching the branches brush against the window as the clouds keep piling, dark and heavy, above us.

There's soup for lunch that she's left boiling on the cooker. She scratches the raw piece of skin below her eye. You are strong enough, Missy, to find your own way. Not Ruby though, for all the noise she makes she's quite collapsible. You must care for her when I go.

I nod my head.

Good, she says, holding the soup spoon with a shaking hand.

I watch my fingers curling one around the other until they've woven together like a basket of reeds. There's the story of the baby in the basket of reeds. His mother put him in it and pushed him off. He floated down the river until someone found him. He lay in that basket, good as gold, and waited to be saved.

I shall leave you one day because there are children that need me, poor ones, in Africa. Do you understand?

I nod my head, again. My fingers are so tight together they don't look like fingers at all.

*T*HE WHOLE WORLD is a windstorm but she sends me out anyway. The brown buttons on my coat won't stay shut from the pulling and tugging. The grasses whip across my face feeling like the licking of tiny animals. I catch the wind in my open mouth, it moans low and hollow.

Piggy finds me in the grasses.

Who have we here? He rolls his cigarette back and forth between his fingers and thumb. Up close he's red-faced, his nose bulges like a poisonous mushroom.

Missy, I say, backing away, Missy Sandhouse.

Is that right? He keeps coming closer. Peculiar name, he says. His lips are wet.

It's not a real name, I say.

That makes him laugh. He flicks his cigarette into the grasses and rubs his hands together. My real name's Joanne. I'm called Missy because I'm sensible. I take a step back and then another.

More sensible than some, he says, looking over me towards the house.

I nod my head, to be polite. Under my feet the ground wobbles. I feel I might tip.

You live here, don't you? He points at my house and I nod my head. Your mother's a crazy broad. But you know that, I suppose. His eyes are wet but he's not crying.

What's that? I ask, meaning "crazy broad," but I don't wait for an answer, I back far enough away to turn and run. I hear him laughing until I turn the corner of the house.

What Piggy said bounces around in my head, bounces around like a bruise or an ache. Crazy broad. Whatever it is, I think it might be true.

LUCKY RUBY LIES inside under her blankets, twisting in her sleep. She doesn't know anything yet. Doesn't know how to stay outside alone, letting the clouds tell her stories so the time goes quicker. Doesn't know that Mummy's going off to Africa to help the children. Doesn't know that Mummy runs off at night, disappearing into the dark.

Daddy comes home on his bicycle as the sun is trying to burn its way out of the clouds. I hear his bike spitting on the dirt road and then I see him waving, both hands flapping above his head like a circus clown doing tricks. I think he doesn't know those things either even though he's older and bigger.

He picks me up and swings me. How's my big girl? He asks this every time and every time I lie.

I'm fine, I say, putting on a smile that's good enough for the Queen.

We laugh and go inside for tea. It waits in the kitchen where Ruby sits on the floor and the eggs have gone cold. She sits on the carpet drawing circles. It's all she likes to do, holding the crayon so tight her knuckles go white. Mummy has locked herself in the bathroom with her cigarillos and book.

After tea Daddy clears his throat and knocks on the bathroom door. There is no answer. Gillian, he calls. Gillian, come out. I've something to tell you. I hear her turn the page of her book. I smell the cigarillos from under the door. Gillian, I think we'll be moving. When he says it he winks at me.

She opens the door. Hair is covering her eyes. Where? she asks, with her finger stuck in the book so she won't lose her place.

Canada. Daddy tips back on his heels and smiles.

Where? she asks again.

The bush, he says. The bush in Canada.

four

We're high up on Bruised Fell where it rounds against the sky like the top of the world. From here we see everything. Each tiny farmer's house and field. Each white dot of sheep. Each dark cloud as it gathers over the ocean and starts crawling towards us.

Say your goodbyes, Mummy whispers.

I take Ruby's hand, pulling her close to me.

There's no room to move up here. The edge comes so close.

It's the edge that makes it worth the climb, Mummy says, kicking at anything that will come loose and go over. We can hear the bits tumble; a sort of scurrying and tossing that gets quicker and quicker. Then, smash; everything splits apart at the bottom. Ruby laughs at the sounds.

Let me go, she says, I want to see them falling. Her hand is hot inside mine as she pulls and squirms.

No, I say, stay with me. But she wants to go. She wants to wriggle free to the edge.

Say your goodbyes, Mummy says, this time louder. This is the last glimpse, the last breath of civilization. Soon we walk into the Wild West.

She splits apart the words with her teeth as she talks.

Go on, she says almost shouting, say goodbye. Her mouth twitches as she wipes at it with the back of her hand.

Goodbye, we say, feeling silly talking into nothing. Ruby bites her lip. Perhaps she'll laugh. Or cry. With Ruby you never know. Our little storm cloud, Daddy calls her.

Come then, Mummy says, pulling Ruby's hand out of mine. Let's consider our choices. She swings Ruby up into her arms and walks towards the edge.

Choice one, she says. The Wild West. Go like a good wife and mother. The fussing and cleaning. The deadening of the soul.

They stop where the earth ends. Mummy lifts one leg, slowly, then puts it back down. Ruby giggles. She stretches her hands out, wiping them across the sky as if she could fly.

Choice two, Mummy says. Hide. Run away. Be forgotten.

Mummy lets one of her arms fall away from Ruby. Ruby rolls forward. Her face stretches with surprise and she grabs at Mummy's neck.

Choice three. Jump. She tips onto her toes, spreads her free arm out to her side like a wing and jumps. Once. On the spot.

Don't, I scream. Ruby screams higher and louder than me, both arms wrapped around Mummy's neck now. Mummy starts to howl.

A dark wind blows the hair back, blows the sounds out of our mouths and rolls the howl through the air like thunder. Her free arm wanders back and forth trying to catch her balance. I grab it, grab her cardigan too, and pull them back. Ruby slips to the ground, crying, and Mummy starts to laugh.

Missy, she laughs, her mouth full of shadows, her eyes slits of black. Fear will ruin your life. Ruin it just as it has ruined your father's. Do you understand?

I shake my head. No. This makes her laugh again.

She gets down on her knees, her cardigan flapping in the

breeze. Her fingers are nervous, they pick up a stone and play with it.

My, my, she says, this is just right. She tosses it in the air. Heads or tails, she shouts. We stare. Heads or tails, she shouts again, spinning around to face us.

Heads, I say.

She throws it straight up, catches it. Heads it is then, lucky girl. But she doesn't give it over.

Please, I say, reaching out my hand.

She slaps it back.

*T*HE AIR HAS gone thick over the hills. It sticks to my skin. It curls my breath into clouds. And the sky is blowing up browns and greys. The sea air is pushing it.

The sea brings storms to punish us, Mummy says, shaking as she pulls her cardigan to her throat. To brood over us. To clean us out.

The wind is tossing her hair. Her blue eyes have gone dull in the grey day. Come on, before the rain comes, before the dark, she says, grabbing my hand, squeezing my fingers too tight when they start to slip.

Ouch, I say, but the wind grabs the sounds so I can't be heard.

I drag Ruby with me and the edge shrinks away, becoming nothing but a thin line, something that I dreamed up, something that was never there.

The heathers are all purple down the fell. Mummy calls this place Bruised Fell because of the colour. I don't like that name; it makes my tummy turn to think I'm walking on something hurt, something soft and purple that has fallen.

We squeeze a path through the heathers, jumping from rock to rock. Sometimes my legs can't stretch from one to the other.

Sometimes my ankle turns and twinges. But we don't slow down.

Quick, she says, grabbing me by the elbow, the sky's getting darker.

I can feel my insides stretch with Mummy pulling forward and Ruby pulling back. I can hear Ruby's quick breath and feel her wobble on the tops of rocks.

If the sun sets, Mummy calls out, we'll lose our way in the dark. And then she grabs at me with both hands, and I feel ripped in half.

That's when I fall; looking up at the sky where it's been grey all day and now the smallest splash of pink peeks over the hilltops. The first drop of rain runs down my cheek as I start to slide. Mummy's fingers are like dog's teeth around my arm as it tears out of hers.

Mummy, I scream, tipping off my balance. Mummy, I say again, crying before I even hit the ground. My mouth snaps shut. My arm twists. The earth shakes underneath. And as Ruby lands on top of me I hear my arm crack.

Pick yourselves up, she says. I can hear her playing with the stones in her pocket. They kick and roll in there between her fingers.

You made us fall, I say. But only a heather, which bends to touch my cheek, listens.

My one arm carries the other. She can't pull me now with my two arms wrapped up like this. I tiptoe on the soft moss between the rocks.

You didn't stop me from falling, I say in a whisper. I know she hears. My bones ache and my fingers don't want to move.

I think it's broken, I say, it's your fault. She turns around and looks at me, a little blue still in her eyes though it's almost dark.

One day you'll know how hard it is to be a mother, she says.

It makes my cheeks burn.

five

W E'LL NEED TO put her under to fix it, the doctor says.
It will mean a night's stay. Daddy holds my good
hand in both of his and says that's okay because I'm a brave girl.
I'm not, I want to say. But the rain is streaming down the
window behind the doctor's head and his mouth moves like a
jellyfish over his teeth and I can't really breathe enough to speak
in the thick underwater air.

There's no room on the children's ward, I'm afraid, he says,
adding a twisty smile.

I WAKE UP IN a strange room with a dry mouth and wet eyes.

Why am I crying? I ask. It's odd because I don't feel sad.
I don't feel anything at all. Daddy sits close beside me, slipping
his fingers through my hair.

It's just the anaesthetic, he says. It's all fixed now. Go to sleep
and I'll come and get you in the morning.

There's only the smallest light in my room, everything else is
shadows. There's a cracked voice of a woman coming from the
doorway.

Jesus, she's saying, oh sweet Jesus.

Do you hear what she's saying? I ask Daddy.

Just her prayers, he says.

But it's Jesus, I say, the one that Mummy knows. He shakes his head and starts to stand. It might be, I say, it might be the same.

Nighty-night, he says and slips through the door like a shadow, his head falling forward off his shoulders so he looks like a headless man.

WHEN I COME home the next day Mummy is sitting at the kitchen table smoking a cigarillo and polishing the smooth black stones from our walk.

Look, she says, and passes me one that is perfectly round and shiny. From Bruised Fell, she whispers, as if it's a secret, from as high up as we got.

I roll it against my cheek. She always finds the best stones, this one is cool and silky.

I heard someone calling to Jesus, I tell her. She smiles; her cool blue eyes flash a little in the sunlight, but she doesn't speak.

Perhaps there's someone else that knows him, I say. She polishes on as if I haven't spoken. Don't you want to know? I ask her. Her eyes are empty, like a spring sky without clouds.

All I need to know, Missy, is right here. She pulls the cigarillo out to speak then puts it back in like a plug. She points to the bones of her chest. She points hard so I hear her hitting them. Thud. Thud. It sounds like stones falling on the hard earth.

We sit quietly across the table from each other while Mummy finishes her polishing. Please, she says, when she's finished. Her hand stretches across the table towards me and I have to give the stone back.

six

*T*HE BOXES PILE high in the moving van and the floors are bare, and then, just as we're ready to close the doors of our empty house, we can't find Mummy.

Gillian? Daddy calls, his footsteps taking the last trip round the house. Gillian?

In the bathroom there are piles of her hair, some of it pulled all straight from worry. There are cigarillo ashes by the toilet and a torn paper bookmark. She should have cleaned, Daddy says, running a finger through a pile of dust.

Gillian?

In the cupboard under the sink, where the last things are left. A broken sieve. A two-pronged fork. A doll's head. That's where she hides, squished in so tight she can hardly breathe.

Her skirt gives her away. A small flowery piece of it escaping under the door. Daddy points at it, gives me a smile and a wink.

Gillian? he calls, knocking lightly.

We hear her sucking in her breath. The piece of skirt disappears.

Gillian? Daddy tugs at the doors.

I won't go, Mummy says. I won't go, you can't make me.

Daddy gets a door open, she slaps at his hand. Leave me, she says, leave me be.

We are all standing around her. Three pairs of shoes are all she sees. Daddy's proper polished ones, Ruby's tiny red ones and mine brown and scuffed.

We're waiting, Gillian, Daddy says, frowning now, not smiling. Gillian, the taxi's waiting.

Her head's against the drainpipe.

Close the front door behind you, she hisses. She bats away our feet and tries to close the door. Go on, she shouts, leave me.

Mummy, Ruby whispers in a small voice. Mummy claps her hands to her ears and squeezes her eyes shut.

Hide in the cupboard! Mummy shouts. Run! They'll find you, fool! They'll drag you out! They'll pull you, push you, make you!

Gillian! Daddy grabs her arm and pulls. Gillian! The children! Behave yourself!

She's kicking as he drags her out and pulls her to her feet. But once she's standing she stays standing. She doesn't fall back down or try to hide. She brushes off the dust and bits and pieces.

Well, she says, looking down at herself, making sure everything is straight. I suppose the world is expecting me to show, I suppose the world is waiting.

And she's the first through the front door, her chin held high. She's the first into the taxi, chatting all the way, as we go to catch the boat to Canada. All of us.

AUNTIE MARGARET is there to see us off, wearing her favourite wide hat that tries to lift off in the wind. There are red rings around her eyes. Her lips shake when she speaks and it's hard to hear what she's saying with the wind and the slapping of the water against the dock.

Lucky girl, she bends down and whispers in my ear. Her cheeks are wet with tears. Her hands grip my shoulders.

Don't cry, I say. She's looking past me to the sea, her eyes are dark and still. But the wind is dancing, the air is warm, and the seagulls scream and float above us.

It's not a sad day, I say. Perhaps you could come too, we'll have a big enough house. She shakes her head and straightens up, holding on tight to the top of her hat as if it were her whole head that might fly off.

Rocks and trees and lakes, Daddy says, looking tall in his new blue suit. We'll be pioneers in a new land. He hugs Auntie Margaret and tickles her under her chin.

We'll be fine, all of us, he says. He bends to pick up Ruby and he takes my hand and we walk up the gangplank and onto the boat.

Mummy's arms are empty. She stays a long time holding onto the railing of the gangplank. She holds on tight as if someone might come to drag her away. Her mouth is open. The wind is whistling through it, moaning.

Gillian, Daddy calls to her. Gillian come on. But she isn't listening. The boat is rocking. Other people start calling to her, too. A man in a uniform tries taking her hand. She shakes him off and pulls herself closer to the railing. Everyone is watching.

Then Auntie Margaret walks over. She takes both her hands and holds Mummy's face, turning it around to look at her. Even when the wind picks her hat up and tosses it into the sea she doesn't move. They stay like that, eye to eye, until Mummy takes something from her pocket, a little book, and gives it to Auntie Margaret. She says something, spreads her hands up at the sky and then walks towards us.

Auntie Margaret walks the other way, crying. She stays to watch us disappear. I watch her too until she becomes a dot and then nothing. I watch until the whole of England disappears into the sea.

seven

MORE THAN ANYTHING I like the rocks. We have a big one behind the Canada house, a hill of rock that heaves out of the ground like a monster's belly. The trees across the street are so thick that I'm not allowed in there.

That's the bush, Daddy says, picking me up to get a good view of the danger. Someone got lost in there and died.

The trees sit and stare, and in between every one is an alley of dark. Sometimes I see the small shine of animal eyes.

There are other children on the street, in houses that line up against the bush just like ours. I see them in their back gardens when I stand on our rock. We stare at each other and then turn our backs. Go over, Mummy says, introduce yourself. But I never do.

She goes over instead, knocking on all the doors, holding out her hand and saying, how do you do. Smiling at the strangers until she turns her back to walk away, then she frowns. Uncivilized, she calls them, mannerless, ignorant.

But she asks them over for tea anyway.

The Ladies. She calls them that, like they're all one person. The best dishes come out and lots of cakes. The Ladies sit around in the afternoon with their legs crossed and talk.

All their children go outside to play, but Ruby and I stay in my room. She practises her headstands, leaning herself against the wall for balance. Her face swells, and her eyes bug out. Then she wants my toys. I let her have the Barbie. If I don't she'll scream and Mummy will come stomping in on her high heels, and blame me for spoiling the day. Then she'll notice we're not outside and send us to play with the others and my head will hurt from their screams and shouts.

I am a teacher, I hear Mummy say to the cross-legged ladies when the cakes are mostly gone. I think I'll start a nursery in the fall.

I spy, I say to myself, making sure it stays in my head. And I wait for the rhyme. I wait and wait but not even one word comes.

SHE TELLS DADDY about the nursery school at tea time. He is quiet, and stares at his plate as if the food were doing something interesting. You can't say you're something you're not, Gillian, he says finally.

Well, she says, tipping her head to the side like Ruby would if she's done something naughty. It's true *enough*, Les, about being a teacher. I'm sure I'll be good.

Daddy prods at the peas on his plate. Outside, through the kitchen window, the bush blows about like arms reaching above waves on an ocean.

I'll help you fix the basement up, then, he says.

I spy, I try again. My head is puffed up with a rhyme. I can feel it in there. I can feel it swelling but it won't come out. Nothing but a blank, nothing but a straight black line.

*T*HE SUMMER IS hot, and, aren't we lucky, Daddy says, not far from our house is a little lake. We go there in the afternoons to cool off while Daddy is at work. There are rocks all around it. Round ones like whalebacks. In the sun they are hot and gritty under my bare feet. We go in the car, down a dirt road with the bush pushing against the windows and the bumps banging our teeth together. The air is so still when we step outside, and the trees so close. I want to run, to get to the water, quick, where the air is moving.

Mummy unpacks the car. Her paints, her easel, Ruby's things. Her hat and skirt are wide and snap in the hot breeze when she steps towards the lake. She stands straight and still, even with the wind. She looks across the lake as if nothing could stop her from walking on it, as if she might step straight across it, like a giant, and keep on going.

She never comes in. I kick the water's edge, making tiny waves. I paddle in, up to my tummy, and float, belly pudged above the water like the whaleback rocks. With my ears underwater other children's screams sound like far-off seagulls.

Ruby plays under a tree, a blanket over her legs to keep the sun off. She hates the water. No matter what I do she won't come in. Just a toe, I say, but she looks right through me.

Mummy has her paints out. She paints the rocks on the lake but she makes them look bad, like angry fists.

Those rocks aren't bad, I say, but she keeps on painting. I push my toes in the sand and wiggle. I trace nothing-lines on top of my buried feet.

Why do you paint them like that? I ask.

The lake has gone silent and still. Everyone has gone, everyone but us and something that calls across the water, crying in a sad and lonely way.

You don't understand, Missy. She opens her box to put her

things away. This is my world, when I paint. This is how it is, underneath.

She is quiet as she screws the tops back on the paints. Her hands are muddy with colour.

Perhaps you'll never understand, she says, like your father. She rubs her dirty hands in the sand, digging them in as if she has them in a sink of soapy water.

There's the small life, she says, the things we see floating on the surface. The skin of life. It doesn't mean much to me. It's dull, colourless. It's what we don't see that matters most. That's what I paint.

When she rinses her hands in the lake she leaves tiny oily rainbows swirling on the surface. They wrap around the stones that stick above the water. Look, I say, the water has a rainbow skin. But she doesn't hear me. She's already gathered things up and turns towards the car.

*W*HEN THE SUMMER is over our basement becomes a nursery school. Daddy builds a playhouse and puts down rugs. I hold the boards while he nails. I hold the paint can while he paints.

I'm not putting Missy in school, Mummy says.

Daddy is on his knees with the hammer, tapping at a nail. He stops and closes his eyes.

She can stay home and help me with the children, Mummy says.

No, Daddy says, but we can hardly hear him.

Mummy walks back and forth across the rugs. I'd like a red door on that playhouse, she says, all primary colours, something bold to stimulate the imagination.

We'll have a lot of fun in that house, won't we Missy?

I STAND BY the stairs, on the first day, and watch the children arrive. I watch them pulling off their rain boots and coats. I watch their mummies flatten their hair and dry off their noses. And hug them. Still, they all cry sounding like birds at the seaside. Their mummies pick them up and hold them one last time before they're gone. Everything goes still then and I feel like one of the trees outside the front window, dripping with rain. They stare at me standing above them on the stairs. They have mean, dark eyes that look at me as if I don't belong in my own house.

There are some rules, Mummy says. No pushing or biting, you must share. And then she shows us the playhouse, she gets inside it on her hands and knees and squeals. Everyone laughs. They push to get in first. But she forgets to tell them that I'm the helper, that I'm supposed to be in my own school.

Every day the children come, squeezing into the house in their boots and coats, stomping mud, and then snow, on the floors and stairs. Often Daddy cleans it up when he gets home from work. He gets down on his hands and knees and rubs the dirt out. Mummy chats on about the day, not noticing how she's let the house get so messy.

I GET ITCHY skin behind my ear and on my neck and have to stay in my room during nursery school. I lie on top of the bed, all dressed, and watch snow pile on the twiggy branches. The forest looks friendly with a floor of snow and I know if I went in I could follow my footsteps out.

Because of the itches Mummy stands a long way back from me and raises her voice as if we are in separate rooms. She throws clean clothes at me from my door. She talks to me like a stranger, like a child she has just met and if I come too close she holds up a hand and tells me to stand back. Ruby's not allowed near me and cries when I'm in my room with the door closed. She's stuck all alone with the nursery children.

The doctor calls it something scary: it sounds like an animal, like a tiger, something fierce with teeth.

Impetigo, Daddy says, sitting by my bed. I can't see his face in the dark but his voice has a smile in it. Nothing to be afraid of, he says, stroking my hair back off my face.

But Mummy's afraid, I say. I hear his breathing stop while he thinks.

Yes, he says, I suppose she is.

I can feel the big rock in the backyard breathing in and out like a guard dog ready to pounce.

Once the itch has gone I go back to the basement. It's Thursday, arts and crafts, and Mummy brings out the paints and papers and we all try making flowers. Mine are huge with no colour inside but the outsides of them are every colour we have.

Fill them in, Mummy says. But I don't want to. I shake my head, no.

Fill them in, she says again. She takes a brush and starts to do it herself. They're winter flowers, I say, they'll have colour again in the spring and I push her hand away.

Her paintbrush makes a slash across my flowers.

Don't, I scream and all the children jump in their seats. I grab my picture and put it under the table.

Mummy steps away when I start to cry. She folds her arms across her chest and walks past each of us looking over our shoulders without saying another thing.

*T*HE MUMMIES COME early to get their children. Mummy called each of them, talking in a voice so loud that we could hear her from the basement. It's over, school is over, she said again and again. Each time she put the phone down without saying goodbye.

Mummy stands on one leg, holding the door open and smoking. The ashes of her cigarillo fall in the snow boots and onto the floor. Snow drifts in, and the cold too, but she won't close the door until everyone leaves. When they are all gone she goes to the basement. I sit on the steps and hear her ripping the paintings, each one, even mine, until they are just strips of colour.

Ruby and I play while Mummy is locked in the bathroom. I roll her over and over along the dark blue carpet and she laughs. I roll her to the edge and stop. Then I roll her back, her tiny arms and legs kicking with her giggles. The snow outside the picture window speckles everything with white and even in the dark and quiet of the house, even with Mummy locked away, we laugh.

We stand at the picture window waiting for Daddy and while we wait we watch the woods for eyes or the quick movement of animal bodies. Ruby shivers next to me.

Did you see something? I ask. I don't really need an answer. Both of us know something is lurking out there underneath the shadows of the trees.

eight

M<small>RS. HINCHLEY HASN'T</small> come to church for weeks now, Mummy says, drying the dishes after supper.

Daddy shrugs behind the paper he's reading.

She walks across the living room to the big picture window and peers down the street towards the Hinchley house. There were the first flakes of snow out there, floating. A storm was coming, that's what the forecast said, snow for days and days.

They have a strange man at their house, too, she says.

He's a specialist, from England, Daddy says, here to help us out at the plant. One of the best.

Mummy stares out the window at their house. You can see it by pressing your face to the window. That way you can see their red front door and the few bushes beside it.

Stop spying, Daddy said as Mummy was hopping about by the window, squinting through the snowflakes and the dark.

That man's just come out of the house, I knew it, she said.

Daddy rattled his newspaper to straighten it out. He looked over the tops of his glasses.

Gillian, please, behave yourself.

Mummy took off her shoes and dragged a chair to the window. She stood on it and pressed her whole body against the glass.

What's his name?

Daddy sighed. John Barstoe, he said, folding up the paper and putting it down beside him.

Well, he's watching me, Mummy said.

What? Daddy asked. He walked over to the window and looked out.

Gillian, he's having a cigarette.

Mummy ducked.

See that, he's looking over here. Who in their right mind would be out in the middle of winter smoking?

Daddy ran his fingers through his hair, then he picked Mummy up off the chair and carried her over to the couch. Sit down and read the paper, I've had enough of this foolishness.

I thought of the snow covering us over until we couldn't breathe, until we disappeared under it like dead flowers and popped up later, in the spring.

*T*HE SECOND DAY of the snowstorm, we were all sitting around the table for breakfast, except Daddy who was on his hands and knees wiping up after Ruby. The doorbell rang. Mummy ran to the front window, looked out and then yelped.

It's him!

Daddy hadn't finished on the floor.

Gillian, please, get the door.

But Mummy wouldn't, she stayed in the living room pacing back and forth on the blue carpet.

It was John Barstoe. He needed a lift to the plant because his car wouldn't start. Doug Hinchley had already left.

Fine, Daddy said. I'll be ready in just a minute.

So John Barstoe stayed by the front door while Daddy washed his hands, rubbed Ruby's face clean, and put his boots and coat on. I went with him to the door to say goodbye and look at John Barstoe.

The snow kept falling outside as silent as sleep and when Daddy opened the door some of it drifted inside and I caught it with my tongue. The flakes were huge and floated sideways and down as if they were taking their time so they could stare in at us. It was quieter with the snow and without the nursery children.

He had a nice smile. I ran upstairs after they were gone to tell Mummy this. She was standing on one leg with her back against the wall, smoking.

Looks can be deceiving, she said, the devil can be found in sheep's clothing. She has a lot of sayings. She has lots of things she looks out for. Signs, she calls them. John Barstoe arriving on our doorstep was a sign.

She called over to the Hinchleys'. Betty, she said, I'm going to have to ask you to warn that John to back off or I'll go to the police. Then she hung up. There was a dull black clunk in the kitchen when the phone was put back. It made my head wobble.

Not long after that Daddy called. She hung up on him, too, and then went to the spare room and slammed the door behind her. All her colours and brushes are there. We could hear her pulling them out and setting them up, we could smell her cigarillo and the oily paints that give Ruby a headache.

Daddy came home in the middle of the day and banged on the spare room door. Gillian, come out, he said, still with his coat on and a bit of snow in his hair.

She came bursting through the door tipping on the spikes of her high heels and holding a paintbrush between her fingers as if it were a cigarillo. There was paint across her cheeks that reminded me of shooting stars.

I could be a real artist, she said, if I didn't have to deal with you. She was shaking mad when she said it and dropped her paintbrush on the hardwood floor, leaving a smear of red there in the shape of an eye.

Go to your room, Daddy said to Ruby and me as if it were the two of us that were misbehaving.

*I*T HAD SNOWED for two days and still the sky was overfull with clouds so that it seemed there was very little room to breathe. I lay on my bed and stared out the window. I let Ruby do what she wanted. She pulled all my dolls off their shelf and swung them around by their hair. She opened all my books and left them on the floor. She emptied my wastepaper basket but there were only two used-up Kleenexes in it. She pulled my hair. I didn't care.

Through the door I could hear Daddy talking loudly at Mummy and then using a quiet stern voice. Mummy was silent. When she doesn't speak it means she isn't listening. I could picture her with her eyes closed, sitting on the couch. Or perhaps standing by the window, looking out, just in case. I wasn't sure what she was waiting for or what it was she knew was going to happen. I didn't want to know.

Daddy had never come home in the middle of the day before but for the rest of the day he stayed home because Mummy locked herself in the bathroom. Every so often he went over to the door, knocked on it and called to her. We could hear her moving around in there or going for a pee.

We had pancakes for lunch, spelled out in our names. I could eat pancakes forever, especially with butter and salt, which everyone says is strange but that's how I like them. Mummy wouldn't come out. We pushed a pancake under the door on a piece of paper but she pushed it back. Make one in the shape of the letter M, I suggested, but she pushed that back too, ripping the M in half.

Ruby and I forgot about her. Daddy couldn't concentrate on our games so we forgot about him too. I piggy-backed Ruby around the house till my knees went numb. Then she had a nap and I went to my room and played with my Barbie.

When I came out, after Ruby woke up, the doctor was over, standing at the bathroom door and talking through it. Mummy didn't care, she didn't answer. Then Daddy got an idea and called the minister of Mummy's church.

He cleared his throat and started to speak.

Gillian, dear, Frank Johnston, your Minister, here.

We could hear her moving. Daddy winked at me. The doctor was in the kitchen making tea and getting biscuits. Ruby scratched on the door like a pup.

Gillian do come out and talk with us face to face, we'd like to see you. He lit a cigarette and started to smoke.

Pass me a ciggie, dear, Mummy said, knocking lightly on the door. She must have smelled his.

Why not come out for one, he said. But she wouldn't. Daddy gave in and slid one under the door.

She smoked in there for a while and we waited outside with our tea and biscuits. Daddy and the doctor whispered down the hall.

It had gone dark. Huge fat flakes of snow were falling past the street lamps, twirling and twisting. I got dizzy watching them. Mummy knocked on her side of the door.

Anybody there? she called out and we all answered, yes, tipping our heads towards the door.

Call John over, I wish to talk to him. Daddy and the doctor bent their heads together and whispered, then the doctor went to get him.

JOHN BARSTOE TUGGED on his tie, making it tight around his neck.

Mrs., ahhh, Mrs. . . .

Daddy whispered to him.

Gillian, John Barstoe here. He leaned towards the door and touched it lightly with his fingertips. Mummy's high heels hit the bathroom tiles with sharp steps and the door flung open. John Barstoe fell forward into Mummy, whose hair had gone wild. Her eyes flashed at him.

Stand back, she said, holding the pointed end of a nail file at him.

John Barstoe did a lot of straightening, pulling down his suit jacket and jostling his tie, making it even tighter around his neck. He stepped back as far as he could, right into the Minister. The hallway was dark and Mummy's eyes were all in shadow. She stood tall and proud, her eye hollows staring at John Barstoe.

Gillian, Daddy said softly.

Mummy wasn't listening. Daddy and the doctor stepped forward together, next to John Barstoe, who tipped back and forth on his heels trying to find something to say.

Give me the file, Daddy said, holding out his hand and wiggling his fingers.

Ruby was hanging on to my leg so hard that the skin behind my knee started to burn. I sat down on the floor, on top of the red paint eye, with her on my lap, and whispered in her ear. It's okay, I said. She put her head against my neck.

Why did you come? Mummy asked John Barstoe.

He looked at the doctor.

Who sent you?

It was so quiet, it felt like my ears were plugged.

Gillian, Daddy said, you know John is here to help out at the plant.

Mummy didn't believe him.

He's here to kill me, she said.

Everything happened quickly after that. Mummy moved the nail file through the air and cut John Barstoe across the cheek. They all reached out to her at once and from where Ruby and I sat on the floor all we could see were legs.

I saw Mummy's ankles crumple on their sides and then her knees bend and then her body fell, hard, so the floor shook and her head landed close by and her hair, which was messy, lay across Ruby's bare feet. Ruby kicked it off. Mummy's eyes were open. They looked right past us, through the living-room window, to where the snowflakes fell inside the light of the street lamps.

nine

T HEY TIED HER UP. They lifted her onto the stretcher and walked off with her.

Daddy cried when the ambulance doors closed. He cried holding tight to Ruby. She kicked and screamed to get away, to run after the ambulance that was flashing its red light over their squeezed-up faces.

I didn't cry. I stood at the top of the stairs and watched as the front door opened and the sharp cold came in, as the stretcher bumped and banged against the door frame and almost tipped, as Mummy's lumpy body lay still under the blanket not caring that she was being taken or that she was tipping, or that people were staring from their front windows. The men stepped slowly on the snow with the weight of Mummy between them like something dead.

There were no stars in the sky, just the cold and the snow still falling. I felt like the bush standing there. Like the pin eyes of the animals in between the trees. Like the snowflakes drifting down and peering in from the outside. Just watching. That's all.

AUNTIE MARGARET SAYS it's like a bad dream. She said it at the airport when we went to get her. She says it at night when Ruby cries herself to sleep for Mummy and no one can make her stop. And she's saying it now, fussing in the kitchen with the teacups as she speaks. The cupboards bang open and shut until she finds what she's looking for. The cups rattle and shake from the kitchen to me where I lie on my tummy at my bedroom door, spying. Chairs scrape and I see them walking with their teacups, past the red paint eye and into the living room to sit by the picture window.

I feel responsible, Auntie Margaret says.

What an outrageous thing to say, Daddy says.

All I can see are his legs crossed one over the other and when he speaks they uncross like springs and he leans forward, putting his teacup and saucer on the floor. The snow outside has soaked up all the sound and they sit for a while quiet as trees.

Gillian tried to kill me once, Auntie Margaret says.

There's a jangling in my ears like a thousand bells. There's a cough and a switching of feet.

There, I've said it. It should have been said before you left England, I'm sorry.

Daddy picks up his tea and crosses his legs. I roll onto my back on the floor and stare at the ceiling. I want to plug my ears and hide under my pillow but I'm stuck to the floor listening to every sound.

She took me into the woods, not long after she lost the baby. She was going to kill me. Ask her. I see you don't believe me.

Daddy stands up like a jack-in-the-box.

Quiet, he says, the children. He takes a step or two towards my room.

Don't you want to know? Auntie Margaret asks. I can hear

him on the creaky floorboards, getting closer. Don't you believe me?

You must learn to control your mind, Margaret, Daddy says, his voice is cold and sharp. You're an adult, for God's sake, grow up, stop these wild imaginings.

I can't move to hide myself; it feels like someone is holding me down, pressing me into the floor. But then he doesn't come all the way. He stops and turns back to Auntie Margaret.

Kill? He is whispering the secret across the whole house, across the whole world. You're out of your mind, absolutely out of your mind. His voice is jumping and bouncing about. It's louder than a shout.

Yes, kill, Auntie Margaret says. I wanted you to know before Gillian gets out on the weekend. Perhaps they would keep her in, keep her away from the children if they knew.

There is the slapping sound of Daddy hitting himself. His forehead, perhaps, or the side of his leg. This is absurd, he says, I don't want to hear another word, not one more word of this craziness.

ten

WE DIDN'T SAY goodbye. We ran out the front door in the middle of the day when Auntie Margaret had gone to buy stamps for Mummy.

We'll stay, I said, meaning Ruby and me. Auntie Margaret can take care of us.

But Ruby started crying a sort of yelping puppy cry. She ran to Mummy and grabbed her and Mummy reached over and slapped my face. Snap. It sounded like breaking in my head.

Children are a mother's, she said hard as the snap, and then she finished writing the note on the kitchen table and left it there.

Can I do a picture for Daddy, first? I asked. But she jerked me away. Pulled me like a car was coming or some kind of danger and my sock feet slipped and I fell. This time my arm didn't break.

Mummy turned her back, walked crack, crack, crack across the wood floors, across the red paint eye. Ruby ran after her, not looking back at me. She ran with her hands out trying to catch the bottom of Mummy's skirt.

I got up. I had to.

*O*N THE PLANE, when it was too late anyway, Mummy looked over at me as I was buckling in and setting my chair right.

I thought you weren't coming, she said, pretending she'd just noticed me.

The engine started and the plane jumped forward. Ruby watched Mummy's face as if she were deaf and had to read lips. I turned away and stared out the window, with nothing to say. The runway blurred. We lifted into the sky, then dipped as if we were falling, then lifted up again. Canada became one white sheet of snow with Daddy and Auntie Margaret lost inside it. And then the clouds took even that away and we floated in heaven in the grey and then the dark. There were no stars, nothing, in the floating world.

*N*OBODY WAS ALLOWED to see us, Mummy said, because they all had dangerous minds. Things were falling apart, she said, like biscuits in a closed fist.

Don't talk to anyone. Look sharp! Mummy says, as she locks us out for the afternoon. Her face is just a flash behind the door.

Rain again, tiny whispers of it, ticking off the leaves, ticking into the little stream next to the new house back here in England.

Hold your hand out, Ruby, I say. How many can you catch? She's standing so still, like she's standing up dead.

Ruby, I say, swishing my hand in front of her face, come on.

I take her hand and lead her. She walks along. She'll walk into anything, holes, nettles, puddles, when she's like this. So I have to steer her, move her around like I'm driving her.

We have a little hideaway. I built it from branches and sticks and every day I check it. I walk around it to see if it's been touched. So far so good. That's what Daddy would say if he were here, but he's not, he's still in Canada.

There's two logs, two seats, for Ruby and me. I sit her on hers and she listens to the stream trickle and the rain tick off the roof. It's always raining here in England. Daddy used to laugh about the rain. He'd say, that's England for you. Maybe that's why he doesn't come to get us. Because of the rain. Mummy calls it tears. Look the sky's crying again, she might say, rubbing a finger across the window glass. But she never comes out in it. And Daddy, over there in Canada, he doesn't know we're here in the rain, locked out again, all wet and shivery.

STINGING NETTLES AND dock leaves. It's a game. There are a lot of them near our hideaway. Usually they grow together, but not always. The dock leaves take away the sting. Auntie Margaret said nature does it like that, on purpose, the cure next to the poison. Isn't it amazing, she said, how perfect the world is made.

Stinging nettles and dock leaves. It's a dare game that I play with myself. You have to take a chance. Find a stinging nettle, the first one you see. Rub your hand against it.

Now, is there a dock leaf?

You can't look for one until you feel the sting.

Is there a dock leaf? Is there a dock leaf?

You have to stay calm. You have to feel the sting. And you hear the stream, in the back of your mind, running along cool and slippery. If there's not a dock leaf for three steps, giant ones if you want, then you lose. No dock leaf. Even if it's just four steps away. No dock leaf. I've never cheated, not once, even though the sting stings and you can hardly hear the water running or the leaves moving or even notice Ruby, for the sting.

eleven

SOUTH, IS ALL Mummy says, when we ask.

The car windows are closed because Ruby's ears are delicate and the breeze makes them ache. She sits next to me with her nose plugged, holding her breath and trying to make her ears pop. Mummy says her eardrums will burst if she does it too hard. Ruby doesn't care, she says she can hear without ears.

My legs stick together under my dress and the cheese melts in its plastic in the back window because it's so hot. Mummy sings the *Messiah*, letting her hand float off the steering wheel at her favourite parts, waving it like a wing, like a bird fluttering in a small place. Jesus, the *Messiah*. We know it off by heart because she sings it all the time. All the time she's happy, that is.

SHE HAD WOKEN us early in the morning.

Leave the beds, she said, grabbing underwear and tops and throwing them in a suitcase. All we need in the world we can put in this. She snapped it shut, then checked her hat in the mirror and fixed it. It was her straw hat; she'd pinned daisies to it, from the garden.

Ready? she asked, watching us from the mirror. I shrugged.

You'll spoil everything, young lady, with an attitude like that, she said.

We left before the sun came up, stuffed in the back seat beside the suitcase, a drizzle slapping against the windows. We drove into nowhere with the headlights making circles in the dark. I looked for things hiding in the bushes. I looked for eyes watching us. But no one saw us go, not even animals. The windshield wipers talked back and forth like gnomes with secrets.

Ruby sucked her fingers and reminded me.

Oh no, I said to Mummy, leaning forward so I could whisper in her ear, we forgot Ruby's blanket.

The dark whizzed past us. The hedgerows jumped towards us. Mummy turned a sharp corner and I slid away from her.

It's too late now, Mummy said, that's the peril of adventure. There's no turning back.

The suitcase rolled back and forth beside me, banging at my leg.

In the afternoon there was sun. Sun on the backs of our necks making us dizzy. It bulged on the pavement when we stopped for petrol. We drank with our hands for cups at a dirty sink while the car was being filled.

Hot, for the end of summer, the man said, as he wiped our windows.

Mummy said, yes, it was good weather for adventure.

Where you off to, then? he asked.

South, she said, pushing her hair back under her hat and smoothing out her lips in the mirror. The daisies were wilting.

WHERE ARE WE? I asked, when we got back into the car. She said she didn't know. She laughed when she said it. The hills were disappearing into flatter land. The sky was getting bigger. We ate the rubber cheese, sucking on it to make it last.

We drove all day and into the dark. No one stopped us. No one knew where we were except the strangers that stood back from us as we whizzed past or the people that honked when we didn't stop where we were supposed to.

We stopped beside a field.

Get out and stretch, Mummy said, and then we'll sleep.

There was nothing but stars for light, winking in and out, high above us.

Like a church, she said in a voice that was soft as air and quiet. She leaned back against the car and hugged herself.

Ruby didn't like it in the dark and stayed inside.

Come on out, Ruby, Mummy said loudly to the sky, or the world will pass you by.

She didn't come. I could see the dark bump of her body in the back seat. She looked like a Martian with her knees tucked up to her chin and her head resting on them.

Ruby, I whispered, through a crack in the window, squishing my lips together to get the sound through. She wouldn't listen. She can be like that, like her ears have doors and she can close them.

Pretend we're pioneers, Mummy said, peering at us over the front seat as we were trying to find a comfy place to sleep. Pretend we're the first ones ever to venture this far.

The car felt like a spaceship floating in the blackness between the stars. I waited for Ruby to notice about her blanket. I listened to her sucking on her fingers without it. She didn't say a thing, but I could feel her legs shiver against mine for a long time until I fell asleep.

Mummy sat up most of the night with her head propped against the window and smoked. Each time she lit a match

I thought of flares that signal for help. The car filled with smoke, thicker and thicker, and all night I dreamed I was choking.

In the morning we were crumpled.

I'm supposed to start school, I said. A cool wind was rippling against my face.

There are more important things, Mummy said, in a dreamy way, leaning against a wall and smoking. In the south the cliffs are white and the sea drags itself along the pebbles and into those cliffs. I've always wanted to go there to sing and shout into the wind.

There was a thick sky growing overhead.

Besides, she continued, I know everything you need to know.

WE CARRIED ON until the car broke down. Mummy was delighted.

I've always wanted to be stranded, she said, looking in the glove compartment for her cigarillos. Today is the beginning of the rest of our lives—Goethe, he said that, a great man.

She lit her cigarillo.

See, they wouldn't teach you that in school.

She sat on the edge of the front seat with her legs outside, her high heels balancing on her toes and swaying.

It was cool out. I rummaged through the suitcase to find cardigans but Mummy wouldn't wear hers.

We'll just wait here to be saved, she said, wiggling her toes so her shoes pitched about threatening to fall off. Lovely this air and all this green. She spread her cigarillo hand out in front of her towards the hills and fields.

Who will save us? Come on, who will save us?

She looked over at me as I stood on the road toeing pebbles into a straight line. Her voice had a tease in it. Perhaps it was a question I was supposed to answer. I shrugged. Often she didn't need an answer. Often she talked right over what I was saying.

Ruby lay in a ball in the back seat. Come pick flowers, I suggested to her. She shook her head. Her face was hidden in her cardigan. Up the lane and down there was no sign nor sound of anything. Anyone that came our way would have to stop. The lane was so narrow they couldn't pass by. In the end someone would save us. I tried to explain this to Ruby but she wouldn't listen. Some people think she's rude but it's just because she's afraid to come out and see the world. She stays inside but she's watching.

Around lunch it started to rain. Mummy slammed the car doors shut and rolled up the windows. The flowers I had picked were wilting. The daisies on her hat were dead.

Listen for cars, Mummy said when I tried to speak.

Her eyes didn't open at all. I could feel her heavy breath filling up the car. She struck a match and lit another cigarillo.

Last one, she said looking it up and down as if it were different. The smoke curled and twisted. I made it dance with little puffs of breath. I made it sweep across the windows like it was a genie trying to get out. We sat silent and still for so long that when a car did come by we were hardly able to speak.

I DIDN'T EXPECT to be saved by *her*, Mummy said, as the woman backed her way down the lane to find a place to turn around. She was going back to town to find a breakdown lorry.

Do you know her? I asked.

No, she didn't.

I had imagined a man, she said. I just thought it would be a man.

We sat quietly in the car listening to the steady rain and Mummy's fingers tapping slowly on the steering wheel.

*T*HE BREAKDOWN LORRY was high up and as we drove we could see over the walls and hedges. Mummy had a cigarette with the driver.

So you don't live in these parts?

Every time he shifted gears the lorry hiccuped and our car swayed behind us.

No, no, Mummy said, wiping one of her fingers through the dust on the dashboard.

Where you off to, then? He turned the windshield wipers on and they swept across the huge window like wings. Maybe she had an answer for him.

Well, I'd like to see the cliffs in Dover, she said.

She was drawing flowers in the dust.

We're just adventurers, we'll take what comes. The driver nodded.

Well it looks like you'll be stuck in one place for a few days by the looks of your engine. Not much adventure in that.

*F*IRST WE FOUND more cigarillos, then we found a place to stay not far from the garage. The man drove us up the hill to Mrs. Barker's Bed and Breakfast. There was a picture on the sign of a smiling egg, its little arms and legs waved about like it was falling.

The room was a surprise. The ceilings were high and the wood floor felt like it went on forever. I bent down to touch it. There were cracks between each plank and the lines in it swirled and zagged like waving arms, like tree branches in the wind. Windows spread across one wall, wide windows with white sills. Outside there were trees, tall and old. The grasses were long, just the way I like them for hiding. They whispered in a soft wind. Even Ruby walked around and looked out the window. Mummy sat in the one chair there was and smoked.

Perhaps we'll stay a while, Mummy said, after a long silence. She nodded to herself.

As nice as the room was it wasn't home. Ruby rocked back and forth on her heels then dropped to the floor.

We can't, I said, I'm supposed to go to school.

Mummy's cigarillo was almost burned down to her fingers.

Don't be such a spoilsport; don't spoil our little adventure, Missy. You know how much I want to see those cliffs.

Ruby was starting to cry.

We slept on the pullout chesterfield in our underwear. I wish I had my nightie, I said to Ruby. She was already in bed and curled into her ball. I waited for her to notice that her blanket was missing. But again she said nothing.

The wood floors were cold, and because there were no curtains a slice of moon came in the window and lay across the bed. I told myself it was the same moon I had always known. The same moon as last night through the car window, and the night before that in my own bed. It winked in and out between the clouds. Perhaps Daddy had stepped outside, just now, so far away, and was standing looking up at the same moon.

How will Daddy find us? I spoke across the dark to Mummy but she didn't answer. If he writes we won't get his letters. Mummy was sitting in the window, the moon had turned her face purple and blue. Mummy?

Ruby was crying again. I tried to sing her a song, but each time I opened my mouth nothing came out. There was nothing there in my head. Just a black sky inside me, only emptier because at least the sky has stars. When I fell asleep Mummy was still at the window and she was talking to the moon.

*I*N THE MORNING we went to the garage. We wore trousers and cardigans because the weather had turned.

Don't expect much from the weather, Mrs. Barker said at breakfast, as she served us eggs on toast.

Ruby won't eat eggs, I told her. She got jam instead.

Weather's taking a turn for the worse; don't drag yourselves out too far from here, there'll be storms.

Mummy wasn't paying attention. She sat with her cup of tea and smoked. Her egg went cold and sat on the toast shivering.

*T*HE GARAGE WAS empty so Mummy called out. We didn't know the man's name so she just called out hello, hello, and walked past our broken car to the back where he lived. He was having a cup of tea.

Johnson, he said with a mouth full of biscuit. My name is Johnson. He gave me a wink and pulled a chair out for Mummy. Ruby hid behind her.

Scallywag, Johnson said, shaking his head. Then he just sat and looked at Mummy.

Five days before I can get the part and fix you up, he said finally.

There was an electric heater in the corner and every time it clicked on the lights dimmed. His bed was next to it. Mummy fished in her purse for a cigarillo. Johnson took one and they sat smoking and not speaking.

Shop's closed tomorrow; Dover's not far off, I could drive you down. His eyes twinkled and he tossed a pen up in the air and caught it.

The weather's turned, I said. Johnson laughed and spat bits of biscuit across the table.

I don't think it would be good to stand on the edge of a cliff in a storm, I said, quietly. Johnson gave me another wink.

Pair of scallywags, he said.

Mummy said, yes, we will go, and stood to leave. Nine o'clock then, tomorrow?

Ay, Johnson said, leaning back and putting his feet up on his kitchen table.

MRS. BARKER SHOOK her head when Mummy asked for a packed lunch for all of us. Those cliffs won't be safe in these winds, she said. Johnson's a right character, not an ounce of sense in him, she added. Mummy looked around the kitchen in a nervous way.

A packed lunch, she said, again.

She was holding her purse so tight I could see the bones of her fingers poking through.

Mrs. Barker had her back turned, she shook her head again. I'd hate to see you taken away by the wind, she said scrubbing at something in the sink.

Mummy picked up an egg and threw it. It flew past Mrs. Barker and hit the wall. The cracking sound split open in my head and the yellow insides that dripped down the wall seemed to smother my brain so that I couldn't think.

I am the mother, Mummy said. I can do what I want with my children.

The wind was rattling at the windows and the rain blurred

the trees as they blew outside. We had no raincoats and no wellies. Mrs. Barker was shaking as she wrapped the sandwiches in wax paper and made a thermos of hot chocolate. Now, mind you eat this all up, she said to Ruby and me. Her eyes were wet in the corners.

*W*E WENT IN the breakdown lorry. Johnson was waiting outside Mrs. Barker's with the engine going. He was dressed with a shirt and tie. His woolly pullover smelled of petrol when he lifted us up to the seat.

Mummy got in first saying how nice he looked. How posh, she said, a right gentleman.

I thought a gentleman was like Daddy with proper shiny shoes, soft clean hands and a whispery voice. Johnson was not like that.

Ruby and I took turns by the window. Even in the rain the view was better than in our car.

Let's pretend, Mummy said, that we're all one happy family. Let's pretend we've been travelling for years looking for treasure and we know we're going to find it in Dover.

The wind whipped the rain into us so hard the window wipers couldn't clear it away. Johnson pulled over.

It's worse than I thought, he said. Perhaps today is not the day for this. Mummy slapped her hand on the dusty dashboard, erasing the flower she'd drawn there before.

Nonsense, after we've come all this way, we can't turn back now.

We've only been driving a short time, Johnson pointed out. He didn't realize she was talking about the pretend-years of travel we had just done to get here.

Listen Mrs., this could be dangerous, these young ones could be blown away. Johnson rolled his window down and let the wind in just to show her. I grabbed onto Ruby to keep her in her seat.

See? he said. But I knew Mummy wasn't taking any notice.

She said we would hitchhike the rest of the way if he wasn't man enough to keep his word. She reached across us and opened the door. Johnson slammed his hand on the steering wheel and began to shout. He shouted for a few minutes while Mummy sat looking straight ahead. Only her hands looked nervous as they tugged at a thread that was coming loose from a button. In the corner of her mouth there was a little smile.

By God! he ended, shaking his head like a horse shaking off flies. Then he started up and we drove on.

IN DOVER IT had stopped raining. The winds were still high, though, and the clouds heavy and dark. Johnson knew a road to the cliffs and we stopped at the end of it and ate our lunch with the view of the land going on forever until it fell into the sea.

Yes, Mummy whispered, her voice like an awful chill wind, yes this is it. Who said it? Milton, I think, "Chaos that immeasurable abyss, outrageous as the sea—dark, wasteful, wild."

The lorry bounced in the wind. I didn't know if he'd said it or not. I didn't even know him.

One of them pansies, Johnson said, crumpling his sandwich paper and tossing it out the window. The wind grabbed it, hurled it, smashed it to the ground.

Look at that, Mummy said, her mouth full of sandwich. There was a house in the distance at the edge of the cliffs.

Ay, Johnson said, it's abandoned. No one in it for years. Tiny, it is. One bedroom, only big enough for two.

Something made Ruby shiver just then. The whole of her body moved like someone was shaking her.

Eat up, I said, it'll make you warm. But the jam sandwich that Mrs. Barker had made her sat forgotten on her lap.

Come on, Mummy said to Johnson. Let's peek through the windows.

She didn't ask us to go. We stayed inside the lorry as it rocked back and forth in the wind.

MUMMY WENT RIGHT to the house. We watched her walk in the wind, her arms floating at her side, her hair tossed up into the air swirling above her like it did that time outside the church. *The wind wants me more*, she had said. I hoped Ruby had forgotten.

She walked around it, stopping to look inside, pulling at the door handle, again and again. There was no way in and after a while she walked away. I saw Johnson take her hand and point towards the cliffs. I saw them walking farther and farther and all the time the wind was tearing and pulling and pushing. We could feel it even inside the lorry.

Twice I got down from the lorry to shout to her. But my voice went nowhere but round me in circles like her hair.

We played with the chocolate biscuit animals that Mrs. Barker had packed into our lunches. We put them to bed in the warm pink straw she had wrapped them in. They're cold, Ruby said, wrapping them in the tissue. Sometimes she wrapped them too tight and they lost a head or a leg. Then she got upset. A sweat would rise on her forehead and nose and she would hold her breath.

Ruby, it's just biscuits, I would say, over and over again, until she calmed down.

I finished the hot chocolate but Ruby wouldn't let me eat the biscuits. Not even the broken ones.

We sat for a long time looking towards the sea and the far-off dots that were Mummy and Johnson.

I miss Daddy, Ruby whispered, her voice wobbled as if it were falling apart. I missed him too.

Just think about something else, I said, just pretend.

*T*HEN WE COULDN'T see the dots of their bodies.

Stay here, I said to Ruby.

I jumped from the lorry and ran. The wind blew through my cardigan as if I had nothing on. It pushed at my legs so hard that it knocked my one foot into the other when it came off the ground. As I ran I kicked myself on the insides of my calves.

There was no sound but the storm, howling through everything. The grasses were bent back flat to the ground and the ground was soaking wet. It sucked at my feet. A few times I fell. All the while I was calling and feeling that the wind was keeping me still and silent. Who will save us? I shouted in my head. Who will save us? I tried to see Daddy bending down to pick me up and swing me as I moved, slow motion, towards the edge of the cliff but my head was like a hollow, all full of wind.

They were lying on the ground, past the little house, at the edge, splattered in mud. The wind had blown Mummy's skirt up so her legs were bare and pink with cold. She was staring at the sky and talking to the clouds. Her lips floated on her face along with a smile.

Johnson saw me first and sat up. His tie was loose, his trousers undone. He fixed himself.

Go back, he shouted, pointing to the lorry, his voice just reaching me between the crashes of waves below, and the wind. His face was hot-looking and puffy. I ran, this time it felt like flying, back to Ruby, the heavy clouds above pressing down so I could hardly breathe.

twelve

*C*OULD YOU WATCH the children for me? Mummy asked Mrs. Barker the next day. I've got to check about the car.

She giggled and tucked her hair back behind her ears. Fresh flowers, picked from the garden, jiggled in her straw hat.

Ruby and I stood in the doorway of the kitchen. Come on, she said, pushing us towards the kitchen table and making us sit. Be good for the lady, I won't be long.

Her hands were hot. Her lips on my cheek dry and scratchy. There was a sweet smell on her that I'd never smelled before.

What's that smell? I asked. She gave me a little push away and I bumped against the table.

Nosy Missy, she said, keep your thoughts to yourself.

*T*HE NEXT FIVE days Ruby and I spent mostly with Mrs. Barker. We stayed in the kitchen with her, helping her bake. She taught us how to mix butter and sugar together with a fork. She taught us how to crack eggs. At first Ruby banged the egg too lightly against the bowl and nothing happened. Come on, Mrs. Barker said, you've got more in you than that, give it a real wallop. So

Ruby did and egg flew everywhere. Mrs. Barker laughed so hard she had to sit down.

Right, she said. Now, somewhere in between.

She told us stories about her boys. They had all grown up and lived on their own. She never had daughters, she said, so she was happy to have us.

I would be a Mummy like her when I grew up, I told her. She said she thought I'd be the best Mummy a child could have considering the way I looked out for Ruby.

On our third day at Mrs. Barker's the sun came out. It streamed through the windows where we sat stirring and measuring.

I'm missing school, I said, rolling out dough for cinnamon buns.

That right? Mrs. Barker said. Her hands were in a bowl squishing things together with her fingers.

I told her I was worried about missing school and about missing my Dad.

Where is he then? she asked, sitting down with her hands covered in paste like dainty gloves.

Canada, I said, taking a biscuit from the pile we had just baked.

That's a long way off, she said. I said I knew. I said we'd all lived there once, until we ran back here with Mummy. Mrs. Barker shook her head.

I don't know, she said, leaning over to give me a hug. The flour from her fingers floated down onto my skirt.

Every evening Mummy came back apologizing. Her hair was so wild it looked like it was screaming, like it was shaking hands and fists it was so happy or mad, I couldn't tell which. Mrs. Barker made her sit down for tea. She talked to her quietly and handed her something we had baked, waiting for her to settle.

Now Gillian, she would say, it seems you've had a busy day. Mummy would nod and chew and sip. I could see from her eyes moving back and forth that she was deciding what to say. I kept waiting for her to apologize about throwing the egg but she never did. Usually it was something about the car.

I was in the church praying, she said, for help.

I didn't believe her. She liked churches but that was usually when she was sad, when she was so quiet she couldn't talk.

Well, well dear, Mrs. Barker said, patting Mummy on her bare arm, things will turn out and you'll be out of here in no time. Young Missy will be off to school before you know it.

Mummy shook her head, trying to swallow quickly so she could speak.

I think perhaps we'll stay, she said, for a while, anyway.

I screamed so loud Mummy's mouth fell open and I could see the unswallowed biscuit on her tongue. It looked like throw-up. I remember that but not what it was I screamed. Ruby ran from the kitchen with me, grabbing my hand, and for a minute I think we thought we might run away.

We went to the room instead. There was still light coming through the windows from outside and dust floated lazy and slow through it. It seemed strange that something could be so still at a time like that. I threw everything we had into the suit-case and had Ruby sit on top so I could zip it up. Then we both sat on it and cried.

It was Mrs. Barker who came after us, knocking lightly on the door and peeking around it with a face like the smiling egg on her sign.

Let's get you two washed up for bed, it's been a long day, she said.

She fussed with the bedsheets so they looked like they'd

been made up all day. She ran some warm water in the bathroom sink and washed our hands and faces.

Your Mum's gone out, she said, scrubbing my face a little too hard.

I hope she never comes back, I said, watching the side of Mrs. Barker's face in the mirror. She said nothing, her face didn't even twitch. Once I was washed up she hugged me close, her warm tummy jiggling against my face.

She sang us to sleep, sitting on the one chair there was in the room with her hands held together on her lap. Her voice wobbled like Auntie Margaret's when it got too high and like Auntie Margaret's you couldn't tell if it was tears or happiness making it do that. Even in the dark I could tell she was watching us. Watching us so we wouldn't feel alone. Her voice got softer and softer and Ruby uncurled a little in her ball before she fell asleep.

MUMMY WASN'T THERE in the morning, nor by lunch or tea time. Mrs. Barker called down the hill to Johnson's. She let the phone ring and ring. Ruby and I sat and watched her with her head turned to the window. She was watching the long stringy willow branches outside twisting in the wind. There was no answer.

Try again, Ruby said, when she hung up. But again there was no answer.

Ruby and I sat and watched Mrs. Barker move around the kitchen with the knives and forks and plates. We watched her butter the bread and make a pot of tea. We watched her whip the cream and fill a plate with biscuits and open a jar of peaches. They slid into our bowls like the slippery yellow insides of eggs. The grandfather clock ticked and struck five times. Mummy had been gone a whole day.

After supper we went outside to wait for Mummy. We gathered stones. Shiny ones that reminded me of the ones Mummy found on Bruised Fell. Smooth ones, heart-shaped ones. We picked and sorted. We held them between our fingers, rubbing them, scratching them, wetting them with our spit to see the colours. We lined them up, gathered them like tiny people.

You be the Mummy one, Ruby said, yours is the Mummy Stone. She held a small smooth stone in her hand and stroked it. I held a big one, rough and speckled, I placed it on the ground in front of me and made it talk.

It's time for bed, let's wash your hands and face and have a bedtime story, it said.

Ruby put her stone next to mine so they touched. The Mummy Stone stared off into the distance but she let the baby stay close.

The low sun barely caught our squatting backs. I could feel it like a warm hand holding me still, stopping me from moving. The grass began to hum as evening insects rubbed themselves awake. The outside world was filling up. The sun slanted across the heavy front door, a golden red.

I wanted Mummy to appear behind the door, silent in her chair, ashes fallen to the floor by her side. Or to see her walking up the hill, waving to us, glad to be back. But everything was motionless, waiting to begin. Anything could happen now, all the sounds rising higher and louder like a scream. A strange heat glowed off the red-splashed sky. Something was smashing at my chest, a fast scattered beat catching in my throat, like an animal trapped and running in circles inside me. The warm hand held us down so we couldn't move.

It was Mrs. Barker who came to get us. She took our hands, pulled us up and walked us through the reds of the setting sun and into the house. She walked us into our room where she tucked us under the covers and sang us to sleep. Ruby took Mummy's slip from the suitcase and wrapped it around her neck. She rubbed it between her fingers and across her cheek like she used to do with her blanket.

She's gone to that little house, Ruby whispered into the pillows. I pretended I didn't hear. I didn't want to say yes or no. I didn't want to say anything. I thought I'd never talk again.

MUMMY WAS GONE each day after that. At first, we waited for her to come through the door all in a mess and loud, but she never did. At first, we would wake in the mornings and ask Mrs. Barker: Is she back?

No, she would say, I'm afraid not.

Soon we stopped asking. We were afraid, too. We sat quietly at the table for our tea. We dressed ourselves in the morning without asking. But our minds, no matter what we did, couldn't stop waiting.

thirteen

Your Daddy's on his way, Mrs. Barker says when she hangs up the phone.

This little piggy, is all I can think. This little piggy as my finger gets bigger and spreads out pink and new until it blocks out the view and touches my wet eye.

Careful, I hear behind me.

This little piggy by the window with the rain streaming down the glass like hair. With the day so heavy out there, so lonely. All the people have gone, hiding somewhere. Hiding just like Mummy. In the woods maybe, because of the storms.

This little piggy, it keeps running in my head, faster when I try to stop it. This little piggy ran all the way home.

Daddy's coming but still Ruby sniffs and cries in her ball. Mrs. Barker can't stop her. Nothing can. And so she picks her up, a big round ball, and I think she's going to throw her, toss her over to me as a game. I feel my fingers, all springy, getting ready. I feel the dark outside staring in. I wait for Mrs. Barker to say catch and I worry about the weight of her even though she's so small. I worry about dropping her.

But Mrs. Barker holds her tightly. Holds her on her lap like it's normal for a person to be one big circle. And she strokes her, starting at the head and sliding down her neck to her back. One soft, smooth line.

There, there, Mrs. Barker says, there, there.

I can feel something wet inside, something soft and wet crawling up my throat, crawling through my eyes. Everything starts sticking together. Ruby's red cardigan. The blue stuffed chair. The bedspread full of flowers. Mrs. Barker's pale pink blouse. The shiny wood floors. Everything joined. I lose the face of Mrs. Barker, the lines in the wood. I lose the shadows of the trees outside in the dark and my own fingers. Each finger disappears becoming one pink stub.

There, there, Mrs. Barker says, louder.

Something pink comes out of the ball like a leg about to step. There is something sparkling in the corner, something wild and free behind Mrs. Barker like Christmas lights when you squint.

There, there, Missy. You're crying.

The stepping leg waves free in the air, across the sparkles.

Come here, love, she says. There's room for both of you.

I wobble through the joined-up colours, everything so thick and sticking in my throat. And a strange sound comes with me. A crying animal, a small one. A mouse perhaps, trapped in the wall or huddled in the corner. Mrs. Barker's arm appears, it's not a leg at all. And the poor animal, the poor little thing is getting louder and Mrs. Barker's arm and Ruby's hot red ball so tight against my tummy and my head falling, falling and my legs folding up and my face against something soft, a pink pillow and the sound of the little animal tickling inside me.

There, there, Mrs. Barker says.

Her voice is in my hair making a hot spot on the very top.

There, there, she says, so hot. Let it all out, love. Daddy will be here tomorrow, first thing, to take you back to Canada.

No, Ruby screams, springing from her ball and banging my face. No we can't.

The blur is gone. The red is so sharp. The lamplight, behind Mrs. Barker, stings my eyes.

Mummy will be back, Ruby shouts, running to the bedroom door, slamming it shut, spreading her arms across it so we can't escape. We can go to that little house. We can bring her back.

Mrs. Barker doesn't understand.

It's on a cliff, I say. The windows and doors are all closed up, you can't get in.

Yes, you can, Ruby shouts, as if we're far off. Her whole body curling around the shout. Yes you can. Mummy can. She's there.

*T*HE COLD COMES in on Daddy's dark coat. It pricks at the hot and cozy smells of baking. It sneaks along the stone floor and through our sock feet. He closes the door, coming in like he's swallowed by the puffiness in the room where it sits close against your cheeks like a warm cat.

We stare. He's holding a suitcase which he puts down, slowly. He's pushing at his buttons and his coat falls open. There's his tie that I remember and his dark striped suit. There's his blue eyes and almost invisible lips. He starts to bend and his shoes squeak. He bends and bends till he's on his knees. His eyes don't move from us. His arms start floating forward, his fingers spreading ready to catch.

My, my, he says, so softly that we have to bend towards him to hear, aren't you both beauties.

1971 to 1974

fourteen

A T PARTIES SHE would hang herself from the tops of door frames and do chin-ups. Her hair coiffed, all queenie. Her sleeveless dress barely covering what hid at the top of her legs. The men applauded. Dad blushed, blue eyes turned to the bottom of his empty glass. Years later, when she was gone, he would say: She was stupid but she sure was sexy.

I'M TWELVE WHEN she appears. Ruby is ten. Big girls now, Dad likes to say. What he means is it's been four years since your mother disappeared. Forget her. Ruby says she is Dad's plan to squeeze Mum out.

She squeezed herself out, I say, you know that.

Ruby says we moved to the end of the earth so Mum couldn't find us.

Cape Breton, Nova Scotia, is not the end of the earth, I say. If a mother wants to find her daughters, really wants to, then nothing will stop her.

Ruby sniffs and gives me the evil eye.

*T*HE KITCHEN IN the new house is redone in avocado just for her. The new green carpet, rolled out wall to wall, becomes a threat for spills. Curtains appear in the window over the sink, hanging on thick brass rails and blocking the view to cliffs in the distance.

You'll call her Mum, Dad says, his arms around her.

They whisper a lot. Her brilliant lips pushing air across his face, her green eyes glinting at us, watching from the other room. Cocktail hour has replaced horsing around, has replaced riding Dad through the house on all fours. They drink drinks with small sips and giggle as dinner sizzles and hisses in the oven.

Ruby and I whisper too, in our bedroom with the door closed. She squeezes her pixie face up close to mine. I can feel her hot breath on my cheeks.

I hate her, Ruby snickers.

How can you hate her, you don't even know her? I ask.

She rolls her eyes to make me look stupid.

If she's here, she says, guess who isn't.

We invent stories about where she came from. Dad found her in a grocery store next to the lemons, Ruby says, squeezing her mouth into a sour circle. I like to think he found her at the beach, in a bikini, drinking her crème de menthe and smoking cigarettes. Ruby says that's boring because it's too close to the truth.

But we don't know what the truth is, I say.

Idiot, she replies, open your eyes.

*T*HE FIRST WE knew of her was when he brought her home. He had been on a business trip out west. They came back, married.

We stood in the living room to meet her. The backs of our knees knocking against the couch. Our hands were held behind us like we were chained up. Outside a bird sat on a branch, its head tucked to one side watching us.

He said her name.

Cerise.

Cerise, I repeated back to him, looking closely to see if he was joking. He wasn't.

We'd never heard that kind of name before. It sounded like tearing, like something sharp that you shouldn't touch.

Hello, we said, staring at her feet. They were pinched into pink high heels.

So you're Joanne, she said, looking me up and down. You're big for your age. I tried to smile. I couldn't remember the last time anyone had called me by my proper name. My mother, perhaps, in one of her fuzzy periods or teachers before they got to know me.

Missy, Ruby said, we call her Missy. I could feel the couch tremble from Ruby's nervous knees banging against it.

And Ruby, was the reply. A peculiar name, we don't have it over here. A stone, isn't it?

A jewel, really, Dad said, though his voice didn't sound so sure.

He held her hand and kissed it between sentences. There were the words "happy" and "home" and "family," but none of them fit together with the way he held her close on the other side of the room. Once the introduction was over we sprinted up the stairs to get away.

You'll call her Mum, Dad shouted, not bothering to chase after us.

*T*HAT'S WHEN RUBY put the photo up over her bed. The three of us, Mum, Ruby and me, sitting on the beach. Mum in the middle with the wind blowing. Her dress full of flowers. Large open ones, spread across her body like mouths. The wind is blowing through her hair. It blows sand over the sandwiches near Ruby's feet and it blows the dry grasses behind us almost flat. She is lifting her face to the wind, lifting it upwards to the sky. Threads of hair are catching in her mouth.

Ruby and I are on either side, shivering. Each of us has grabbed a fistful of her dress. Ruby sits like a doll would, all crooked and tipped to one side. One foot off the ground. Fingers and toes spread like she's startled. And I have a broken arm, I'm holding it to my chest as if it might fall off.

When I look at that picture I try to figure out why Ruby doesn't fall over. But I can't. It's an optical illusion, I guess, it looks like something it's not. I try to tell Ruby that about Mum.

She wasn't a good Mum, she wasn't like she looks in the picture, I tell her. Forget about her. But Ruby can close her ears whenever she wants.

Later I tried taking the picture down. I couldn't stand it there each time I came into the room. Ruby went mental. She scratched my face and bit my shoulder. The whole time I stayed quiet. We both did. All you could hear was our breathing and the sounds of our bodies moving against each other and the bed banging against the wall.

Ruby, I whispered into her face, once I'd pinned her down. She didn't look right. She was red. Even her eyes were red, broken with blood vessels and her lips so swollen they were almost purple. Just the tip of her nose and the outside edges of her ears were white. It looked like someone had taken white crayon and drawn a line around the outside of her as if she were in a bubble.

I'm sorry, I said. She lay quiet underneath me, her heart pumping through her wrists under my hands. I held a corner of the picture. She had the rest.

I taped the picture back together. It had torn so most of me was ripped out. All of me but my one good hand holding the edge of Mum's skirt. I suggested cutting the hand out so it could be just a picture of the two of them. But that's not what she wanted.

I want it the way it's supposed to be, she said.

AFTER THAT FIGHT we tried not to think. We tried not to think about the move to the East Coast, to this little town where down the hill there was a small lake sitting in a hollow. It was a pond, really. Our little pond, Dad said with a smile, trying to ignore its sickly look. It was nothing like the lake in the bush. There were no rocks or trees around it. There was no sand. I wouldn't want you swimming in it, Dad said, but it's better than nothing. It's something to look at.

There were the cliffs, though, their red gash startling next to the blue-greens of the ocean. I could see them best from the bathroom window. Though I didn't know how to get to them I was sure I could find out.

We tried not to think about Mum; at least I did. No one mentioned her anyway. Though Ruby thought she heard Cerise on the phone talking about her. Put away, she heard Cerise whisper, where she belongs.

No way, I said.

I couldn't imagine Mum locked away. I couldn't picture her squashed into a small space without the fells and the sea and the wind.

Maybe it's against the law to leave your children, Ruby said.

When I laughed it came out nasty. Ruby stared at me as if I were a stranger. Then she walked from the room, closing the door so quietly she made no sound at all.

Sometimes Ruby called to Mum in her sleep but I never told her.

Sometimes Ruby tore things up. First Mum's slip that she'd slept with for years, then the hair out of her best doll. I tried to stop her.

Leave me alone, she said, through gritted teeth. I knew she didn't mean it. She meant shut up, which I did, and stayed sitting with her while she destroyed most of the things she liked.

THEN THERE WAS my Mummy Stone. She kept taking it from my dresser and putting it under her pillow at night. She wouldn't ask because she knew I'd say no.

What do you care? she'd say when I demanded it back.

It was a good question. I never knew the real answer to it.

I don't care, I'd say. But it's mine. Give it.

I held out my hand until she passed it over and each time, as I waited with my hand out, I felt mixed up, like on a roller coaster, like I could see the hill coming and I was rushing up it and all that was at the other end was a long drop and there was nothing to do but hang on, eyes closed, and seal my mouth closed against the screams.

WHEN SUMMER VACATION came I lay on my bed and read. Ruby started going out. Cerise didn't know. She thought Ruby was with me upstairs, neatly locked away.

Ruby started having adventures. There was a long stretch of uninterrupted time after lunch and that's when Ruby ran. She'd sneak down the front stairs when Cerise went out the back door to hang the laundry or weed the garden. Monday, Wednesday, Friday—laundry. Tuesday, Thursday—weeding. It never varied.

Ruby, being so tiny and light, made no noise on the stairs when she returned. That was hours later while the dinner pots clanged, Petula Clark sang, and the first martini glass sat empty in the sink.

Sometimes I would watch her go. My room faced the pond and I could see her sprint down the hill without looking back. She dipped into the hollow, running, just under the rim, like a rabbit. And then she'd disappear. Always taking a sudden right turn through the bushes in the direction of the cliffs.

Where'd you go, I asked. The cliffs? She shook her head.

These thongs hurt my feet, she said, trying to change the subject.

So stay home, I said.

I don't belong here, she replied, rubbing at a spot by her big toe where the thongs had made a scab. I've got better places to be.

Sometimes I thought I'd follow her but the thought of going through those bushes gave me the creeps. What if I couldn't find my way out? And the thought of getting caught. Ruby never cared about those sorts of things.

Cerise joined three clubs halfway through the summer. That cleared the way three days a week. Ruby could run out the front or back then. Or walk. No one was around to stop her except for me lying on my bed threatening to tell. Of course I never would, we both knew that. Be careful, I'd shout from the bedroom window. There was a carelessness in the way she crossed the road without looking.

*B*RIDGE. BAKING. BADMINTON. The three B's. For her badminton club she had to get in shape.

You've got a wonderful shape as far as I can see, Dad said, loosening his tie and tossing it on the couch. She picked the tie up and threw it back at him.

Well, before dinner we shall all go for a run around the pond, get your runners on.

We did as we were told. As I sat on the back steps tying mine I could hear Cerise complaining.

She lies on her bed all day, no wonder she's fat.

The words floated through the screen door. Dad mumbled something but Cerise talked right over whatever it was he was saying.

I don't have time to organize them, what do you think I am? A social convenor? A gym teacher?

There was silence. Perhaps Dad was concentrating on tying his shoes.

And I won't be a mother to a fat girl, she hissed.

CERISE RAN PAST all of us even though we had a head start. As she passed us she shouted, come on you Sandhouses. Lazy things, use your legs.

I could feel my middle dancing. In fact all of me snapped up and down under the looseness of my top.

My God, young lady, Cerise said, looking back at me, look at your breasts!

Ruby and I stared at the mounds that jumped just under my chin. It was one of those hot evenings where you could hear the bugs screaming. My legs rubbed together at the top. My heart pounded in my ears.

Ruby stayed with me, though she could have gone ahead. I cupped my hands under my breasts so they wouldn't move so much. Ruby said that made it look worse. I tried squeezing my arms in to stop them but that didn't help.

Just let them bounce, Ruby said, they're kind of cute.

The pond was a long way around and when we got back to

where we started Cerise was there doing push-ups, her cheeks a little pink, her brow a little damp.

Once again, she said, before we could catch our breath. She tugged at us until we got going at a running pace.

At the end of two Dad insisted that was enough. Cerise went around for one more, prancing like a well-bred horse, tossing her hair back when it fell forward. Dad stood with his arms crossed and legs wide apart and watched her all the way around.

She's nuts, Ruby said, kicking at a tuft of grass.

Now, now, he said, we should all be as fit and trim. He was looking at me out of the corner of his eyes.

Fit and trim, Ruby spat back at me later when we were upstairs. She pranced around my bedroom tossing her pretend hair back from her face and running her hands over her tiny body. I would never have thought to touch myself like that to describe Cerise, but Ruby did it perfectly.

HALFWAY THROUGH THE summer Cerise announced there would be a party. She was inviting the people from her clubs, she said, wiping the counters clean after dinner. Dad nodded, pushing himself back from the table and wiping his mouth free of cake crumbs. He opened his mouth to say something but changed his mind and shut it again. There was an underwater silence. What? I wanted to know. Say it! But whatever was going to come out of him got swallowed along with the mouthfuls of cake.

WE WERE TAKEN out shopping on a Wednesday afternoon. That meant no sneaking out for Ruby.

You'll have to look proper, Cerise said, I'll need you to serve.

Ruby suggested maids' outfits. There was silence in the car. Cerise looked at us through the mirror, squishing her lips together as if she had us in her mouth, chewed and ready to swallow. Ruby glared back. I watched the road skim by under the car and listened to Ruby's quick breathing. She kicked the underside of the empty front seat and whispered something I couldn't hear.

We stayed in the change rooms and tried on what was handed to us. Cerise ran back and forth. The sales girl chattered like a hen behind her. And a bra while we're at it, she shouted, so the whole world could hear. She threw boxes at me with half-naked women on the front.

Gawd, Ruby said, quite loudly, what's her problem.

But I had something there. We'd both seen it bouncing as we ran. In fact, I had a lot and wished I could chop it all off.

My dress was a light blue with black and brown stripes running from top to bottom.

Blue matches your eyes, brings them out, even through those glasses, Cerise said, not looking at me but at the pile of things that hadn't worked. But I heard the real reason she liked the dress as she was paying for it.

Stripes from top to bottom thin a person out, don't you think? She was tilting her head so the cashier would think she was harmless. The cashier laughed. Her eyes flickered over me and back to Cerise. They both nodded.

*T*HE DAY OF the party Ruby and I were held like prisoners in the kitchen. We polished the silverware and china and glass. Dad mowed the lawn, fixed the loose front door handle and bought more outdoor chairs. Cerise hoped the guests would mingle inside and out.

There'll be an interesting comet tonight, Dad said.

Cerise was pounding dough so it lay flat at the bottom of a bowl.

Don't talk about such things with them, they won't be interested in stars. I don't want all my guests standing around and looking up like ridiculous scientists.

But they are scientists, Ruby said. And wives of scientists, she added. Cerise had only invited the "rich people," the husbands who worked at the plant with Dad, and their wives. None of the "real people" as Ruby called them. The people that had lived here all along.

We put the cheeses on the cheese plates, trying not to breathe around the Limburger. We stacked raw meat chunks in pyramids. We tossed small squares of bread into baskets and stuck toothpicks through sausages.

Make sure no one goes hungry, Cerise lectured, her hands covered in flour and grease.

Keep passing the trays about and smile, keep smiling.

She had been going over these things all day.

Men eat more, keep the men fed, keep asking the men.

It was as if she were talking about animals, as if we were preparing for people who had just crossed the desert or climbed Mount Everest and were in danger of dying.

An hour before the guests arrived the flame was turned up under the fondues and Cerise disappeared upstairs to shower and change. Dad finished sorting the bottles of booze and rearranged the last of the glasses, the peanuts and chips. We sat, side by side, on the couch and reviewed the display. Ruby's brown dress was still ugly. Mine was tight around my chest. Even with a bra on it flattened out my puffy breasts so they looked like Cerise's punched-down bread dough.

Good scotch, Dad said, swirling his glass so the ice clinked.

Upstairs the shower ended. Small bottles of perfume and cosmetics made their own glassy sounds.

To the chin-ups, Dad said, raising his glass and bowing his head towards where the "rich people" would soon be standing.

Chin-ups? Ruby asked.

He looked into his empty glass.

You'll see, he said, looking unhappy.

EVERYONE ARRIVED AT once, coming through the front door and going straight to the drinks. We stood around with the sausages and cheeses, getting banged in the face with elbows and stepped on. No one said thank you or sorry or hello.

We are maids, Ruby hissed, her cheeks hot, her forehead sweaty.

Across the room Cerise swanned about in hot pink, busy talking and drinking. She laughed and rubbed up against people. She sat on someone's knee.

Gawd, Ruby rolled her eyes and blushed, let's get out of here.

No one was outside. All the chairs Dad had set up sat in a careful circle. Cerise had complained that no one would sit out there in a circle, because it looked too much like nursery school. She was right. Ruby and I moved them around, scattered them here and there across the lawn.

The sun was setting. We sat, a bowl of chips between us, on the grass where it started to dip downhill. We watched the water in the pond change colour with the sky.

Stupid thing, Ruby said, pointing her foot at the pond. Her cheeks were full of chewed chips.

Swallow, was all I said in return. She spat them out instead.

Don't talk Ruby, please.

I could tell she was upset. I could tell she was about to talk about Mum. I could feel her humming with it.

I'm too tired, I said, to even think.

Out past the pond and through the trees were the cliffs. I couldn't see them from where we sat but I felt them humming just like Ruby.

SHARE YOUR CHIPS?

The soft voice startled both of us.

I'm afraid I need a bit of a break from the hullabaloo, mind if I join you?

She lowered herself slowly, leaning on my shoulder, complaining about her knees, laughing about the effort it took to get herself down. Even in the dark I could tell she was fat. Her hand, on my shoulder, felt spongy. Her breathing was short. She wheezed.

I'm Marla, she said, reaching across me to get at the chips, and you must be Missy and Ruby.

I nodded. She ate like a cow, sloppily, her mouth partially open.

We're just up from Halifax for the weekend. Ben, my husband, is a friend of your Dad's.

I nodded again.

I'd never met your Mum before.

She's not our Mum, Ruby said.

There was silence for a moment.

Yes, Marla said, I suspected as much.

Ruby laughed an odd laugh that sounded more like a squeak. Marla covered her mouth with one of her hands.

Ooops, she said, perhaps not the proper thing to say.

Ruby took a chip and ate it. There was a definite smile on her face.

So, how old are you both?

Silence.

Let me guess, then, I love to guess. Ummm, twelve and eight?

I shook my head. No one ever gets Ruby's age right. They always think she's younger. Even though I couldn't see it in the dark I knew Ruby would be smirking.

Thirteen and eight?

I shook my head again. Ten, I said.

Ten and eight? Impossible!

Twelve and ten, I said, trying not to smile at her reaction.

She laughed. She hit the side of her fat leg with one hand. You win, she said. You'd make a lot of money at the circus, wouldn't you? At one of those age-guessing games.

I've stopped growing, Ruby said.

Marla stopped laughing; she sat still, turned her head and looked at Ruby.

I don't want to, Ruby said, staring back.

Don't want to grow?

Ruby nodded.

I have a son, Marla said, a few years older than you. He won't be growing up, he's dying. Be careful what you wish for.

We sat silent a long time after that listening to Marla breathe and swallow. I was afraid she might start to cry if I said anything. And I was afraid that if she started to cry I would too. Mostly, I was afraid that Ruby wouldn't, that she would stand up and walk away from us as if we were idiots.

So we just sat until the noise of cheering pulled Ruby and me back inside. Dad was on his way out as we were going in. He waved to Marla, she motioned for him to go and sit beside her.

What's going on? I asked. He didn't answer. He just moved aside so we could go in and see for ourselves.

CERISE DANGLED FROM the top of the kitchen door frame doing chin-ups. We could see the small white edges of her underpants and hear someone counting. Her arms bulged, her toes curled, but her face was smiling, her face was happier than I had ever seen it. She bit her lip and neon lipstick smudged across her teeth.

Thirty-five, someone shouted.

She stayed hanging.

Chips, she said.

Someone stood on a chair with a bowl of chips and held one out for her. She pushed her hips forward, swinging over to get it.

When she nodded her head a man grabbed her around her hips and lifted her down.

Well? she asked breathlessly, looking around at the crowd and pushing back hair from her face. She wore a sleeveless dress. We could see the perspiration glisten in her armpits.

Gawd, she's so naked, Ruby whispered.

It was true. I blushed for her.

Well? Cerise said again, this time like a teacher with her hands on her hips. No one took the challenge. Ruby said no one else wanted to look so stupid. Even so, the men had applauded.

THE REST OF that party Ruby, Dad, Marla and I sat on the back steps watching for the comet in the darkening sky. Occasionally someone came out to sniff the air but we were quiet and boring and no match for the excitement inside.

fifteen

ARE YOU AMERICAN? Auntie Margaret asked at the airport, reaching out to shake Cerise's hand. Ruby kicked me in the shin when Cerise, keeping her hands to herself, lowered her sunglasses and asked, no, why do you ask? There were creases around Cerise's mouth, like we'd seen a few weeks before, at the end of her party when she'd found us on the back steps. Oh, she had said, so this is where you're hiding. Was it too much for you?

We sit in the front room when we get back from the airport. Ruby and I with our knees together and hands on our laps, as Cerise has taught us. Auntie Margaret squints at us from across the room.

My, my, so grown up. Such young ladies, she says, shaking her head and smiling.

The mole by the side of her mouth twitches when she smiles. If you look at it up close you'll see two tiny hairs moving like alien antennae. Ruby used to love that mole. She would sit on Auntie Margaret's knee and stroke it as if it were the Queen's finest diamond. But now we sit too far away to see the hairs. We sit where Cerise put us, where we feel we're at the far end of a telescope and everything around us is tiny and far off.

Dad talks about the neighbourhood and his new job.

A fine opportunity, he says, his arm resting along Cerise's shoulders. A real step up.

Cerise, looking like a Popsicle in neon lime green, smiles in that way she does where her lips flatten out into a perfect straight line.

And a pond down the hill, Dad continues, and the ocean not far off. He points through the living-room window at the dark outside. We follow his finger, leaning forward and squinting. In the glass is the green glow of Cerise, the white of Dad's trousers and socks, the pale of Auntie Margaret's face but nothing of us in our browns and greys, sitting in the corner, too far off to make a reflection.

My! My! Auntie Margaret shrieks. What a wonderful life!

Her enthusiasm catches us all off guard. Ruby and I let our hands fly off our laps and our knees come unglued. Dad and Cerise, each holding a tiny glass of crème de menthe, jolt back into their seats. The brilliant green sprays across their clothes like tie-dye.

Not to worry, Dad says, as Cerise runs from the room, sprinting up the stairs and slamming her bedroom door. But he looks worried. He stands up, pulling his wet trousers from his legs, and produces an awkward smile.

Well, he says, I suppose this is goodnight.

*I*N THE MORNING we sneak into Auntie Margaret's room and get into her bed. You've grown, she says, giving each of us a poke.

Not me, Ruby says, I don't want to. Auntie Margaret looks at her like she's seeing her for the first time. Then she brushes a few hairs away from Ruby's eyes.

Yes, Auntie Margaret says, I think I can understand that.

Ruby leaps up and starts bouncing on the bed.

Why is your hair so short? she asks. Her arms are floating at her sides as she hovers in mid-air. Auntie Margaret's hair is short and cut in an odd way so that it won't stay flat on her head but sticks out here and there in tufts.

Well, Auntie Margaret replies, I forget to take care of it so the shorter it is the less noticeable the mess. I giggle but Ruby comes crashing down on her knees, all serious. The bed shakes as she comes to a full stop.

You forget? Ruby asks, running her hands over Auntie Margaret's hair as if it were breakable.

I don't like mirrors, Auntie Margaret says. Ruby continues to stroke her hair as if she were a child. I don't like what I see, Auntie Margaret says, pulling the blanket up over her head.

You don't like yourself? Ruby asks, trying to pull the blanket down. We can see her shaking her head under there.

It feels like one of those mixed-up moments when everything is turned around. When it should be the kids hiding under the blanket and the adult up above asking the questions.

Come out, I say to Auntie Margaret. Nothing happens. Auntie Margaret! I say, almost shouting. But she stays underneath.

And you don't look like Mum, do you? I thought you would. Ruby is staring at her almost accusingly. You're not as pretty, she continues, she likes to look in the mirror, doesn't she?

This makes Auntie Margaret laugh. She pulls the blanket off and lies back on the bed and can't stop laughing.

That's only the beginning, she says, only the very beginning. And before we can ask her what she means she's started a pillow fight.

*W*HEN CERISE APPEARS in the doorway I have a pillow over my head and I'm growling. Ruby has kicked the sheets off and is hopping around the bed.

Stop this foolishness, Cerise says, picking the stray sheets off the floor. Your Aunt's too old for all this. You're not babies.

Our heads snap around.

No, no, Auntie Margaret protests but Cerise has already walked over and is pulling us away.

Breakfast is waiting, she says, turning to Auntie Margaret, it's already cold.

*N*OVA SCOTIA! New Scotland! Dad sings after breakfast, standing at the front door and spreading his arms across the garden. A new life in a new land! Ruby scowls, she hates these little pep talks of Dad's.

There's not a flower in sight. All we stare at is the pond sitting in its hollow, still and grey as a puddle.

Are there fish? Auntie Margaret asks. She puckers her mouth so her lips form a perfect "o" and her cheeks hollow in. She gives us a wink. We try doing the same, our cheeks collapsed against our teeth and our lips sucking in and out.

We were all fish lips when Cerise came to the door, purse in hand, sunglasses on. We couldn't see her eyes but she was surely startled because her head jerked back and a strange oh! peeped from her lips.

Auntie Margaret, I say, seeing Cerise is not amused, come and see our rooms.

I TOOK THAT picture, Auntie Margaret tells Ruby and me when she sees the photo over Ruby's bed. Her voice trembles a little. Ruby's eyes widen with interest.

You were both so little. Look at you. I was down for a visit. It was just before you left for Canada. Ruby squints, hoping to see something she's never seen before.

Your mother hadn't been well that day. We could hardly get her out of the house, your Dad and I.

I feel dizzy when she speaks.

I think your Dad put the camera in my hands so I would have something to do, so we'd all look normal. A happy family having a happy day at the seaside.

Her voice is suddenly so far away. And Ruby beside me is starting to shrink.

It was a cold day but your mother insisted we sit there and have our lunch. Look, you can see the goosebumps. She looks closely and smiles. And Missy's broken arm. You had fallen, I think, on a walk. I nod, wanting her to stop. She's going to say too much and upset Ruby.

She looks fine to me, Ruby says, running her hand over Mum. She's just thinking, that's all. She's got a lot to think about.

sixteen

D O YOU MIND if Cerise and I go off for a few days? Dad asks one morning at breakfast. Auntie Margaret has been staring into her cup of coffee, watching the cream gather on the top.

Absolutely not, she said. How long? Where do you think you'll go?

Dad held up his hand and stopped her questions.

I'm not sure, to both those questions, he said, but we'll call when we get there.

They were gone that very evening. Dad hugged us, sweeping us off our feet and giving us a twirl.

You be good for Auntie Margaret, he said, tickling us under the chin.

Cerise waved from the car. She couldn't get away quick enough. Just put white gloves on her and she'd look like Jackie Onassis pulling out of the harbour on one of her yachts.

CORNFLAKES FOR SUPPER. Salmon sandwiches for breakfast, at least that's what I had the first day. Ruby ate toast and jam and stared a lot at her fingernails. Auntie Margaret made tea and put away all the fancy glasses that were for the fancy drinks.

A lot of nonsense, she called it. Your father has never been bothered with this before, she said. He's always been so sensible.

We spent most of our time traipsing back and forth to the mall for groceries. My, the sun is hot! Auntie Margaret would say every time we stepped outside. She'd open her umbrella and walk with it under the perfectly blue sky. Her mole, she said, was oversensitive to sun and her heart became swollen in the heat.

One evening, around dusk, coming through the mall parking lot licking ice cream, I whispered, I thought I saw a UFO here once. Auntie Margaret searched the sky.

There's something about this parking lot and the treelessness, something space-agey, that makes me believe you did, she said.

I felt thrilled that she believed me but scared, too. We laughed uneasy laughs, hearing our voices bouncing in the dark.

Ruby began making choking sounds, a sort of crying, and we stopped. I hate it here, she said. Perhaps I could go back with you, Auntie Margaret.

Auntie Margaret's closed umbrella swung on her arm. I could feel the day's heat, trapped in the asphalt, shimmering up my legs.

Don't be silly Ruby, what would Dad do without us?

Where's Mummy? Ruby lets her ice cream drop at her feet. Auntie Margaret doesn't move, doesn't even look to be breathing.

Where? Ruby demanded. You know, don't you? You're her sister, you should know.

Auntie Margaret shook her head and took a step back.

Is she even alive, then?

Auntie Margaret nodded, yes.

Does she have another family? Other children?

Auntie Margaret shook her head. No. And then she held up her hands.

Stop Ruby, it's not my place to talk to you about these things. Your father doesn't want it. He doesn't want you bothering with the past. A new life in a new land, that's what he says, that's what he wants for you both. Please, don't ask any more, I've promised not to say.

I could feel my heart and Ruby's beating the same beat, though mine was monstrously loud and Ruby's was so quiet it was hardly there.

Has she gone to Africa? I ask. The word "Africa" feeling secretive, something that shouldn't be spoken.

What? Auntie Margaret seemed to laugh. Africa?

I nod. To care for the starving children, I said.

Listen, Auntie Margaret said prodding the ground with the pointy end of her umbrella, your mother has only ever really thought about one person and that's herself. She didn't go to Africa, nothing as heroic as that.

You have to tell, Ruby hissed. You have to break your promise.

Auntie Margaret shook her head. She couldn't look at us. Please Ruby, I can't. Your father knows what's best, not me.

We could hear her breathing; it sounded urgent, animal-like. Her own heart was terrified, beating twice the speed of ours.

I thought you were on our side, Ruby shouted, her voice ringing across the empty parking lot. I thought you cared.

Auntie Margaret has nothing to say. She knows she's wrong. I can see it in her crumpled mouth, in the way her cheeks have hollowed.

I hate you, Ruby screams. Her eyes dagger in the dark.

Don't Ruby, I say, and as I say it I feel our heartbeats scatter

across the asphalt and spin out into the night becoming as cold
and distant as the stars. And all that's left is the bang, bang, bang
of my own heart gnawing away at my chest.

I WAS WRONG, Auntie Margaret said the next morning at breakfast, to promise what I did to your father. She held her hands in
her lap and stared at her empty bowl.

I'm sorry, but I have promised and that's all there is to it.

And then she reached into her pocket, bringing out a small
pocket-sized version of the New Testament.

This was your mother's, she said, you can have it now. She
placed it on the table between us.

It had a ripped leather cover and shiny red-gold paper edges.
We took turns opening it, turning it over and over in our hands,
rubbing the thin paper between our fingers. Ruby held it to her
nose and gave it a sniff.

Inside were handwritten words, pencilled in on the front
page in tiny adult writing. "Actions are what we believe." They
were Mum's words. And in faded blue ink it said: "Gillian Hurst.
Given me before going to France 1952." Dotted here and there,
again in tiny pencil writing, were the names of people and the
dates of their death. Churchill, it said, 1965. He was the only one
I'd heard of.

Where'd you get it? Ruby asked. She looked small and delicate.

She left it with me when you went to Canada, the day you
left, actually, Auntie Margaret said. She said she'd lost her faith,
lost everything, when she was made to leave. She wanted me to
hold on to it. "Guard my faith," those were her words. Well, you
can have it now.

Auntie Margaret ran a finger around the lip of her empty
cereal bowl.

What was she doing in France? I asked. Auntie Margaret shook her head as if she were about to say she couldn't answer me, but she did.

Art school, she said, but it didn't last long. She hated France. She hates leaving England, really. It sets her off. She was back in less than a month, moved back in with Mum and Dad, set herself up in her old room with her easel and paints. That's where your Dad found her. He'd always lived next door, but he'd been away at university. When he came home that spring he came to call. Mum pushed Gillian out the front door, literally. Forced her off for a walk with him. I remember Mum actually placing a hat on Gillian's head, wrapping a scarf round her neck and giving her a shove through the door towards your waiting father. But she married him, didn't she? It was her and no one else that said yes at the altar. Never mind. She's a puzzle, your Mum, she's her own person, unpredictable.

Ruby and I sat stunned. Ruby took the Bible, put it in her pocket and closed her eyes. Auntie Margaret looked at Ruby, nervously.

There, there, she said, I've said enough, more than enough.

Nothing more was said. Breakfast stretched on without words. Each of my swallows bringing a glare from Ruby. Each of Ruby's kicks on her chair leg bringing a flinch from Auntie Margaret. The heartbeats were gone. I couldn't tell what theirs were doing; my own heart felt lodged in my head, swelling there and threatening to burst.

In the end I spoke first, saying, shall we go shopping for dolls?

Ruby perked up. She said she needed a new one because hers had lost its hair. And I forgot I'd outgrown them. At least Cerise said I should have when she gave mine away to someone less fortunate during her spring cleaning.

*T*HERE WAS NOTHING at the mall.

Crowells Department Store, a shop clerk said, you'll have to catch the bus into town. He told us how to get there. I wrote it all down and we caught a bus across the street.

I sat beside Auntie Margaret swinging my legs, watching each building as it whizzed by. Ruby sat across from us, eyes closed. Her fingers and toes looked unreal, like porcelain, or something liquid and see-through. It scared me when she looked that way, like she had no blood. And she sat so still. I watched her chest to try to see her breathing, but all that moved were her eyes under her eyelids.

*W*E FOUND THE perfect dolls. I chose one with curly light brown hair and eyes that closed. Ruby's was different. Straight dark hair; a strange doll with a weird look. It was called Sarah. Mine I called Adrian.

But it's a girl, Ruby said. She was holding hers by the hair and swinging it. No, it's a boy. I don't want a girl, I said.

Adrienne can also be a girl's name, Auntie Margaret whispered to Ruby. I pretended I didn't hear.

Why don't you buy yourself something? I asked, holding Adrian over my shoulder and burping him.

Buy me something, surprise me, she said, handing us her change purse.

*A*UNTIE MARGARET WAS wandering through the furniture department, running her hands over chesterfields and chairs, when we brought her the present. It was wrapped in pink tissue paper and sat in a pale blue box.

Oh my, she wailed when she opened it. She truly wailed. So

loud I thought she might be crying. Are you all right? I asked, getting her to sit down on a nearby chesterfield.

No one has ever given me such a perfect present, she said.

It was just a fish, made of blown glass of all colours. And inside it there was nothing.

Glorious, she said, over and over again. She held it in her hands all the way home, stroking it. So comforting in this never-ending heat, she said, more than once.

Aᴛ ᴅɪɴɴᴇʀ ᴛʜᴇ six of us, I'm including Sarah, Adrian and the fish, sat on a blanket at the edge of the pond. I fed Adrian. Sarah starved. Ruby didn't consider food. We ate sandwiches: cucumber, peanut butter and salmon. And Sarah stared her mad looks over all of it, including the raspberry Kool-Aid and the marshmallow and jam biscuits.

Sarah had the tidiest and then the messiest hair. Ruby spent her time dragging her around by the hair and then brushing it whenever they settled. During supper Ruby mostly brushed and hardly ate. She kept her eyes away from us, staring into Sarah's eyes, or far off towards the cliffs. At least she was sitting with us; I was glad for that.

Once the salmon sandwiches were finished I lay on my back with Adrian in my arms. I enjoyed having a doll again.

It hasn't rained much this summer, I said, deciding not to mention Cerise not wanting me to have a doll.

The darkening sky spread out above us.

These are huge skies here, I said. When you lie like this it feels like that's all there is, sky.

Auntie Margaret agreed.

I felt dreamy, my eyes wanted to close.

Ruby had Sarah on her back and was brushing out her hair

so it lay on the blanket above her head.

Sometimes with the stars, when it's dark, I get scared. Sometimes I think I might disappear, she says. Her voice is curious, not scared-sounding at all.

Auntie Margaret gives a little hiccup of a laugh. The fish, in the middle of the blanket, shimmers. Auntie Margaret's hand lies beside it. Fish loves the sky, Fish might never come back if I let her go, Auntie Margaret says, sounding dreamy, sounding more like Ruby than an adult.

Shall I tell you about my fish dreams, before we go in? We nod, yes, in the darkness. Ruby stops combing and reaches over to stroke the fish.

All my dreams are underwater, she says, it's the strangest thing. I am always swimming in my dreams. Swimming through a thick jelly liquid and without fins. Imagine! And my body is a sort of translucent jelly too, like Fish here. Isn't it amazing that you bought her for me?

Auntie Margaret's face is as smooth as a baby's, her lips move like kisses across it. Fish lips, the way a fish comes up to the glass of an aquarium, its little lips puckering so delicately.

All I do is swim through this unformed world. Sometimes the jelly liquid is thicker, sometimes thinner. And as I move, snaking my body along, nudging through this world headfirst, I feel a sort of ecstasy, a sort of joy and I have this feeling when I wake up that I have seen mysterious things but I can never remember what. I could cry for the beauty of it.

Ruby is staring up at the sky, a smile on her face. When you have ecstasy are you floating? Do you think you're in the stars? Auntie Margaret's eyes pop open. Yes! she says, absolutely! They are both silent, both with their faces turned upwards and all I know is that I'm getting cold. I can feel a chill coming off the pond, a sort of fog crawling along my legs.

I've been there then, in ecstasy, Ruby says. With Mum. I didn't know it had a name.

*T*HE FOLLOWING DAY, around suppertime, Dad, Cerise and Rand arrived. He was a small, pouting boy. We were having sandwiches again, this time on the front lawn and when they pulled up none of us moved. We sat there, continuing to chew and watched them wave at us and then slowly step from the car.

Who are you? Ruby asked the little boy. He kicked at stones on the driveway and they skidded towards us.

Don't, I said, that's rude. I hugged Adrian, protecting him from danger. Ruby stood up, with Sarah by the hair, and spat.

Ruby! Cerise leaped forward and Rand grabbed her around the legs.

Girls, she said, this is my son Rand.

seventeen

RAND LIKES THE Beatles.

He puts on his best pants and tie, and pushes the couch out from the wall. Cerise moves the record player so he can reach it from there. He plays the same record over and over, it's the only one we have. Dancing behind the couch, his good shoes whisper over the parquet floor as he twists and slides. His little hands are clamped into fists and his crewcut shows a small dent on the side of his head. We don't know how it got there but Ruby says it's affected his personality for sure. When he dances he stares at the wall, perhaps at the tiny circle and cross Ruby drew there once, when she was trying to curse Cerise.

BEFORE AUNTIE MARGARET left to go back to England she tried making friends with Rand. She tried going behind the couch to dance with him.

Bad idea, Ruby whispered to me as we watched. It was. First Rand's face went purple, all except the dent which stayed white and looked like a quarter moon in the setting sun. Auntie Margaret didn't notice, she had her eyes closed and her arms spread out. She moved her body in a snaky way. Her arms moved up above her head, and then they swam down and stayed flat to her body. She smiled a twisty little smile and her head nudged about like she was a dog looking for a scratch or a pat on the head.

Fish, Ruby whispered, watching seriously. I wanted to laugh but it was true, she moved like a fish.

Ecstasy, Ruby said, giving me a nudge and sounding like an expert.

Auntie Margaret's sock feet squirmed like fins along the floor until Rand took one of the heels of his best shoes and jammed it into her toes.

Uh-oh, Ruby said, quite loudly, when Auntie Margaret's eyes flew open with surprise. Nothing happened for a second or two and everything was perfectly silent until Auntie Margaret began to cry.

We'd never heard an adult cry. It sounded just like Ruby. A sort of siren wail, the sound of emergency, it went low then high, low then high and the whole time her eyes stayed wide open and her mouth too. Like a caught fish.

I ran over to drag her away before Rand did it again. I wanted to get him back, to hit him or stamp on his feet, but Cerise had already come running in and was scooping him up as if it were him that was hurt.

THEY DIDN'T COME to the airport to say goodbye, Rand and Cerise. Ruby had cried, grabbing onto Auntie Margaret and begging to go with her until Dad peeled her off. We waved to her as she hobbled out of sight. It felt like she was going forever.

IF RAND CATCHES us watching him dance he screams. He screams as if we're torturing him, as if I have him pinned to the ground and Ruby is jumping up and down on his head. Cerise comes running from the kitchen, steamy and pink, wooden spoon dripping something gooey. Ruby and I stand by the window with our hands behind our backs and our mouths open. Rand is nuts, screaming with his eyes squeezed shut and pointing at nothing, as if he's seen a ghost.

Spaz, Ruby mouths to me, her mouth stretching over her face like one of those talking puppets.

There is nothing Cerise can do but pick him up, the wooden spoon resting along the back of his best pants and oozing its way down to his shoes. This is revenge enough, he'll have a fit when he sees it. He hates dirt. He hates anything messy and out of order.

Leave him alone, Cerise says, he's having a hard time. I shrug. Ruby doesn't move but I suspect she's projecting another hex, something deadly, for the two of them.

Luckily we are at school most of the day so we can avoid him. He should be in school too but he won't stop crying. Cerise had to take him out the first day, kicking and biting, past my class where everyone watched, out through the front doors and home again. So far, he hasn't gone back. At home the fridge door is full of his drawings. At supper he counts the peas on his plate. In the car he points out letters on signs. He's smart enough, Cerise says, I'll teach him at home.

He holds on to her leg as if he were permanently glued and she walks around the house like Long John Silver acting as if it were normal. Dad says he's traumatized. He says he'll come out of his shell when he's ready.

Gawd, Ruby says, when Rand has been obnoxious, just wait till he's out of his shell!

ONE SATURDAY MORNING Cerise manages to unglue Rand from her leg and go grocery shopping alone. She slips out the front door with her coat undone and her shoelaces whipping around her ankles as she dashes to the car.

Rand was at the kitchen table finishing his French toast when he heard the door click shut. Dad was in the backyard raking leaves. I could see him from the kitchen window, stopping every so often to look up at the sky, or off into the distance at the cliffs.

At the sound of the click Rand throws his spoon down, pushes his chair aside and heads for the stairs leading down to the front door. Out of the corner of my eye I catch Ruby's leg disappearing inside the hall closet. Rand's dancing shoes have no grips and the stairs have no treads. Down he goes, landing at the bottom in a silent pile. I am amazed at the silence and at the pile he makes. It doesn't occur to me that he might be dead until Ruby reaches out from the closet not far from where he lies and grabs at his clothing. Still he doesn't move. She starts hauling him towards her and he lets her. She pulls him right into the closet and closes the door. Outside the car is coughing as it makes its way out of the driveway and down the road to the mall.

I know he's not dead when I hear kicking at the door. One of Rand's shiny dancing feet appears then disappears back inside. There's a bit of scuffling and a rumbling of voices and then it all quiets to whispers. I creep down the stairs to listen in.

Neither of us has had a conversation with him before but it seems Ruby's got the right idea, talking to him in the dark.

Look, she's saying, you've got another dent on your head. On the other side. Move your opposite arm, go on. Move it, I said. There. See. You're fine. That part of your brain moves the other side of your body.

I guess she has a flashlight in there.

Sometimes mums don't come back, you know. Ruby whispers.

There's a little gasp from Rand.

Don't be such a baby, Ruby says. Do you see me running around crying, ever? No. Do you see me grabbing on to my mother's leg? No. Even if she was here I wouldn't do it. Grabbing on like that scares them off, you know. That's why yours just ran away.

There's a struggle inside. One of the doors starts to shake but I'm on the other side blocking it from opening.

Ouch, Rand says. It's his first word in the closet. Don't pinch.

Cold air sneaks under the front door and creeps towards me.

Shhh, Ruby says, be quiet and I'll make a magic spell to get your mother back.

I listen for a while to the sounds of their breathing.

Are you making the spell? Rand asks.

A whole sentence! No answer.

Ruby! Are you?

Shhh, Ruby hisses. Rand pushes at the door again but I'm in the way.

Perhaps I'll make a spell to keep her away, Ruby says. See what I'm drawing here? See this circle? I'm putting this cross inside it here. It keeps away evil. That's your mother, she's a witch.

There is wild banging inside the closet. Don't kick you stupid baby, Ruby says.

The door digs into my shoulder. It trembles with their struggles.

Ouch, I hear. Stop it.

Dad is whistling near the back door. There is the scrape of the rake against the concrete steps.

She's already left you once, Ruby hisses.

I can feel my face getting hot as Rand starts to cry.

Okay, okay, Ruby says, forgetting to whisper. I'll erase it.

Look. There. Silence in the dark in there as Ruby rubs it out.

It's not fair, though. You getting your mother back.

There's a quiver in her words. I can picture her lip trembling and her eyes disappearing up under her eyelids. I can hear Dad coming up the back steps, kicking his feet against the house to get the leaves off. The whistling is loud like a warning.

I run. Up the stairs to the couch where I grab a book and look like I'm reading. Rand isn't long behind me. I can hear his dancing shoes tap and slide up each step quick and crisp. He flings me a nasty glare before he starts to scream. And just as the first sounds escape Dad arrives pushing his hair off his face, his cheeks pink from the fresh air, his face shifting about in surprise.

Hey, hey. What have we here? he says, starting to bend down to try to catch Rand's eye. He reaches out to touch Rand's almost bald head. He does have another dent, perfectly matching, on the other side, flared in reds.

Rand doesn't speak but continues to howl, slapping Dad's hand away, kicking at his knees so furiously that Dad has to jump up and back as if away from a wild animal. Rand lunges at a lamp. Dad manages to catch it. He flips the dining-room chairs. Dad lets him. And then he heads for the kitchen. One plate shatters before Dad grabs him, lifts him up and plasters his arms to his sides. His legs carry on. No one can do anything about them and as they fling about Dad squints with pain.

Ruby watches from the doorway looking at Rand like he's from Mars.

I think your Mum's here, she says.

There's a car coming up the driveway. Rand goes perfectly still as if he were playing Statues and Dad puts him down.

Careful on the stairs, he calls after Rand, but it's too late. There's the same banging and clattering as before and when Cerise opens the front door there's Rand in a heap at her feet.

MY BIRTHDAY WAS a week later. At breakfast I opened my present, a transistor radio, bright green, small enough to fit in my hand.

Thank you, I said. Dad beamed.

Cerise chose it. He gave me a look that said wasn't she special.

Thank you, I said again, turning to face Cerise. But it's just her small, flat back working at the kitchen sink that greets me.

Across the table Rand glared, his little head barely visible above his plate of pancakes. And Ruby looked bored, slicing her food into tiny squares and piling them into a tower.

Happy Birthday, Dad said, not seeming to notice the flatness in the room, a coolness and a quiet that had nothing to do with happy.

You girls, Cerise said, her voice bouncing off the dishes and into the awful stillness, must change your attitude about a few things.

Ruby shoved the tower with the back of her hand, it fell over in one sticky clump.

Rand tells me you trapped him in the hall closet, hit him on the the head, told him lies.

Ruby's eyes were beginning to roll. Dad was placing his fingers together, tip to tip, as if they needed exercise.

Les, Cerise said, turning around to face Dad. He was watching his fingers touch. Les, she said again, this time louder.

Yes, he said, finally.

Cerise was drying her hands against her apron, front to back, front to back, like sharpening a knife.

You haven't tried to help Rand feel at home, he says. We'd like you to try harder.

Ruby was mouthing something at me from across the table. I stared at her long and hard. "Happy Birthday," her lips said. Her jaws were clenched like fists around the silent words.

The butter was forming a hard cool layer over my pancakes. For once I wasn't hungry.

Why do you do these things? Cerise asks.

Behind her, outside the kitchen window, a neighbour has climbed a ladder. He's reaching into the eavestroughs with his gloved hands and is pulling and pushing at the piles of leaves trapped inside. They come out in wet clumps and fall past him to the ground.

I guess we're jealous, I hear myself say. It feels disconnected from everything.

Ruby shoves her plate towards me. It slides across the table banging my green transistor radio.

I am not, she shouts. I've got a mother of my own. Who needs you.

She looks at me accusingly. Dad's fingers are white with pressure and Cerise's face is a cool, porcelain blue. Rand tips back on his chair with a satisfied smile, chewing ever so slowly on the last bite of his pancake.

THE REST OF my birthday I stayed in my room, lying on my bed with the transistor radio hidden under my pillow. Flicking channels, I hear music I've never heard before. With my eyes closed I listen carefully to every song, stunned by the beauty of the words. Jumping from channel to channel feels like sailing through the night sky. I am light-headed and empty.

Happy Birthday, Dad called through the closed door as he went to bed. The sound of his voice is far off and, without the sight of his face, I can believe he doesn't exist at all. I can believe that none of them do.

eighteen

ONE SATURDAY MORNING Dad and Ruby took off, before the rest of us were out of our pyjamas. Cerise said what about the groceries. Dad said the groceries could wait. There was a long look between them. The sky, full of grey, pressed down on us as we stood shivering on the front steps to wave them off. There was all this space between Dad in the car and Cerise on the front steps. It looked like the earth had split open and pulled them apart.

Ruby is going to hatch chicks for the science fair. She's taken bird books out of the library. She's made calls to farmers to find eggs she can hatch. She's drawn diagrams of wood frames with Plexiglas sides and light bulbs for heat.

Incubator for my babies, she said, running her tongue along her lips slowly, in concentration, as she made her plans and drew her lines.

Ruby looked funny sitting in the front seat, serious and proud. She put her change purse on the dashboard and held a shoebox on her lap. It was full of soft cottony things that would keep the eggs warm. I waved as they pulled away. One corner of Ruby's mouth turned up just enough to show me she was pleased. She looked like a princess then, someone distant and sombre and sure of where she was going.

AN HOUR LATER, Ruby dashed from the car curling her body around the shoebox like she had stomach flu. I held the door open, then followed her down the basement stairs two at a time.

Shhh, she said, opening the lid and placing the shoebox under the lights. She closed the Plexiglas door and waited.

I hope it's warm enough, was all she said.

We sat on the cold cement floor, putting our hands under our bums because of the chill and waited.

Ruby was wearing Dad's watch which she kept on by holding her arm up like she was wanting to answer a question. She looked at it constantly. Dad popped his head in.

It'll be a long time yet, he said, and then disappeared. Ruby rolled her eyes. Idiot, she said, what does he know?

We heard Cerise and Rand come in from shopping. We heard her high heels and his sock feet and the rumble of voices. But nothing was real to us, sitting so far below. The furnace clicking on and off. The chairs in the corner with missing legs looked like old people hidden away. The packing boxes piled along one wall up to the ceiling looking anxious to go.

I'll take care of you little ones, Ruby whispered, rubbing the Plexiglas with just one finger.

The light at the small windows greyed and blurred, and when Dad said time for dinner I was still in my pyjamas. Ruby could stay with her eggs, Dad said, but I had to eat upstairs.

After dinner I went back downstairs. Ruby was lying on the basement floor with a pillow over her tummy.

An experiment, she said when I asked. She had an egg on her tummy, right against her skin, with the pillow keeping the heat in.

You'll get pecked when it hatches, I said, but she didn't care.

We had just studied about Gandhi in history and that's who Ruby reminded me of. She refused to move when it was bedtime and lay on the cold floor, perfectly still, like she was lying on a bed of nails. There was a darkness in her eyes, pure points of black, and when I said goodnight she looked past me as if there were someone behind me who held her attention. If there was something she wanted bad enough, I thought, she would hold on forever.

She was still there in the morning, a blanket over her, the pillow puffing her belly out so she looked pregnant. She hadn't slept. In case she rolled over in her sleep, she said. And in case the others hatched first.

Nothing had hatched.

Sunday moved like we were under water. The windows were washed through with a grey rain all day. I brought an electric heater down and got it as close to Ruby as I could. And my transistor radio. But Ruby wouldn't allow it. She wanted silence, she said, the way it was supposed to be.

There was nothing much but the ordinary house sounds until Ruby whispered. It moved!

Her eyes shifted back and forth under the surface of her lids as if she were scanning for something.

Missy, check the others.

Nothing. We waited. The house carried on above us like another planet. The phone rang. Rand's quick footsteps moved towards it. The smell of dinner cooking. The hum of the mixer. A knife chopping.

The egg on Ruby's tummy moved again and then again. She stuck her hand under the pillow.

Take notes, Missy, she said. Say four oh-five, first movement. Four twenty-five, second, third and fourth. She thought for a while, her hands still under the pillow. Feels like a crack. Four twenty-seven, first crack. Nothing was happening in the incubator.

When the chick was born she pinched the soft skin of Ruby's

belly and made her laugh. I lifted the pillow off slowly and helped Ruby sit up. The small chick in her hands reached with its beak.

Oh Gawd, Ruby cried, worms!

I searched in the dark for worms. I dug in the flower beds with the rain running down my back and the wind pushing up my coat. Two worms were all I could find. Ruby was in her bed with the chick asleep in her armpit.

Wave it by its face, she said. I'm sure it's starving. But it wouldn't wake.

We made a home for the worms, because they had to be fresh, putting dirt in a bowl with a lid on it. Ruby lay in bed singing softly. Her voice was high and quivery, making every molecule shake in the air. The chick slept with her head tucked under her wing, shivering occasionally as if she were dreaming.

You'll have to name her, I whispered, sitting on the end of the bed and picking at the dirt under my nails.

How about Raindrop because of the weather? Ruby shook her head.

After someone strong and famous then, I suggested.

We let the ideas float silently in the dark room.

Gandhi, I said. He was strong. He stood up for what he believed in by refusing to move. That's who you reminded me of last night. Ruby smiled and then laughed.

I like that, she said, I really do.

Gandhi slept with Ruby and after everyone had gone to sleep I snuck into the basement with my blankets to be with the other eggs. Dad and Cerise had said no sleeping in the basement because it was a school night, but Ruby went nuts about them being alone, so I did it.

They sat under the bright lights like movie stars, their white china shells perfectly still. I looked for cracks and any signs of movement but there were none. I had Dad's watch and a paper and pen. "Twelve A.M.," I wrote, "nothing." I wondered how Ruby had lasted the night before. I drifted in and out of sleep, waking often to the spooky glare of the incubator. It looked like a space-ship in an empty field, the eggs a strange kind of Martian.

GANDHI ATE BOTH worms during the night and by morning was cheeping for more.

You get them this time, I'm frozen from sleeping on that floor, I said to Ruby. She held Gandhi like she was afraid she would explode.

She's just hungry, I said. That's good, that's healthy.

Ruby wasn't convinced. She dressed quickly, forgetting I was there.

I couldn't remember the last time I had seen her without clothes. She was tiny, like a porcelain doll. Even her skin looked unreal. It shined as if it had just been polished.

Gandhi ate all three worms, which were all Ruby could find. Still, she was desperate for more. I tried. Six A.M. with a flashlight in the drizzle. I found one more. All the flower beds turned under and even some grass. Cerise would go nuts when she looked out the kitchen window.

We'll have to buy some, I said, dropping the last one into her mouth.

Gandhi went to school hungry. Dad drove us, along with the incubator and unhatched eggs, and then went to buy worms. No one could get any work done in Ruby's class because of Gandhi's screaming so they were sent outside to dig for worms. I could see them from my desk, bent over, shivering. They found a few, but because of the cold, worm season was mostly over.

Dad didn't find any either. We tried hamburger meat but

Gandhi ignored it. We tried grass, lettuce, apple, nuts. Rand thought maybe spaghetti because it looked like worms. Gandhi refused.

She's dying, Ruby said, which I told her was ridiculous. If she had a Mum she would live, she continued, holding poor Gandhi tight in both hands. She'd know what to do.

The next day she carried Gandhi to school, tucked next to her skin and wrapped in a towel. She smashed the unhatched eggs against a toilet seat and flushed them. Above the toilet, on the wall, she drew a cross, scratched in pencil over the bumps of concrete, pushed in so hard it was black. Around it she drew an egg. Looking at it was like biting down on a stone found inside something soft. It made your teeth turn on their edges.

Ruby kept Gandhi next to her body all that day and by evening she was dead. Her little body covered in fuzz, not even old enough to have feathers.

*I*T'S MY FAULT, Ruby said, at the funeral, for being so stupid and selfish.

Leaves blew into the hole we'd dug. The maple leaves each carried a black spot. Ruby said it was a sign for sure, God's way of saying we'd gone against nature.

It's not natural, she said, kicking dirt at the hole, to try to live without a mother. Ruby clenched her jaws. And I felt myself float away over the housetops where I could see across everything.

Nothing looked familiar. The trees like black pencil lines without their leaves. The rooftops flat and colourless. Ruby's shoulders were bent forward, compressed towards the ground. She became smaller and smaller as I lifted through the clouds, looking like she had flattened herself out into Gandhi's grave, to be buried too.

Missy, what about the Mummy Stone?

She was stroking the earth, picking away anything sharp or hard and rounding out the hole so it looked like cupped hands.

We could bury it with her, she said looking up at me.

At first I didn't understand.

The Mummy Stone, that one we found, you know. She gave me a fierce look.

No, I said, before I knew what I was saying, before I might change my mind and let Ruby's sad face get to me.

Please, she said, so she won't be alone.

I don't know why, it was only a stone, just a thing I kept on my dresser but I couldn't say yes. I just couldn't.

I need it, I heard myself say. I heard it far off, as if in a tunnel, as if someone else spoke it.

Gandhi disappeared, all alone, under a few spadefuls of dirt. We marked her spot with a heart-shaped stone that Ruby had saved from that same time we found the Mummy Stone. When I touched it I could still feel the heat of that sunset and the redness of it, as we had squatted in front of the house, waiting.

Ruby pulled the New Testament Auntie Margaret had given us out from her coat pocket and flipped through the small, thin pages.

"And the rain descended," she began, her voice quivering, her tiny pink translucent finger tracing a line under each word.

". . . and the floods came, and the winds blew, and beat upon that house; and it fell . . ."

I didn't stay for the rest. I ran into the house letting the screen door speak out behind me, a nasty metallic snap into the frozen air.

IT WAS A CURSE. Ruby's voice had been sour. I could feel my mouth pucker up with its bitterness. I ran to my room as if being chased, as if I could get away from the words. And I lay on my bed feeling like a frog turned inside out, heart beating fast and wild on the surface of my skin.

nineteen

JESUS WAS A carpenter and Ruby says that's good enough for her. Good enough reason to be working with wood. Leftover scraps of Plexiglas and wood, from the incubator, are being turned into altars. Strange ones. Barbie dressed in a white robe stuffed inside a little wood box with a Plexiglas front. That alone would be bad enough. But that's not all. She painted eyes all over the inside of the box, she wrapped a snakeskin around her feet, she glued flower petals to her eyes.

Why? I ask.

None of your business, she says.

She hides them under her bed when they're done.

In another altar there's a pile of stones and on top of the stones sits a candy heart. The inside of that box is painted gold. The redness of the heart, that's what you notice most in that one.

Another Barbie, in a black box wearing a miniskirt. Around her neck a rope. She's dangling from the rope. Her mouth is tied up. She's blindfolded.

I'm not stupid, I tell her, I can see who that is and it's sick.

Tough, she says. She makes a knife-cutting motion across her neck, drops her tongue from her mouth and then laughs.

twenty

OUR SECOND Nova Scotia summer with Cerise was the hottest anyone could remember. They spoke about it in the lineups at the Sobeys, wafting their shopping lists back and forth across their faces and throats, trying to cool off. They talked about it over the fences in the backyards while hanging up the wash. The sea wind snapping at the clothes and conversation both. The neighbourhood women were in curlers, faces with no distinct shapes, no lipstick, eyeliner or blush. Not Cerise. She never steps out of her room without war paint, Ruby observes. Cerise, glowing like a neon sign, thought the neighbours were ignorant, she thought they didn't speak right.

What she really means, Ruby says, dabbing a dot of Cerise's lipstick on her cheeks and rubbing it in, is that they're stupid because they aren't rich.

We whisper in the bathroom where it's private and we can lock ourselves in.

The wind never stopped its wailing off the ocean that summer. It flung dust off the dry roads, into our noses, and along the floors of our house where Cerise chased it, wicked with her broom. And when she wasn't chasing dust she was chasing us. She waited to catch us in the bathroom more than the allowed few minutes.

No need to lock the door, she'd say. But we did anyway.

And there was her hovering in the hall outside our bedroom door hoping to hear us saying things. We could hear her shifting on the floorboards.

You'd think the sourness would sweeten at least once in a while, Ruby said, referring to Cerise's mouth which had recently begun to gather in a permanent pucker. She knew Cerise was there, spying.

I could feel the summer snap. I could feel an electric hum and then a rush of heat as it split open like the naked insides of fruit. Cerise appeared in the doorway, her puckered mouth dropped at the edges. I waited for her to explode. I waited to see her cracked open like a watermelon rocking on its rounded back, fleshy red like brains. But there were only words.

One day, young lady, Cerise began, lighting a cigarette without taking her eyes off Ruby, you'll learn that there's not much in this life to be happy about.

Her cat eyes pin on Ruby until Ruby lifts her hands in front of her face, palms out, as if a slap were coming.

SHE CURSED ME, Ruby said that night as we lay awake in the dark. She was fascinated by the idea. Her mouth seemed to linger on the words like she was licking at the icing on a chocolate cake.

I woke up in the middle of that night to see Ruby kneeling on the floor beside her bed, a small flashlight in one of her hands and in the other an altar. I pretended to be asleep. She looked so private, so perfectly peaceful. She had removed the Plexiglas front from one of the boxes and was snipping at something with scissors. It sounded like hair. And then she was drawing on something with a marker. I could smell its chemical smell and hear it squeaking.

When she had finished she replaced the Plexiglas and put the altar on her bed and began to pray on her knees, on the floor. A slight breeze came through the window and the sound of insects calling and leaves moving. Please, I heard her whisper.

$\mathcal{T}$HOU SHALT NOT lock the bathroom door and stay in there too long. Sooner or later she is out there, the knob struggling, her sharp knuckles knocking on the dark wood.

Open up, she shouts.

But I have another pimple to squeeze and a blackhead by the base of my nostril and then three washes with hot water and one with cool to calm the flared red spots where I have been working.

Get out of there, she yells, taking her fist to the door. Go get your sister out of her bed. Get some fresh air.

A dusky light presses through the bathroom window. The trees are bursting with their brilliant greens, bowing and bending in the wind. There is a small square of sea visible from the window. Whitecaps skid its dark surface and hit the cliffs.

Don't go near them, she commands, when I mention them.

They crumble at the edges, at least that's what she says, and their sandy-red soil will give way and heave you into the waves. Her back is turned to me as she talks, beating butter and brown sugar together until they cream.

She has more commandments than you can imagine. No jeans to school, that's another. She spends the summer sewing pink polyester pantsuits on her old Singer that sometimes screws up and gags out a pink bunch in a visible place.

Her outfits will be the wonder of the school, Ruby says

sarcastically, they'll be brilliant among the faded denims and T-shirts.

We try to laugh. The pale green hallways will be dangerous places to be seen. I imagine spending my free time in the washroom, sitting on the toilet reading, or when no one is around, at the mirror squeezing pimples.

CERISE SAYS IF she has to look at that puddle down the hill one more time she's going to die. She hates the whole place, in fact. No real mountains, she says. She claims the Pacific doesn't smell like the Atlantic.

Why not Vancouver? she asks, her back to us as she cuts the Sunday roast. We sit silent and stunned, watching the sinews in her neck work as she digs the carving knife into the meat.

Not like the West Coast. Even the children are not the same out here, she says. That includes Ruby and me with our strange names and ugly looks. Ruby says it's all movie stars on the West Coast. She says we'll never live up to them so why even try.

PLEASE, RUBY SAYS, please, please, please. She gets down on her knees in our room and prays for it to happen. The three altars before her seem to listen carefully. I take a close look at them to see what she was doing the other night. The Barbie in the black box, the one that's supposed to be Cerise, has had her hair chopped off here and there and her lips are black. Black and sour, jagged and down-turned.

Please, please, please, Ruby is whispering, hands clasped together in prayer. She's rocking back and forth as if she were rocking a baby.

What? I ask.

That she'll die from looking at the pond like she said, she says, continuing to rock, keeping her hands together. Or that she'll die from anything, I don't care.

I tell her nothing good ever comes from wishing someone dead.

You don't know anything, she hisses back at me. You put up with too much, like Dad.

And she leaps to her feet and shoves me. I can't believe it. I stand there like a dummy and stare.

Get out, she screams. Get out.

And I do, walking out of the bedroom and into the bathroom, slamming both doors behind me, and locking myself in.

WITH THE BEDROOM a battleground, the bathroom's the only place to go. Throughout my barricades in there I become attached to the acid smells of urine that gather at the base of the toilet. I love the cool bone feeling of the tub against my hot legs. The cracks near the ceiling become crooked smiles. Out past the small square window of my bathroom territory is the cool slice of ocean and cliff that, as the summer progresses and the battles intensify, pulls at me more and more until I can resist it no longer.

Secretly, in the privacy of the bathroom, where I can mouth it out, I say, go, go, go. Meaning she should take her kid and leave. She should go back to the West Coast where everyone is perfect and beautiful, where the sea smells right and hills have the guts to be mountains, and ponds to be lakes.

But every morning there she is at the kitchen table with her sour red mouth and bitter green eyes tossing the dishes and cereal spoons at Ruby and me as if we were seals at the zoo.

AUGUST IS ALMOST over and an ultimatum is issued once again.

Open up, Cerise shouts.

I pause too long at the bathroom door and open it just as her fist flies through the air to knock again. It lands sharply on my skull. I yelp and dash down the stairs while she stands speechless.

There is a still moment, a small dance, as I push past her. Her body twirls, light as a child's. Her long hair following.

Go, I scream. Go, go, go. It comes out loud.

But it is me who goes, skimming over the stairs, the concrete steps and sidewalks, past the pond, through the bush, through the harsh windblown grasses to the cliffs. After all this time of wondering about the cliffs I arrive without thinking or fear.

THE SKY IS a sharp solid blue and it stretches down to the white-capped ocean as it rolls against the cliffs. Fifteen feet or so from the edge, I lie on my belly and pull myself slowly forward. The wind swirls in the hollow of my open mouth. I let it speak for me, shaping my lips against it, making the strangest sounds, deep and sad.

The earthy edge crumbles. Soft chunks of soil splat into the swell below. It's the only sound but for the cold cries of gulls and the rustle of their wings as they settle on the ledges below. No thunder or rush from the waves as I had imagined, just a huge silence, a giant rolling over and over, so sure of itself in its sleep.

I hold still. The whitecaps are nothing but a white wisp on the surface of this massive grey monster.

If Ruby were here she'd run along the edge, she'd spread her arms out to feel the first cool air of the summer, the first real breathing for months. Scream, she'd say, nudging me. Do something.

I have done something. I ran, like Ruby did last summer, along the edge of the pond. Like Mum, on the cliffs, in the wind, so long ago that it's only a dream. I've run away to the edge where I can go no farther. No farther, that is, unless I want to go over.

The sun stings the backs of my legs and the grass prickles but I don't move. And even when the sun slides low to the water and the grass sings with crickets, still I don't move. The body-thick saltwater giant rolls on and on below me, swelling against the darkening cliffs like the softest, hugest body I could imagine. It's at moments like this that Ruby would talk about Mum and I would hum till my throat ached trying to shut her out.

*T*HE VOICE THAT came from behind was so soft it was unrecognizable. It trembled a little, then repeated itself.

Truce, she said, a second time.

I kept my eyes on the heaving water. Truce. A stupid relief, like being picked up and carried, washed over me.

She came to lie beside me. I could smell her perfume. The three-quarter moon that lay across the water also lay across her face and I saw the lines in it and the pockmarks around her chin. She watched the ocean awhile.

Things will be cooling off, she said, summer's almost over.

The giant swelled below us, murmuring in the dark. I closed my eyes to listen.

My mother loved cliffs, I said, without thinking.

It's the kind of thing Ruby would say, not me. Cerise tossed a stone over the edge.

It would be so easy to go over, I carried on, speaking with my eyes closed. Perhaps it was the dark tempting me. It was like

going over an edge just talking. Cerise was quiet. My cheeks
burned with the embarrassment of having spoken.

Not for you, she said, finally. For some maybe, but not you.

When I opened my eyes she was standing, hands on her
tiny hips.

Come on, she said, dinner's waiting, we're holding everyone up.

twenty-one

T HE SPRINKLER HISSES in the early evening of the last day of summer vacation. There are the hollow sounds of dusk: children squealing, bicycles kicking up stones, the screen door complaining and springing shut as Cerise waltzes in and out with trays. I sit at the picnic table watching a mosquito gorge itself on the soft inside of my arm. Dad prods the barbecue coals until they're red hot.

Ready? he asks, following Cerise back to the house with his eyes.

When there is no answer from her I snap my arm shut at the elbow, leaving the mosquito dead in its own fat pool of blood.

Ruby has locked herself in our room all day. Hours ago Dad lay a ladder against the house and peered in. She was half off her bed, he said, head on the floor, arms out from her sides.

Crucified, Cerise said, when he told us, and she laughed a wicked laugh as she wiped her hands on her apron.

When Dad had knocked on the window and waved, Ruby leaped up and pulled the curtains closed. That's the last anybody has seen of her. Even me she won't answer. I've slipped her notes, which she hasn't picked up. I can see them there by the door if I lie with my face flat to the floor and look under. We can smell incense. We can hear clicking and whispering and page-turning.

Religious bullshit, Cerise hissed. The swearing made me sweat.

Dad suggested we call the fire department. They could break the door down, he said, or smash in the window.

Can't you handle this yourself? Cerise shouted, kicking a basket of laundry down the basement steps. It was clean and neatly folded. The arms and legs unfolded as it fell, reaching out like falling children.

THERE'S ANOTHER THING going on that's the cause of all this. Rand's dad showed up yesterday, just after lunch. I still had some toasted cheese sandwich in my mouth when he knocked. I thought it might have been those Jehovah's Witnesses. I don't like the way Dad treats them, closing the door before they get to speak. It's embarrassing. He's not like that, usually, I want to tell them, but of course I never do. I ran to the door thinking, if it was them, I'd let them speak and I'd take their little books.

But it was a man in glasses, wearing a striped shirt and tie.

Hi, he said, I'm Randy's father.

Randy! I had never thought of that. Rand had seemed such a strange name, now he was just another kid with a normal name.

He held out his hand for me to shake. My mouth, still full, fell open, like in the cartoons. I'd never thought of Rand having a dad. No one ever mentioned him. Rand's dad stood, with his hand out, and smiled. He smiled until Cerise's head appeared around the kitchen door. Then his face fell and that's when I decided I liked him. We were on the same side, I figured.

Cerise's head disappeared. Rand's dad looked at me.

I shrugged, the sort of shrug that means: Oh her, what do you expect? He winked.

Come in, I said, feeling thrilled and bad, and anxious about what would happen next.

The back door slammed shut. Rand's dad, hearing it, dashed out the front and stood in the driveway. She had locked herself and Rand in our car but she was going nowhere because Rand's dad's car was parked behind. That's when she jerked forward in the car and sped into the backyard. Ruby was just stepping out the back door. Dad was standing on the steps behind her with a tea towel in his hands. Their mouths dropped open just like mine had. Just wait, I thought to myself, there's more surprises where that came from.

Cerise didn't have the courage to plough right through the fence. That was a disappointment. I had hoped she would burst out, leaving splintered wood and pulled-up grass. I had hoped she would spin down the hill, out to the highway and go on forever. It didn't happen. One perfect circle was all, pressed into the grass as if a UFO had landed.

She returned, parking nose to nose with Rand's dad's car and lay her forehead down on the steering wheel. Rand let himself out. He walked, like a little man, hands in his shorts' pockets, towards his dad. It was the first independent thing I'd seen him do.

Who's that? Ruby asked. She had come around to the front and stood in the shade with me. I told her.

The sun was hot and shimmered on the driveway. Rand stood there barefoot, toes curled up tight trying to grab on as if the world had tipped.

Dada, he said, as if he were just learning to speak. His dad bent down, one knee on the ground, then the other. He held out his arms.

Randy, he said. My little guy.

I looked at Ruby, she rolled her eyes up into her head. She was feeling uneasy.

Dad was tapping on the car window but Cerise wouldn't look up. Rand was being lifted up by his dad, legs swinging loosely as if they were not attached to the rest of him. Rand's dad laughed, then cried, and a cool breeze blew up from the ocean, salty and fresh.

Dad introduced himself. Rand's dad wiped at tears under his glasses. It was strange that they didn't know each other, what with the crying and hugging and such.

Leslie, Dad said, Les.

Rand's dad nodded. He had put Rand down but kept a hand on the top of his head.

Randall, he said, Randall Swain.

We sat around the picnic table. Dad and Randall drank beer. Rand stared at Ruby and me across the table as if we'd just met. Dad drew a map, in his careful way, with his well-sharpened pencil, and explained to Randall where the best beaches were and the hotels. Then he went in and packed a suitcase for Rand and we were left alone, at the picnic table, with the two Randys.

Ruby had her eyes half closed. She was rolling her eyeballs up into her head so only the whites showed. It was making Randall nervous.

Where do you live? I asked, surprising myself by asking an adult a question. He turned away from Ruby.

Vancouver, he smiled, hugging Rand and then tickling him under the chin.

Will you take him away? I asked. Ruby's eyes flew open and positioned themselves to normal. Neither of us could quite believe I was asking these things.

No, he said, just visiting. The little guy needs his mum.

He had a sad smile.

Sherry didn't let me know where they'd gone, it's taken me a while to track you down. We'll have to talk, she and I. He pointed his head towards our car, all we could see was the top of her head lowered to the steering wheel.

Sherry? I blurted out. That's her name?

Why, what do you call her? he asked.

To her face? Mum. They make us. In my head, Cerise. That's what Dad calls her.

Randall laughed and laughed. My, how things change, was all he said, picking Rand up and dancing him around the lawn following the fresh-pressed circle the car had made.

*T*HEY LEFT ON vacation around the Cabot Trail. Cerise had tried to stop them. When she saw Dad coming out of the house with the packed suitcase she had jumped from the car. She had tried to pull Rand from his dad's arms. But Rand hid his face in his dad's neck. Cerise must have pulled hard because Rand cried out. He looked like a doll, sort of limp. Then Dad grabbed Cerise from behind. He told her it was okay. He handed over the suitcase with one hand and held Cerise back with the other. She slapped him and he squinted against the pain.

Randall slammed the car doors shut and started the engine. He held his hand up in a still wave. He looked right at me like it was our secret or a private joke. As if we'd planned it. Rand was invisible. I thought of him curled under the dashboard like a stowaway and smiled.

Ruby and I stood side by side and watched them go.

Lucky him missing the beginning of school, I said, feeling Ruby swell up dark like a storm cloud.

I wish that was me being taken away, she said, twirling a long grass around her finger until the blood was cut off. I'd go anywhere to get away from this. She spoke loud, not caring.

How could you, Cerise screamed, as they headed down the hill and disappeared. You gave away my only child.

Dad explained it was just a vacation. His voice was patient and a long way off.

A lot you know, Cerise shouted. You're the man who gave his children away to a crazy. She almost . . .

Dad put his hand over her mouth and glared at her. Enough, he said. Enough.

A boy needs his father, too, Dad said after we had all been standing there stupidly looking at the empty road and trying not to think about what Cerise had almost said.

That's when Ruby ran.

She disappeared down the hill in just her flip-flops, running in that awkward way you have to run when you're scrunching your toes to keep them on. She ran past the pond and into the woods. It was her old route.

I'll go get her, I said, I know where she's going.

I FOUND HER at the cliffs, tearing at chunks of the edge and throwing them over. Ruby, I whispered, not wanting to scare her. She was so close to the edge that it seemed a sudden noise might tip her.

Come away from there, I said, trying to stay calm.

The crickets were rubbing their legs and getting anxious in the grass. My heart was wild. I could feel it in my throat, in my fingertips, behind my eyes.

Ruby, I whispered. Please.

Remember how we ran away to the cliffs, Missy?

The ocean holds its breath.

Remember that little house?

The whole world is holding its breath. Birds pause mid-flight, beaks frozen open, and the sea wind stops its whistle and tug.

Missy?

I cannot answer. The waves have paused, have stopped at their very peaks. The whole height of a roller coaster waits below us.

I wish Mummy would come and get us, she said, leaning farther to watch the bits bounce their way to the bottom. I could hear them thud, thud, thud all the way down. One of her feet dug into the ground to hold her back. It was eating away at the grass, making a raw, bald patch of dirt.

But she won't, she continued. We have to get rid of Cerise, Missy, it's the only way. Mummy can't come back otherwise.

Come on, I said, holding out my hand to her. Please.

I stood waiting, long enough and still enough for mosquitoes to start biting behind my knees.

What if I went over, she asked in a suddenly cheery voice. What if we both went over? She pushed herself up on one arm and turned for the first time to look at me.

I don't know her. That was my first thought as she cocked her head to the side and started to giggle. Her face was all wrong. It was pinched in, each piece of it small and angular and nasty.

Come on, Missy, we wouldn't be missed. Her free arm arcs upwards, delicate as a bird.

Then her hand slipped on the grass or the edge gave way. Whatever it was caused the arm she was leaning on to go over and she fell flat to the ground with a scream. Her arms and head dangled. Her toes clung but they were useless.

Idiot, I shouted, hating her, truly hating her for a split second. And then the hate blew off, just as quick as it came, and I lurched forward to pull her back.

*W*E WERE PARTWAY home, still in the trees, when Ruby spoke next. You don't care, do you? She stopped to pick up a stick.

What? I asked.

About Mum. You don't care if you never see her again.

Though it was late August the bugs were still bad in the trees. I slapped at one. It made a huge bloody splat on my arm.

I don't know, I said, hoping the answer wouldn't bother her too much.

She was silent after that except for the whap, whap of her stick against each tree as she passed it.

We stopped at the pond and stared at its stupid rippleless surface.

Sit down, Ruby said, I want to tell you something.

We sat. Ruby took her flip-flops off and put them in the water. We watched them float.

I spied on Dad and Cerise the other night, she whispered.

There was excitement in her voice. We watched the ripples made by her toes as they wiggled in the water. Each of those ripples she broke apart with her stick until the water was jarred with a chaos of waves.

Watched them have sex, she continued. Snuck out of the house, late, and saw them with the curtains open. They started off cuddly but something got Cerise mad. You know how she can look, throwing her hair back, her chin coming sharp forward, her hands on her hips.

Ruby snickered.

Her boobs sure are small, not like yours at all.

She stretched forward and dipped her toes farther into the water.

Let's go, I said, it's getting dark. The pinks had almost gone, leaving shadows in the bushes.

She hit him, that's the best part. Took her fist and smashed him in the back.

Ruby stood up, holding a shoe in each hand. He doesn't fight back, you know. He's a wimp.

I stood up and looked at her.

You shouldn't spy like that, Ruby, I said.

She slashed me on the back of my legs with the stick. I didn't move.

You're a wimp like Dad, she screamed, dropping the stick and sprinting the rest of the way home.

*T*HAT WAS YESTERDAY and now she's locked herself in. I sit alone on my side of the picnic table feeling weird without her and Rand. It's hard to swallow, watching Cerise's orange lips circling the food and trapping it in her mouth. The meat mixing with the bun until it's all one pale paste. And the martini on top of that before it's gone down.

I'm not hungry. It's something new that keeps happening, this thickness in my throat when I look at food, this sick feeling when I think of chewing the food and swallowing it. I think of it sitting in my body and rotting.

Then the slapping begins. A blood splat on the thigh, a welt by the neck. She swills down the rest of her drink and piles the plates.

Take that, she says, eat it with your hands.

I shake my head, no, expecting an argument but there is none. The last of my burger floats away. The table is cleared. A stain of ketchup, a sprinkle of salt is all that remains. We run to the house, the screen door snapping shut behind us, my skin hot and itchy in the places that mosquitoes like.

Because we are so fast coming in we catch Ruby in the

kitchen pulling something from the cupboard. Cerise is quick. She runs down the hall into our room. She lies on Ruby's bed. Ruby goes mental; she can't stand being outsmarted, she can't stand anyone on her bed, even me. She takes the closest thing, a mirror, and hurls it. It skims above Cerise's forehead, smashing into a thousand pieces against the wall, slashing into the picture of Mum and us and spraying across the pillow and Cerise. This time Mum is torn, her face frayed and unrecognizable. Each of our hands still grasps a side of her skirt and it looks as if Ruby and I have ripped her in half.

I head for the basement, stepping over the thrown laundry, hearing Cerise wail and Ruby screech and Dad's voice rumbling under both, trying to calm them.

I don't go upstairs until morning. No one asks me to. No one even notices I've gone.

And no one hears me when I go to the laundry tub, stick my fingers down my throat and throw up. The small bit of pink meat and pale bun. It burns, it rips at my throat as everything is hauled out and sits in a neat thick pile on the perfectly clean sink bottom.

I sleep on the basement couch, feeling wonderfully empty. Rolled up in a winter coat I try not to think about the seven years of bad luck to come and the fact that the glass cut into the picture, splitting Mum in half.

twenty-two

*T*HE CAR COUGHS a time or two in the early-morning chill. Onward! Dad calls, looking at us three in the back seat through his rear-view mirror. We are perched like china dolls on a fireplace mantel, afraid of touching.

Forward ho! he carries on, raising his left arm in the air as if about to do battle. As if we were all prepared to charge forward with him, all the way. His other hand rests on Cerise's leg.

Enough nonsense, she says, and brushes it off.

We have rented a cottage on a lake for Thanksgiving weekend. A chance to get away from it all, Dad said when he told us.

You'd think he'd know by now that what's wrong with this family can't be got away from, Ruby said back in our room, as she punched at the pillows on her bed. You'd think he'd know by now that he's made a big mistake. She looked at me to see if I'd say anything. Well?

I don't know Ruby, I said, I guess he's trying.

Wimp, she'd hissed and jumped on her bed, grabbing her pillow like a weapon. You're both the same, afraid to see the truth, afraid of the mess it'll make.

*T*HE SKY IS A perfect fall blue. The trees are electric with reds, yellows and oranges, but our steamy breath dulls the sharp edges of colour as the car windows fog up, and we see everything melted together, as if we were looking through squinting eyes, as if we can't quite focus.

The water looks chilly, Cerise says, peering through a patch she's cleared in her window. We slip past a view of the white-capped ocean. The waves are high, churned up by the winds we've been having.

The lake will be fine though, Dad says, the brave and the hearty will rise to the challenge.

Almost immediately we rise and fall through the colours. We stop at a high spot where there's a lookout. Dad and Cerise get out, but the three of us don't budge. We sit in the back feeling the car rock in the wind. Rand is torn. He holds his hands on his lap nervously, not knowing what to say to us. Since his dad appeared he's been suspicious of Cerise. He's been keeping his distance from her by pouting and pulling away, but that means he's stuck with us.

I've been here with my dad, he whispers. We already did the Cabot Trail, he adds, picking at something invisible under his fingernails.

Wow, Ruby says sarcastically, aren't you special?

Dad and Cerise point into the distance, rocking back and forth on their heels and nodding. Dad turns, calls out to us and waves. His waving, calling hand against the perfect blue sky is a fragment, caught like a snapshot in my mind.

Come on, it says, follow me, come on. I wish someone would pick me up, force me to join them, but nothing happens. I am stuck in the back seat, held down by invisible hands. Dad turns back to the view when we don't respond, his hair lifting in the wind, dancing.

We drive on, hills swelling up around us. They're not mountains, Cerise points out, certainly not the West Coast, though I suppose they're better than nothing at all. Travelling puts her in a good mood. She opens her window and lets her fingers play in the rush of air.

The whole day of driving is like watching a long dance without music. The world waltzes by. Flashes of colour, someone's arm sweeping through air, a dog chasing its tail, a tree bent in the wind. The road below us is a dull grey blur, and in front, the back of Cerise's head. Strands of her hair escape from her French bun and curl. I want to touch them, to tuck them back up where they belong. For a second I wonder what I could do to make her like me, but the thought breaks apart as soon as it comes.

Mummy, Ruby mumbles. She's talking in her sleep. Everyone in the car hears. Cerise turns around and pokes her in the ribs to wake her up. Nobody says anything. Even Ruby, who seems stunned from her dream, doesn't fight back.

We STOP FOR supplies, all piling out to use the washroom. Behind the counter an old man stares at us, chewing on the inside of his mouth.

Hurricane weather, he says to Cerise, unusual this late in the season. He gives her a satisfied smile as if they'd been arguing and he'd just won.

I know, she says, her nails drumming nervously on the countertop, we live on the other side of the island.

Not from here, though, he says looking her up and down, his eyes getting caught on the redness of her lips. There's a gap where his teeth are missing and behind that a bloody mouth.

No, she says, pushing a bit of hair from her face, her back going rigid. Certainly not!

Jane Finlay-Young

Lovely spot you've got here though, Dad says, nudging Cerise aside to gather up the groceries.

If you like storms, he laughs. A month or more, we've had, of winds wandering up the coast, blowing out windows, breaking limbs. He tallies our bill on the back of an old paper bag. And it's not over yet, he adds. I've seen this once before, the worst is yet to come, he says, stopping the chewing to gulp down a breath.

He looks back at Ruby, Rand and me, where we stand by the door. The wind could do it tonight, he says, pointing a finger at us, could snatch something away, just like that.

I'LL FIND US a spot of ocean to walk along, Dad says, once we're back in the car loaded with groceries. He starts whistling tunes we've never heard and pretends to scout the horizon, pretends the old man has said nothing at all.

No, I just want to get there, Cerise says, looking up at the sky for signs of a storm. Dad drums his fingers on the steering wheel.

I need a rest, darling, he says. Just a few minutes' fresh air to clear my head.

Get out then, Cerise says. Go around, I'll drive.

And drive she does. Rand says it's too twisty, he's feeling sick. Ruby needs to pee. But Cerise presses on, going too fast, I can tell, because Dad keeps raising his hand, hesitating, then putting it back down on his lap where he knows it belongs.

We drive in silence, as if we're thieves or intruders, looking for something to take, something we want. We watch the sky, driving through dinner, through the sunset and into the dark. And when we finally come to the cottage there's nothing to see but patches of water shining in the half-moon light.

We sit without speaking until Ruby opens the car door. It's

dark but we can hear waves licking at the shore and wind rustling in the trees. And then, without a word, we all spill out and run squealing along the beach to the water. Ruby wails like an ambulance, a bit of the moonlight catches her somersaulting, her small legs and feet tumbling over her head and spraying sand across the dark sky.

In the morning, Dad says, as we unpack the car and fill the tiny cabin with our things, we shall all go for a swim. No one says a thing.

THE UNLIT ROOM. I have to feel my way along the walls, walk with my fingers, find the corners. And all the time the whispering of the wind through the cracks, through the hollow room and chill air. The curtains ripple. Ruby's bed is empty.

Walking the walls. The light switch doesn't work. Wallpaper curls off in tongues and catches under my fingernails. A scurry. Mice, perhaps, or Ruby. The wind is aching in the trees. There's a big tree out front, mostly dead. Its creaking and heaving reminds me of the old man at the store. The wind could do it tonight, snatch something away, he said. Or heave the dead tree down onto us, yank it, roots and all, from the earth and send it flying.

The doorknob. I turn it, open the door. The first crack of lightning explodes inside the living room and there they all are, their silhouettes by the window, looking out at the storm.

Hi, I whisper, and they turn in unison, look at me and turn back.

The room is splashed with light again, the thunder pounding right inside it. And lit up outside, beyond the lake, are bending trees, some almost touching their tops to the ground, as if praying. Everything out there is tipping over.

I step towards them, towards the window. They are wrapped in blankets and have moved the couch to the centre of the room where they sit side by side.

Stay back, Cerise says, the window might blow in. Get yourself a blanket, come and sit.

I find a place beside Ruby who is curled into a ball and staring blank-faced out the window.

You're shaking, I say, are you okay? She shrugs.

Those trees look so weird bent over like that, she whispers, they don't look right.

A lightning stab, a fist of thunder.

You can see the front of the storm, Dad says leaning towards the window. It looks so solid, like mountains, something you could touch, don't you think? It does.

We nod.

But it's only clouds, bits of water, nothing much at all, he says, his words full of wonder. A lot of fuss from nothing at all, I'd say.

No one laughs.

Mummy says storms are sent to punish us, Ruby whispers, loud enough for everyone to hear. Remember, Missy?

I shrug.

Remember? Up on that hill?

A fine thread of lightning splits through the sky.

That one touched down, Rand says, I saw it, I saw it. He tries to leap from his seat but Cerise holds him back. He pushes her away.

Storms to punish us, Ruby repeats. Her voice is dreamy, far-off-sounding. We left her, Missy, we left her all alone. Now she can't find us.

Dad is pacing behind the couch, checking his watch. Ruby, he says, the past is past. Your mother can look after herself.

Silence for a split second until the next shock of light and sound. The windows rattle, the glass wobbles. Branches bounce off the roof and spring at us like leaping animals.

Storms to punish us, Ruby says again. Louder. And I smile, a secret sort of smile because suddenly I don't care what Ruby says. In fact, I have the feeling that the more she says the better I'll feel. I bite my bottom lip to keep from smirking.

The dead tree is moving. We watch it shifting, side to side. Each of its movements brings with it a cracking, creaking sound.

Les, Cerise whispers, perhaps we should go.

We all turn to Dad. He's pulling his sleeves down and buttoning the top button of his sweater.

We're safer here, he says, but perhaps sitting behind the couch, covering ourselves with blankets in case of flying glass would be a good idea.

No one argues. We all stand and start moving towards the back of the couch. Outside the treetops whip and bend. A pounding begins on the roof, so loud we all drop to the floor. Rain! The air outside is white with it. Sheet after sheet charges over us. Ruby, crouched down beside me, is screaming, though I can't hear her. Just her face shows it; her mouth is stretched full open and her eyes are black and dance with excitement.

Suddenly the window explodes inwards. Ribbons of glass stream across the room. Lightning catches it sailing like stardust in all directions.

Blankets, Dad shouts, cover yourself!

Around us the tiny tinkling of falling glass. So delicate a sound, and so perfectly still and silent when it stops. I am rocked by my own heartbeat and drowned in the sound of my own quick breath.

Mummy, Ruby whimpers into the silence. Her voice is rich and full and trembling.

Don't move, Dad calls from under his blanket, not an inch until I check things out.

We're moles in our own little burrows. The dark is perfect, though my eyes are wide open there's not the slightest hint of light.

Rand, Cerise calls out, are you okay?

Yes, he says, so muffled I imagine his face in his hands and his hands wet with fear.

Mummy, Ruby calls again. There's a shifting of glass when she speaks.

I said don't move, you'll cut yourself. Dad's voice is firm.

Mu— Ruby starts again.

Shut up, Cerise shouts. Her voice is clear, unmuffled, she's uncovered her head.

Your mother was a crazy woman. She was a lunatic, dangerous. Forget about her, she's not worth another thought.

Cerise! Dad shouts. There's something else he says, but it's drowned out in a clap of thunder.

And then Ruby escapes her blanket. She sprints barefoot across the glass and out the back door. There is the smallest of yelps as her feet are cut and a hissing of her breath as she lets it go.

Stop, Dad shouts, come back! The back door snaps shut. I don't come out from under the blanket, though I know I should. I should call out to her, say something to help her. But I don't. I stay underneath holding myself still.

Dad starts to shuffle, through the shards of glass, on his blanket. Leave her be, Cerise says, you'll cut yourself, she wants you to follow, don't you see? Don't let her manipulate you like this, for God's sake. The shuffling stops.

twenty-three

*I*T'S ANOTHER WORLD in the morning. Wet steps after the storm, a swell in the lake, not quite a wave, something more human than that, something like a sigh. A cricket calls out from under a leaf. How small its lungs must be, how tender its lips. And the water carries on swelling and the steps are slick, dangerous, on their way towards the water's edge.

Passing by, Dad could be anyone. Wrapped in a robe, walking barefoot. Swim? he asks, patting me on the bum. I shake my head, no. I shiver at the thought of it.

Come on, he says, throwing his hands out in front of him, it's a new day.

Barefoot, after all that glass. After the hospital and the bleeding and the bandages. Each shard pulled from her feet by the doctor, with Ruby shouting, Mummy.

Hush now, he said so kindly, your Mummy's home cleaning up the mess so this doesn't happen again. Ruby howled all the more and the doctor shook his head and carried on pulling, then stitching.

Ruby tossed the rest of the night in her sleep and though the wind had quieted, our room felt wild with danger.

DAD TIPTOES DOWN the stairs, holding both arms out for balance, flapping like a bird looking for worms.

Oh! he yelps, it's almost warm.

And then he's in, the swell coming up to meet him, the damp air closing around him. Arm over arm he cuts through the water. A bird calls. The last drops of rain fall from the roof.

The best, he shouts, catching a mouthful of water and spraying it fountain-like around him. One hand is raised and cupped in an almost salute as if he were going under, never to return. There are the long stretched seconds of his disappearance until he appears closer in, bursting through the surface, triumphant. But his smiling face is pinched.

Something about the day after a storm, he says as he labours out of the water grabbing the towel I hand him. Something brand new, another chance to start again. His pink face appears from under the towel.

Don't you think? he asks, his eyes so blue and full of hope.

We'll fix your sister up, Missy, don't you worry. It's her age, just a stage. We'll let her run her course, get it out of her system.

Yes, I say, but I don't believe it.

This is a new day, but it's black around the edges. The clouds have cleared in the centre, but the ones before and the ones to come still hover.

twenty-four

SHE HAS PUSHED him out. The slow, slushy roll of winter ocean takes him.

Quick, quick throw him the rope, I shout. His heavy booted feet, steel-toed Kodiaks, gleaming a perfect fall ochre against the white ice he floats away on.

You pushed him out, you pushed him out, Ruby accuses, from the car, opening the back window where she sits and screams it towards us. Cerise turns towards her and glares. Ruby stares back, the Bible resting across her chest, looking at us as if we were all mad.

I try to unravel the thick rope. Gloves off, my pink fingers are hopeless in the cold.

Kodiaks on the ice, placed apart, absolutely still. Arms outstretched for balance. His baby blue eyes so pale against all that white.

Rand is silent, standing back behind us as if we were unrelated. And Ruby, fogging up the windows, has refused to come out of the car. She had tried refusing to come at all. She was going to go to church, she said, but, at the mention of church, Dad picked her up and swung her over his shoulders, without saying a word. "Actions are what we believe," I thought to myself. It was a thought that came to me pale as winter sunlight, slowly curling itself over everything as I watched Ruby hit and kick to get free.

Dad had walked slowly down the icy front stairs towards the car with Ruby upside down and kicking while Cerise scanned the street nervously for signs of neighbours watching. They stuffed her into the back seat of the car next to me who sat like an idiot pretending nothing was happening.

Churches, Dad said clutching the steering wheel, almost shouting above Ruby's curses, are a scar on the corner of civilization.

It was the most interesting thing I'd ever heard him say though I didn't know what it meant.

The car had purred out of the driveway, then spun its wheels on a patch of ice.

They swallowed your mother, he said, his hot breath puffing out of him and fogging in the frozen air, I'll not let them get you.

That got Ruby's attention and she went suddenly quiet. Cerise was quiet, too. And we drove on, our gloved hands jammed between our thighs for warmth. Dad's words dangled as thick and formless as our breath in the closed-in car.

THE ROPE, DAD shouts as I try to unravel enough to make a length to reach him. But Cerise grabs at it, her green cat eyes too sharp, the red gash of her lips too red, in all this snow. The cliffs rise up behind her like a huge hand about to slap.

The rope, Dad shouts again, a little louder, but his voice is weak. Airy, forceless, trying not to rock himself from his tiny balance on the floating ice. He doesn't look like a dad, not like this, helpless as a child.

CERISE PUSHED HIM out. I saw her small foot do it. Pointy-toed leather boot. A delicate push was all it needed and he was out there floating, the heavy green-grey water, twenty feet deep, below him. Seconds in there and you're dead. I know that, just like Dad knows it, motionless on that piece of ice.

The rope is yellow, brand new, never used, and she flings it through the air, a knot on one end thick enough for him to grasp. She is laughing. She misses and slowly hauls it back through the water, a coating of ice on it as it hits the frozen air. Again she throws it.

A yellow cord tossed against a grey sky. If he dies I will have nothing.

The icy end of it hits him near the neck and slides back into the water. She starts to jeer.

Come on, Sandhouse, grab it!

She hauls it back like a fishing net. Empty. Another layer of ice building up a thickness.

You know, he used to be a lot of fun, she says. When I met him he made me laugh.

It sounds like a eulogy. There's something secretive and prayerful about it. But it's all gone wrong. It's all hard work and crisis now. She screws up her face in concentration, slowly rewinding the rope.

If I had the guts I'd shut her up. Push her in without a thing to float on. But I am silent and still and stare out past my father into the endless greys.

I HAVE MY OWN prayer. Please, please, please, I shout in my head, not daring to utter anything else or even think it for fear I'll make it happen. For fear that he'll sink, drown, die.

Use the other end, I say, handing it to her, but she doesn't listen.

This time, I chant in my head. This time. I will the rope to land in his outstretched hand. He has thrown his gloves away in order to catch, they float on the slushy water then fill up and go under. His long fingers are pinched pale by the cold, he moves them like a small child wanting candy.

The rope lands in his hands. He tilts forward, bends his knees, compressing his tall, thin frame into a ball around his hands, around the rope.

She hesitates. I see the ruts around her mouth carved deep. She bites her lower lip and I see a smudge of lipstick smeared across her teeth. There is a tear frozen on her cheek. From laughter, I think, despising her until I see it's the kind of laughter that's really crying. Her breath is jagged. Slowly she draws him in.

Faster, I say, leaning towards her and touching her arm.

He'll tip, she says, shaking me off.

I know she's right. She keeps biting her lower lip in concentration, leaning back into nothing to gather her strength. Ruby has come to join us, standing next to me with the Bible pressed to her chest. Her lips are moving, reciting something that I hope is helpful.

He glides across the last foot of open water and bumps against the shore. She holds out her shaking hand and he takes it, pulling himself carefully towards her, stiff from standing so still. Her cat eyes look straight at him, electric in all the white. But his eyes are lowered.

I WIND THE YELLOW rope in perfect circles. The ice coating cracks and snaps in puzzle pieces, falling to the ground. A few warm months from now there will be nothing here to stand on. It will be surf we jump into, salty as tears and strong enough to carry us away.

They have turned towards the car and walk ahead. I pull Ruby along the frozen ground. She has curled herself into a ball around the rope and slides along on her rounded back. The rope digs into my shoulder as I drag her behind me. Ahead, they are two dark surfaces on a sheet of white. Rand walks behind them like their shadow. And Ruby and I follow, paler than the snow.

twenty-five

ICICLES JAM THE way, long-toothed and glassy. The stream is frozen but for the tiniest trickle, muffled under layers of ice. Dad kicks an ice mound until it flies free, jagged edge up, skidding along the other icy surfaces. It has been a treacherous Sunday-afternoon walk and we have to take the longest way home.

There are tears in his eyes. I swear I can hear them crystallize and drop to the ground with the smallest of sounds. From under his knit wool hat a few curls of hair, cheeks pinked up by cold, blue eyes watery pools.

We should get going, I say.

The sky is turning over grey and dull. He nods, jabbing at another ice ball with his steel-toed boot, the soft leather almost untouched, until now. Now, the ice edges cut the ochre skin, slit it open revealing a shiny metal glare.

They are the same boots he wore last weekend as he teetered on the ice, the same ochre against white glare, the same frozen sky.

It's strange, I say, but I can't remember getting here. How did we come? We are surrounded by trees that are coated with ice. There is no path. And there are no footprints because the snow sits under a thick crust of ice, too. Even Dad's steps have skimmed the surface without leaving a trace.

It's as if we've been plopped down into a foreign land, I say. Like another planet.

Dad likes this idea. He doesn't laugh exactly, it's more like a cough, but he lifts his head, he stops kicking and flashes a shy look at me.

It's getting late, he says, pulling his scarf tighter, stretching his arm from its winter sleeve to find the time. We must keep going.

But neither of us wants to go. Dinner will be sitting fat and hot in the oven, waiting for our return. The curtains above the sink open to a snow-engorged sky that presses in, presses down, on the full house. The kitchen window will be icing up from cooking steam so that the light that comes through is fractured and faint. The dark will bulge through the window as we sit, shoulder to shoulder, at the table, at the end of another day.

MY HEART IS racing again, I say, as we take our first steps forward.

It's been beating wildly in fits and starts since the Thanksgiving weekend.

Did you ask the doctor when you were there this week, he asks.

No, I say, he was in such a rush. Dad nods.

We two are not much for asking, are we? He's not proud when he says it. He's pulling himself along the icy path holding on to anything that will hold him. Small baby steps, ready to fall each time the foot touches down.

Yeah, I say, in response to his question, I suppose. I have a tentative grip on a silver birch, a sapling. If I move too quick and slip I'll take it with me, snapping it in half. It's doing its best to hold me. The air is disturbed with our breathing and moving. The sun is going down, the temperature dropping, thickening what we breathe and dulling our voices.

THE DOCTOR HAD taken my blood.

Not anemic, he said, finishing me off with a flourish of ink across the page. He placed the cap back on the pen and folded his fingers in a tight weave.

Now, he said, his eyes catching on the full waiting room outside his open office door.

Now, he said, again, unaware he had said it before. You must eat, you must eat more. And he stood up before I could lie that I would.

Cerise, in the waiting room, stared at a magazine, bouncing one leg against the other. Rand, at the other end of the room, was reading a book and picking at a scab on his hand.

Ruby had refused to come to let the doctor check her feet. She had squeezed under the bed and held on to its legs and screamed. Cerise couldn't get her out. Enough of this, she kept shouting. As if Ruby had ever had too much of anything. Finally, after poking her with a broom handle, after slapping her hands and threatening to call Dad home from work, she had shouted, fine, you can die under there for all I care. It sounded like another curse.

All is in order, the doctor had said to Cerise. I caught his wink and her flashing eyes. I saw the brush of his hairy arm against hers as he turned towards his next patient. She must eat, he said, from the corner of his mouth. A fierce whisper that the whole room heard.

I won't eat but for the small sticks of carrots, and things I have studied that don't count too much. I won't eat anything without suspicion. The smallest crumb an enemy. The awful heat that food builds in the body. The terrible fatty tissues and sinews of meat and cheese. The globs of food gag in my throat and refuse to be swallowed.

*W*E WALK ON awhile in silence, the iced-up trees looking magic, the grey sky reaching down so close. It feels like a small, private world we're walking through.

Remember when you read us *The Lion, the Witch, and the Wardrobe*? I ask. Those kids that ran through the wardrobe and into that winter world?

He nods.

This is it. It feels just like that place. We are quiet for a while, concentrating on moving forward.

I read that to you before Cerise. He says it like a confession, as if "before Cerise" was something I never knew.

I remember, I say, wanting to say more, to tell him there is nothing I've forgotten. I want to talk to him about Ruby. How worried I am about her nastiness. How small she is. How she doesn't seem to have grown for years. And the cliffs. How close she sat to the edge. How she almost went over. And her alone-ness. How day after day she's alone in our room with her altars and incense and prayers. How dark her eyes have become.

I open my mouth, sure that something will happen. But he seems so small. His skin is pinked up like a child's and soft. And his eyes are wet. The cold, perhaps, but I can't tell.

Do you think there is one thing you could do or say that could make a person happy? The question escapes my mouth before the thought is even in my head. It's a shock in the thick chill air.

Sorry? Dad asks, turning his wet eyes on me.

Do you think there is one thing you could do or say that could make a person happy? I repeat, feeling suddenly stupid for asking the question. If you could figure out what that was, I mean, like a spell, perhaps, some sort of magical thing. Well, not magical, but it might feel magical if it happened. Do you know what I mean?

He is silent. I know he heard me and I wait for him to laugh. There is the hiss of my heavy breath as we walk on, listening to each footstep hitting the hard ground, as we get closer and closer to where we don't want to be.

I think, he says finally, and pauses. There is no hint of laughter in his voice. I think, I wish, I wish it were possible, he says, almost coughing or stuttering the words out as if starting something up that hasn't been used for a long time.

Perhaps it is possible, he continues, I'd like to think it were, but . . . his voice trails off, wobbles before us and then behind us as we walk on.

No, I don't think so Missy, he finally says with more conviction. No, unfortunately life is more complicated than that.

And then suddenly we are through the trees and by the cliffs. I let out a gasp of surprise and Dad grabs my hand and pulls me towards him.

So, you're afraid of heights too, he says. I shrug and try to pull my hand back, but he doesn't let go.

I didn't know that about you, Missy. I suppose there's a lot I don't know. Mum was saying you've become so silent. We were wondering if anything is wrong. He's taken my gloved hand in both of his and is staring at it.

She's not my Mum, I say.

From below there is the suck and pull of water and ice, the occasional thud of something huge flung against the rocks, and then the deep, thick sigh of withdrawal.

Won't you ever get used to her? He grips my hand tighter. Won't you ever give her a break?

A break? I yank my hand away, and as I do I slip and fall. There's a crack as my elbow hits first, but it's the ice, not my bones, that breaks.

Missy, he shouts, grabbing my sleeve as I slide from him towards the edge of the cliff. He slips, too, and falls beside me.

The sky is pinking up through the greys. Both of us are lying on our backs and staring at it as if waiting for something to descend.

What's wrong, Missy? Please tell me. His voice is tiny under all that sky, insignificant. We are almost invisible under its weight.

Nothing, I say. The ocean heaves another sigh and then pauses. Through the corner of my eye I see him nod to himself, perhaps relieved there is nothing I have said.

I THOUGHT PERHAPS England for this summer, Dad says, as we make our way back towards the trees on our hands and knees. Just the three of us. A little break from it all. Your grandparents would love to see you.

Ruby will be pleased, I say.

But not you? Dad asks.

I guess so, I say. But really, I don't know.

twenty-six

AFTER THE RAIN we are suffocated. The damp dripping from trees and rooftops has chased worms up from below. They slide thick and certain across the flagstones and grasses, across the squat black road and stone walls. The clouds dull down on us, heavier than we can bear. The greens are impossible. The bark dark and swollen. We can't stay in and we can't go out.

Grandma is in the kitchen, fussing with pots. Biscuits? she calls out, pretending food is our friend. If we answer, if we say no, there will be questions, we will have to repeat over and over the "no thank yous" and the "we're fines." So we stay still by the window; breathing on the glass, making foggy patches from the puffs of our breath, pretending we've not heard.

Grandpa turns the pages of his book. The dictionary by his side is as heavy as the clouds past our hands on the window glass.

If only we had a destination. If only we had somewhere to go. But we stay here trapped by rain; something sizzles in the kitchen that we will have to refuse.

And outside the damp and crawling make us itch. Make us terrified to place a foot or touch a thing, for fear of the small and the slimy, anything at all that scurries.

We circle around the table placing the plates and knives. We settle the cups and smooth the serviettes as the rain tears off the sky and drips through the trees. We are dripping too, feeling no more substantial than the moist air around us. Our thin bodies slip, invisible as fairies, as we set the table we do not wish to sit at.

The fried mushroom lies on toast, limp from fat and heat. Brown like bark with crevices for worms. We use the fork prongs to pry apart the folds. Grandma's head wobbles on her fleshy shoulders. Her breasts heave with enjoyment and a drop of juice escapes her mouth, beading in its corner.

AFTER LUNCH, A SPLASH of sun spills over the clouds. Everything is brimful of water and sparkles. The damp comes up at us as we step outside. The thick air steaming in the sun.

How lovely, Grandpa says, swinging his walking stick each time his bad leg sails above the ground.

The post office: three miles there, three miles back. The afternoon has an itch to it; something caught under the skin, a little breathless.

Settle down, girls, Grandpa says, brushing absently at flies that have lost their way from cows. He laughs at us, perhaps a bit uneasy, perhaps a bit unsettled himself from the days of rain we have just endured.

THE POSTMASTER FINGERS the few pieces of mail with his blue-veined hands. Canada, this one, he says, stroking the stamp, his own Queen's head, and passing it to Grandpa.

Followed my granddaughters over, I suppose, Grandpa says, winking at us.

We can't stand still on either foot and hop and wiggle in the tiny room that smells of damp paper and old skin. We politely refuse the offer of chocolate and ask, instead, for the toilets where we whisper and whine to each other about the oldness and the boredom as we tear the letter open.

It says: "Can't come. So sorry." It says he's busy, had to cancel his flight, there's been some problems. "See you in a few weeks. Have a wonderful time. Love Dad."

We throw it in the fire when we get back. It moves in the heat like a human, like someone ashamed and trying to get away. It chars up, black then grey, and disappears.

Figures, Ruby says, poking at the thin black flakes till they're gone. Good riddance.

THE WORLD HAS conspired to trap us here in England. Has shut us up in this slow-moving place, with the watchful eyes and smiles of our grandparents. And Auntie Margaret has gone home for the week. Aunt Fish . . . swum away while we drown, as Ruby puts it, chewing on her fingernails and reading our futures in the cards she's laid out across her bed. Sometimes she's up all night, predicting.

THERE HAD BEEN a fuss the night before Auntie Margaret left when Ruby announced she wanted to see Mum. Dinner was on our plates, untouched.

Where is she? Ruby asked. Her arms were folded against her chest, her cheeks were flushed.

Grandma got up to clear the table though we hadn't even started.

Where is she? she asked, again. Grandpa straightened his

knife and fork. No one had to ask who. No one wanted to answer. Grandma stayed hidden in the kitchen.

Well, Auntie Margaret had said, we don't know.

That's a lie, Ruby said. How can you just lose a person? She's your sister! It's impossible. Auntie Margaret nodded, understanding.

What about your parents? Ruby asked. They would know.

Auntie Margaret had seemed suddenly upset. She had passed a serviette across her mouth, had dabbed at the corners of her eyes.

They're dead, she said. That's the last time I saw your mother. At the funeral. I thought you would have known. Ruby was glaring at her. Giving her the evil eye.

How? she asks, her voice nasty, as if it were Auntie Margaret's fault.

A car accident, last year. Coming home from the pub.

Something was rocking us on an edge, something taut and wound up. The grandfather clock squeezed all the space out of the room with its ticking.

Perhaps your father will help you find her, Grandpa said, breaking through the silence. His voice had wobbled as he spoke. His words came out squeaky and weak. And I felt at that moment that I could have shoved him across the room and through the huge front window.

Yeah, right, Ruby spat. He's given us so much information already, obviously.

A twitch had started at the corner of her mouth, it ran into her shoulder. Three or four times it happened until she put her hand to her face to stop it. Her eyes slid up into her head and her eyelids fluttered.

Stop that, I said.

Just the whites of her eyes peered out at us.

Stop. It looks like your insides are coming out. Like you're dead.

Auntie Margaret had gone over to Ruby. She had held her face in her hands. Ruby, she whispered, I hate secrets as much as you. I'm sorry. Your mother isn't well. She can't be with you. I'm not at liberty to say more.

Ruby's eyes had come back as she shoved Auntie Margaret away.

I know about you and secrets, she spat. She'd pushed herself away from the table. Her chair up-ended and lay stranded on its back on the floor.

We could die and it wouldn't matter, no one would even talk about it, she shouted when she had reached the top of the stairs.

I had held my breath, thinking she might throw herself down, but all was silence after that.

As we were getting into bed that night Ruby took a Bible from the bedside table and flipped through its pages. Here's that quote again, she said. I was only half listening as I rearranged my pillows behind me.

"And the rain descended and the floods came and the winds . . ." She stood up on her bed to read, holding one of her arms out like a preacher.

Stop it, I said.

". . . blew and beat upon that house . . ." she continued.

Shut up, I hissed through my teeth. Then, as if it were a dream, I leaped at her as she continued to read and I shoved her off the bed. She lay still on the floor for a moment and then I heard her flipping the pages.

"And it fell: and great was the fall of it," she said, and began to laugh hysterically.

I let her laugh. I didn't plug my ears or cover my head with a pillow. I listened until she stopped.

Missy, she whispered. Do you know why the house fell?

I didn't answer and she began to snicker.

Because it was built on sand. Get it? Sandhouse.

twenty-seven

BUT WHAT WILL we do now, we whine at breakfast the morning after we receive the letter. Each of us slices a thin piece of bread and eats it without butter. We were going to go climbing with Dad, we say.

The day is brilliant, wind fluffs at the bushes by the kitchen window.

Can you read a map? Grandpa asks. Can you stay on a well-worn path? We say yes, yes to both questions and wait for his idea.

Well then, he says. Perhaps you are ready for an adventure of your own.

EACH TIME WE turn back they are waving. Grandma's worried head tipped to one side keeping us in full view. When finally we turn a corner, they disappear, and a wide wasteland of hill stretches above us. We climb, not caring for the view or the coolness of the air. We climb to feel the burning in our legs and exhaustion in our lungs.

I have an idea about Dad, Ruby calls to me over her shoulder. The house will be empty when we get back. Empty of them. It'll just be us and Dad.

It's something I have thought about, dreamed about for the past few years.

Are you sure?

Ruby nods her head wildly, her body ripples with it. We will her to leave. I can feel Ruby making it happen with her mind.

The trail we take rises and falls the whole day. No sooner are we getting to the top than we're on our way down. The fells are a peculiar grey, rising from the mist, then disappearing again. Ahead of me Ruby's shoulders slide like blocks, like something mechanical beneath her shirt.

Slow down, I shout out, thinking I've pushed my voice too far, but the fog seems to catch it. She's pumped up like a steam engine but she stops, turns in slow motion and glares. Come on.

We stride on in silence, side by side. The packed lunch on my back digs at my shoulders. Next to Ruby I feel like a giant. Even her ears are miniature and her lips, a pale pink, seem doll-sized and plastic.

As the fog lifts the colours poke out at us, bits of surprises that we can't ignore. Look, I whisper to Ruby, pointing below us, straight down. We are high up, above a tarn, a perfect blue-green. Between us and it, the screes. If you fall, Dad said, in his stories about climbing, you won't stop. He didn't say more than that, but of course he never does.

Scree: a beautiful word for a fell-side full of small loose rocks.

Scree, I say, standing with my feet planted apart. Standing a distance from the edge.

Screeee, I say again, louder. The sound bounces off the sides of the fells. Ruby shifts on her feet and glances around. We are alone, except for sheep.

Sssssscreee, we both say, our words tumbling down the loose rocks till they find the cool waters.

You can start an avalanche with sound.

We carry on, checking our map now and then as if we had a choice of paths. But there is only one and we stick to it as we had promised.

Coming down we jam our heels into the hard fell-side. Digging sharply without mercy so our bones bump and shake. Ankles wobbling on the wrong sides of rocks, feet slipping on moss, but nothing slows us. We are like machines set in motion without brakes. I feel I could plough through anything and not be stopped.

I could go on forever, I shout out, not caring who might hear me. I let my jaw go loose so each heel hitting the well-worn path makes my teeth smash together.

Ruby is ahead, again. The sun is hot and her shoulder skin, where the bones poke through, is red.

You've got a sunburn, I shout, but she doesn't seem to hear.

Her hair bounces on her head like it's not a part of her. Our arms swing. I time mine so they move with hers. We look like toy soldiers going to battle. We look like we might lose our arms right out of their sockets if we go any faster.

Halfway down we stop and take out our lunch.

Let's feed the birds, she says, unwrapping the sandwiches from the wax paper.

We tear off small bits.

Delicious, I whisper as I toss the first piece.

Superb, she says, and throws it so it sails a long time through the air. We attract the attention of birds. We become louder.

Eat, we scream in unison, ripping apart the sandwiches, spraying them across the grasses and rocks. The biscuits too. We squeeze them in our fists until they're powder and toss them like confetti.

Eat, we scream, over and over until everything is gone.

I can't believe it, Ruby whispers, her voice loose and edgy. I can't believe that I've waited for her my whole life, every day, and here we are, so close and . . .

Our fists are clenched. I don't notice mine until I see Ruby's, white around her knuckles even through her tan.

I thought we'd see her. I thought being here, so close, that you know . . . she'd be here, with us.

I feel myself backing away, each step onto unseen ground. The rubble underfoot, the way my feet are tipped off-centre, off the sides of stones, makes me feel I am walking a tightrope or cliff edge.

Shut up, I hiss, through clenched jaws. She looks up at me. Shut up. She's gone. She doesn't want us. She never did.

I've said too much. Her face is unbelieving, her tiny mouth ajar, her eyes dark shocks of surprise. Her fingers fly apart from their fists as if she were falling backwards with no hope of being caught.

No, she says, before I can say I'm sorry. You're wrong, Missy.

It's a small, uncertain whisper; the voice of a ghost, of something almost invisible.

I'll get her to come back, she says, somehow I will, you'll see.

I turn and run, not looking back, not even wondering if she follows and when I reach the car where Grandma and Grandpa wait I get inside and can't stop crying.

twenty-eight

CERISE WASN'T GONE.
    We hadn't asked at the airport about her, we had decided on the plane that we wouldn't. We had decided that if Dad wanted to say something it was up to him. We saw him first, hands in his pockets, staring at the ceiling as if something curious were up there. But there was nothing, just a ceiling.

Figures, Ruby said after we'd both looked up. He can't stand to watch us coming, he can't stand to see anything before it's right on top of him and he has no choice.

I don't know where she gets these ideas but there's always something right about them. He looked down when we called him. His face warmed and then flickered like a TV having reception problems. I hugged him, quick, so I wouldn't have to think about what the look meant but Ruby stood back with her arms wrapped around herself and just said, hi.

He said nothing but the polite things as we drove home. How's your Auntie Margaret? Are Grandma and Grandpa well? I sat in the front passing raised-eyebrow looks to Ruby through the side mirror. It was okay with me if Cerise's name was never mentioned again. I had no interest in explanations. It was enough that she was gone.

We felt ahead of the game, for once. After the letter Ruby had checked our suspicions with her magic. She hadn't let me watch but I stood guard outside our room at Grandma and Grandpa's listening to her bumping around and mumbling. Sure enough, according to "things," Cerise was gone.

You're too thin, Dad said, looking ahead at the road. Both hands clamped around the wheel as if we were spinning out of control on a patch of ice.

Your clothes hang off you. It's not becoming.

It didn't seem like Dad who was speaking. It sounded like someone had told him to say these things and he had been practising all the way down in the car. I imagined his soft, shapeless lips practising. Too thin, he might have repeated, over and over, trying to make it harsh.

Ruby and I said nothing. But I could have said a lot. I could have said I didn't know what I was supposed to be: first too fat, now too thin. Somewhere in there I must have been just right, somewhere, sliding from one to the other I must have been perfect, for him anyway. Maybe even for Cerise. Perfect. That one word, if I said it out loud, would make me scream. I could feel it splitting me apart just thinking about it.

RAND'S BICYCLE LAY in the driveway. There was a shadow in the house by the front window. And then, when Dad honked, we had to face it. I looked back at Ruby through the mirror but she had her head down as if she were too exhausted to keep it up. She told me, sometime later, that she had decided at this moment that it was all-out war, that if no one else was going to do anything about the mess in our lives, she would.

Cerise came out, a cigarette between the fingers of her waving hand, a smile pressed onto her face. She had been practising too.

Then it hit me. They had had the whole month together, without us. They were tanned, they had been away. Dad had probably never even bought a ticket to England, had never planned to go in the first place.

Please try, Dad said. It was a whisper. I had my hand on the door handle and he was begging. I nodded. What else could I do? I stayed in the car until his hands slid off the wheel like little rivulets petering out after a rainstorm, slow and unwilling. I stayed in the car and felt it rock as he lifted his weight from it. I stayed while he dragged the cases from the trunk and slammed it shut again. Rand peered in at Ruby and me without coming too close. I gave him a half wave. He gave me a half smile.

Come on, I heard Dad call through the closed windows. Then he turned his back on us and walked into the house with Cerise.

Ruby stayed in the car, her head still down. No one said hello to her or touched her but me.

Ruby, was all I said, reaching back to touch the top of her head.

Don't, she said shaking me off.

She seemed to be filling herself up with something nuclear, something strong enough to blow everything apart and leave nothing recognizable.

Go, she said. Leave me. It was a whisper, a harsh one.

*T*HE KITCHEN WAS full of pans of rising bread, cookies cooling on racks, and warm sticky smells. I knew what they were saying, what they had been saying all summer: this is our happy home, don't destroy it.

I wanted it destroyed. I wanted it obliterated. Fingers flying loose, Cerise's crinkled eyes exploding in the heat. Body shards:

hair singed and then melted, everything incinerated until it didn't exist.

The edges of things started forming doubled lines. Cerise moved in front of me in a blur.

Suitcases in your room, Dad said, patting me on the bum as he passed through the kitchen and out the back door, grabbing a cookie on the way and whistling.

What he whistled stuck inside my head through the rest of that day and all through the night. The words came along with it, bouncing and taunting as if there were two of me, face to face, warring.

"Oh what a beautiful mornin', oh what a beautiful day, I got a beautiful feelin' everything's goin' my way."

Those were the words. They wouldn't stop.

The beds weren't made up but sheets sat on each of them neatly folded into small sharp squares, pillowcases on top. They had been pressed and smoothed by anxious hands so that the corners were exact.

Ruby and I were the cause of the anxiety. I'd never seen that before but I saw it now in the way the corners looked like knife edges and the white looked like ice. We were the start of all the trouble.

Try hard, try harder, be good, Dad had said so many times. But it was never enough. Without us things could have been perfect.

". . . Oh what a beautiful mornin' . . ."

I FAKED SLEEP WHEN I was called for dinner. I heard Dad come up the stairs like he was carrying three of himself; one on top of another in a pyramid. He stood in the doorway, breath trembling from the weight of all those selves. He stayed a long time, staring at me as if I were a sleeping baby.

Missy, he whispered. I crossed my eyes inside my head. I felt a long way off and sort of dizzy and dreamy.

Missy, he tried again.

". . . Oh what a beautiful day, I got a . . ."

I disappeared down a tunnel and through glass doors that snapped shut behind me. My crossed eyes strained and I could feel my brain twist. I could see him back there. A shadowy form leaning against the door frame.

". . . beautiful feelin' everything's goin' my way."

He leaves.

It's cold between the sheets, under the pale fuzzy moon appearing outside the window. Someone's on the stairs, some-one light and quick. Cerise.

Close your eyes, Missy, I say to myself. Close your ears. There's heat behind my eyelids, a squeal inside my head. The door swings open and bangs against the wall.

Missy, she says. Her hair is in a bun, I can see its shadowy bump through my eyelid slits. Get up. Come down for dinner.

I am nothing but a log of wood.

She rips the sheets back.

Enough of this, she says. Get downstairs. Eat.

I can picture her mouth, her teeth as they grab at the words before they're all out. We stay like this: me a lump of something dead, she holding the sheet back like a bullfighter.

Your first day back, she says.

It makes me ache the way her voice has softened.

Don't start off this way, Missy.

But I'm too far away now to answer. Fine, she says, your father will carry you down. Fine, I think to myself, I'll store it all in my cheeks and spit it out later. I'll store it all in my belly and bring it up.

But Dad never comes and the door stays open, the door handle impaled in the wall from Cerise's forceful fling.

AFTER DARK RUBY creeps in. I hear her getting into bed. It must be a full moon because she's all lit up grey.

Are you okay? I ask.

She looks like a ghost with the moonlight caught in the crinkles of her clothes. She gets into bed fully dressed and pulls the covers up over her head.

They don't want us here, she says from underneath.

I know.

Even Dad, she says.

I can tell she's talking into her pillow because her words sound choked.

Maybe, I say. But not in his heart, not if he really had to choose. As soon as I say it I'm unsure, but Ruby doesn't disagree.

We'll see, she says, turning onto her stomach and putting the pillow over her head. We'll put him to the test.

I watch her almost invisible form under the sheets, the moonlight glaring down on her like headlights. All night she doesn't move. She's as still as a rabbit in that glare, waiting. I know she never slept because all night her breathing was quick and uneven and sometimes I could hear her blinking. Her damp eyelids flicking off tears.

twenty-nine

RUBY IS IN OUR room, on her knees. She's set a cross up on the wall with the altars underneath. She's burning incense and praying. Praying so loud I can hear her, here in the bathroom, even with the door locked and cotton batten in my ears.

If Cerise hears her she'll tell her to stop, to get outside and be useful, but she's in the garden ripping out raspberry canes. She has tied her hair back with a scarf and put Dad's work gloves on her hands and stands with her legs apart, pulling. Her body is one tight muscle. Her jaw and her calves, her arms and her throat.

The roots come out whole. She jiggles them till they loosen, sometimes using the spade, and when they're ready she pulls. She doesn't care that they still have fruit on them, lots of it that is turning her gloves purple. Each time I hope for her to tumble back but her balance is perfect.

Ruby is punching at her mattress, she's screaming into her pillows and as long as Cerise is out there pulling she can carry on. I keep one eye out the bathroom window on her strong back and the other on the cliffs. If she heads for the house I'll bang on the bedroom wall to warn Ruby. Not that she cares, not that she's asked me to watch out for her. Most of the time she's itching to fight Cerise but if I can stop her, I will.

Dad's gone, again. Locked away in his office where he can't see the leaves beginning to turn colour against the blue sky. He was gone before breakfast. The car rolling out, silent, like a submarine, past my bedroom window. Sneaking out. A pinch of fall air coming through the window with the spit of his tires on gravel. Five minutes later Cerise swore because she'd woken to find him gone. Perhaps I should feel sorry for her but if I were him, if I could drive off, I'd do it too to get away.

CERISE TAKES THE ripped-out canes and piles them together. Some strands of hair are loose from her scarf, her back must ache because she's holding it.

Ruby is silent in the next room.

Cerise strikes a match and holds it to the pile of canes. It goes out. She lights another and bends herself around it, crouching like a caveman. There's a wind working against her. It rubs the oak tree against the house, bending its branches so the leaves brush against the window. I have the binoculars with me. I use them to see her face now that the wind is making trouble for her.

A bedroom door slams shut.

Clouds are coming in off the ocean, heavy ones clamping the sky shut, pulling it down so it looks like there'll be only inches to move in. Her back is to me, I can see each rib push out and squeeze shut. She's breathing hard. I can see anger in the way she strikes another match; the sharp ending of the outward stroke, the effort of her arm muscles.

Someone's rattling at the bathroom door.

The clouds have dark undersides and rush towards us like moving mountains, like something unstoppable that will plough us under. The binoculars bring them so close that I feel I will have to lie flat to the ground to save myself. Like a war. Like the pictures Rand draws of planes diving at people. Bullets spitting from their bellies. Hit the decks, he calls to the people as he draws them flat on the bottom of the page.

Someone is kicking at the bathroom door. I don't answer.

The canes have caught. Cerise's loose strands of hair are sucked up by the wind and look like tentacles trying to grab at something. The flames whip at the edges of the cane pile like brandy lit over Christmas pudding, hungry and devilish. The clouds are gods, watching, they are another world bearing down on us.

DAD LOVES STORMS. He loves watching them blow in off the sea. Sometimes he'll get up on the roof. We can go up too if we promise to sit still. Up the ladder, with someone holding it at the bottom, then scrambling on all fours up the rough shingled roof. Up where there's nothing to protect us. Up where we are nobody to the sky, where we are specks sitting on a black roof, blown at by the wind.

OPEN UP, RAND SCREAMS, I've got to go.

I've got to go. I've got to go. People scream that in their heads, to themselves, when they can't take it any more. Maybe that's what's in Dad's head when he wakes in the morning next to her.

The clouds are now solid overhead and colliding with each other so that they appear to be boiling. Cerise is watching the fire not the sky. Through the binoculars I can see the creases in the corners of her eyes. She is squinting at the flames which have started to leap in the wind like clothes snapping and jumping on a clothesline.

Rand kicks and pounds. His jaw will be set and his hazel eyes pinched into slits.

Wait, I answer.

The fire slips along the grass, burning a wide black lip. The wind pushes it towards the oak tree, it could lick itself around that tree and crawl up the trunk. In no time the fire could be at the windows, its heat cracking through the glass. She looks around, sweeping her gaze into the neighbours' yards and then towards the house, looking for help. I duck, feeling nasty and pleased. I don't care. I don't care if it all burns down, the whole house, the whole town.

She starts to toss spadefuls of dirt at the fire. It makes no difference. She starts a ditch, digging furiously, her free hair washing around her face. Les should be here, she must be thinking. Bastard. Asshole. Wimp. Each thrust of the spade is like a knife in his throat. I can feel it.

The bathroom door swings open and bangs against the tub.

Bastard, Rand shouts. The lock has been heaved from the door.

I'm not leaving, I say. I'm busy. I won't look.

Because he's so desperate he doesn't argue, doesn't notice the binoculars in my hand.

I hear Ruby on the stairs, going down each step slowly.

The clouds let loose. Cerise stops her digging, as if someone has called her, and looks up. She reminds me of a farmer, rocking on her spade, one foot resting on it, the handle digging into her belly. She shakes her head and then lets it drop. Through my binoculars I see her back quiver and her neck go loose. I turn the binoculars around so she's far, far away and stands all alone under the thunderheads, crying.

RUBY WON'T COME DOWN. She's on the roof, on her knees. The rain has plastered her hair back, the strange light has marked her pixie face with shadows. Depending on whether you want to see her face or her back, you stand in the middle of the road or in the garden where the raspberry canes used to be. Thunder and lightning, sitting one on top of the other, don't scare her, don't even make her flinch.

Each time we have tried to get up to her she has kicked the ladder off. Each time we speak to her there is no response. She has marked me the same way she marks Cerise. I am an enemy, I am someone who has betrayed her and let her down. Her mind is made up about something, you can see it in the way her eyes stay steady ahead of her. In the way she doesn't shiver in the cold and wet.

Four, nine, two, oh, oh, seven, one, Cerise shouts at me, the wind whipping around her mouth so her words come to me as if through a tunnel.

Tell him to get home, fast.

There's a neighbour looking out her window. There's a car stopped on the street with its window rolled down. Cerise sends it away. She won't let me call for help, she says Dad will deal with it. She says this is Dad's doing, Dad's mess, and he can clean it up.

Ruby sways on her knees, her arms spread out like Jesus on the cross.

For Chrissake, Cerise wheezes under her breath, such a spectacle, such a show. She glances up the street and down. That wimp, she says, can't face up to anything.

WHEN DAD ARRIVES he calls the fire department. Ruby can't push their ladders away. A fireman picks her up and carries her down over his shoulder. She lies limp and upside-down, her hands dangling by his knees. Her knees are bleeding. Streams of blood trickle to her feet and spread out like the Mississippi Delta.

On the stretcher she stares right past us like we're not her family. There's something in her eyes that reminds me of someone, but I can't recall who.

Later, when he's home from the hospital, I ask Dad. Did you think Ruby looked like someone we know? He was undoing his tie at the bedroom mirror.

Yes, he says, your mother.

*T*HE PSYCHIATRIST AT the hospital says Ruby won't come home because of Cerise. She thinks Ruby may be irrational again if she is forced back. Cerise thinks she should be sent to England for a year or two, where she can get all the attention she wants.

Cerise says it's all over town, she says people are talking and passing nasty rumours. Her friends hear things.

My name is mud, she says at dinner, throwing the mashed potatoes on each of our plates with the ice-cream scooper. Rand thinks this is funny.

Hey, Mud, he says, pass the potatoes. He starts to laugh. She sends him to his room which Dad says is ridiculous.

Cerise stares at him as if he were a Martian that had suddenly popped in for dinner. As if she'd never heard him speak up before. Perhaps she hasn't. Rand gets sent anyway, howling up the stairs and slamming his door against the unfairness. And Cerise follows, throwing her lipstick-stained napkin on the table after staring Dad down has not produced an apology.

DAD AND I CLEAR UP. He washes. I dry. The house is quiet, all drifty-feeling in the grey light coming in through the window. He turns the radio on to something classical and when we are done we sit at the table across from each other, our chins resting in our hands.

Quiet, he says.

I agree.

Unusual, he says, raising an eyebrow.

We both start to laugh, snickering at first, then hysterical. His face falls into the table, his lips touch it like a kiss. The laughing bounces up at me sounding hollow and private. Cerise bangs from upstairs, but we can't stop. When Dad looks up he has a twinkle in his eyes that I've never seen before.

Shut up, she shouts down.

We carry on.

Some people have no sense of humour, he snorts. We have tears in our eyes that won't stop. The laughing squeezes them down our faces and onto the table where they glimmer in the little light left.

We carry on until Dad stands up.

Come here, he says, opening his arms. He is breathing hard.

I'm sorry, is all he says. He holds my head to his chest so I can hear his heart pounding and feel his chest heave in and out. His cool fingers rest across my forehead and through my wet eyes I see the back door leading out into the night.

thirty

*D*AD IS LATE coming home from visiting Ruby in the hospital so we start dinner without him. I have planted myself at the far end of the table where I can lean against the wall.

No thank you, I say to each thing Cerise puts on my plate. She carries on as if I haven't spoken. Fried steak, mashed potatoes.

No thank you, I say again, I can serve myself. Peas, carrots.

Rand lifts his head and stares at me. You have to eat, he says, you're getting sick. He says it softly, a pulse beating in the hollow of his dented head.

I can't, I say, speaking just as softly, I can't swallow.

He nods as if he understands.

Cerise chews loudly on a piece of meat.

May I be excused? I ask, already knowing the answer. She shakes her head, points at my plate.

Eat, she says, through a full mouth. I push my plate away.

I said I can't.

My voice is foreign in the kitchen, it has a glow to it like the stove clock.

Six forty-five. I push my chair back and Rand's hands squeeze around his knife and fork.

THE STAIRS COMPLAIN as Dad comes up them. Hello, hello, he calls as he opens the door, I've brought a visitor.

We weren't expecting both of them, but there is Ruby, a small, thin stick standing behind him. Her head looks too big for the rest of her.

Cerise sits up straighter, a sort of shiver runs through her.

Oh, she says, wiping a finger across her lips, putting her knife and fork down and sliding her plate away.

I don't want her back. That is my first awful thought and it makes me sick.

Ruby stands behind Dad staring at us as if we were strangers in her home. As if we were thieves, bad people. I take a mouthful of steak and potato in defiance. I'm not sick like you, I want to tell her. I'm normal, see I'm eating. I chew, work at swallowing, but nothing goes down. So I sit with it in my mouth, soft and warm.

She wanted to come home, Dad says, reaching back behind himself to try to pull Ruby forward. She moves away, drawing her shoulder up in a kind of cat hiss.

Our Ruby's home, he says, trying on a smile that makes him look ridiculous.

Seven o'clock. The dark is crowding through the window above the sink. Outside there's a freezing sky, thick with stars.

Ruby love, Dad says, come and sit down. He pulls a seat out for her like a waiter in a restaurant. Cerise gets up from the table, starts clearing our dishes. Even mine with only one bite gone, though the one bite still sits in my mouth, bulging.

Ruby refuses to sit. She stays standing in the doorway, swaying a little.

Get out, she says, suddenly. Her face is pinched and pale when she speaks. Though her back is turned Cerise knows she's speaking to her. She spins around.

So, she says, you're making the decisions now.

Get out and leave room for my mother, Ruby says, her voice flat and cool.

The chewed food swells in my mouth.

Ahhhh, Cerise says, nodding as if she understands, of course.

She is folding a tea towel against her belly, watching carefully to make sure the edges match up.

I've written to her this summer. I've told her to come. Ruby reaches a hand out to steady herself against the door frame.

And she's written back? Cerise asks.

Dad holds his hand up at Cerise, fingers spread like a traffic cop. But he doesn't speak.

Auntie Margaret sent it to her, she promised she would. Ruby's voice is pitching higher, quivering. Tell her to go, she whispers, staring straight at Dad.

He shakes his head.

If only I could swallow.

When Ruby lurches forward, grabs a bottle and throws it to the floor there is a relief I feel like a gust of cool air. But I can't breathe in, not deeply, because of the food.

Tell her to go, Ruby shouts, toeing at a piece of glass with her boot.

Rand has started to cry.

Tell her! She bends, undoes her boots, and kicks, sending them flying across the room.

Cerise laughs. Go ahead, she says, you're as crazy as your mother. We'll lock you up too, forever, just like your mother. We'll put you away where you can't do any harm.

Ruby steps towards the glass.

Stop, Dad says, grabbing Ruby by the shoulder, please. And then he turns to Cerise.

You'll have to go, he says.

You're joking, she laughs, you're not serious. There's a look between them that's impossible to read. Ruby's eyes dart back and forth from one to the other.

It's Cerise that drops her eyes first. She falls back against the counter, fumbles for her empty martini glass and pitches it to the floor. Walk in that, she screams, lie in it, roll in it for all I care.

As she walks past us she snaps the tea towel in Dad's face and kicks glass shards at Ruby, but neither of them flinch. It's as if she's already gone.

You were always decent to me Missy, she says, turning to face me as she passes out the kitchen door. There are tears pouring down her face. I try to smile her a thank you but my face is frozen still.

You're a wimp, she screams when she gets to the top of the stairs, and you've just been *had*.

Dad starts to drop his head but changes his mind.

Well he says, let's clean up this mess. And he grabs a broom and starts to sweep.

I throw up. Not just the mouthful of steak and potato but whatever else there was, which can't have been much but is enough to look disgusting sitting on the table in front of me. At the sight of it Rand jumps away from the table and stands by the doorway leading into the living room. He looks at us and then towards the stairs.

Go, Ruby shouts, and she takes a run at him, shoving him through the living room and towards the stairs.

Go and pack, she says, your mother needs you.

thirty-one

DAD CARRIES RUBY up the four flights of stairs. I can hear him breathing with the effort, though she's so small. I carry her sandals and purse and watch her legs sway like a rag doll's. We are quiet except for the creak of our feet on the stairs and the brush of my hand against the perfect, white walls.

DAD HAD APOLOGIZED at the front door.

I'm sorry, Ben, showing up like this, unannounced, but my daughter is sick and it's a long drive home. Ben had held his hand up against the apology and coughed out an awkward laugh. Then he called his wife. It was Marla, from the party. She came from the kitchen; short and round and soft, wiping her hands on a tea towel then holding them out in front of her as if she could take Ruby in her arms and heal her with just a touch.

Bring her in, bring her in, she said excitedly, smelling of roses when she came close.

She is paler than I remember. Softer. Quieter.

Missy, she almost whispers, as if it's a secret that we'd met before. She takes my hand and squeezes it.

We were at the circus in Dartmouth, Dad said, and she collapsed.

Marla runs her other hand over Ruby's forehead and mutters something about too much excitement.

We followed Marla up the four flights of stairs. Her hips rolled under her skirt, her bare feet flattened under her weight. She chatted on about how there was only one room on each floor, except theirs, where they slept, which also had a bathroom.

But look on the bright side, she said. I can always use the exercise. She laughed at the thought.

The guest room, at the top, overlooked a stretch of rooftops and part of the harbour. I wondered if it had been Jason's room though there was no trace of a teenager in it. He had died a year or so ago, at sixteen. I remembered Cerise talking about "the tragedy" and Ruby standing behind her as she spoke, bringing the back of her hand to her forehead and pretending to faint. Dad had talked about how they had spent thousands of dollars at a clinic in the U.S. trying to save him. And that night as Ruby and I brushed our teeth together in the bathroom she had said: Big deal. People die all the time, what's so special about Jason? You usually think it's a big deal when someone dies, I had said to her, thinking of Gandhi. She spat into the sink. The toothpaste was pinked up with blood. Your gums are bleeding again, I had said. We stared at the pink gob until she rinsed it away, washed off her brush, banged it against the rim to get the water off and slammed the bathroom door behind her. Big deal, she had shouted through the closed door.

Everything was white. White bedspread, white pillows, white dresser and a deep white carpet that squished between my toes. Marla held the blankets back so the bed looked like a waiting white mouth ready to swallow Ruby. Ruby's head snapped back like a baby's as Dad lowered her in. Along the front of her throat each bit of bone stuck out like the back of a clenched fist.

Marla squeezes out a washcloth and places it on her fore-head slowly, covering her eyes and the front bits of her hair. Dad sits at the foot of the bed and lets Marla take over. He's watching Ruby like he's in a trance; his hands hovering around him, some-times starting out towards Ruby but never getting there, turning instead towards his own hair which he straightens or his glasses which he pushes up or clothing which he tugs at.

All we can see of Ruby is her lips and the little holes of her nose, the rest of her is under blankets and cloths. I clear my throat with a delicate cough.

Are you okay? Marla asks, turning to me, looking concerned. It's the same look she gave Ruby the night of the party when Ruby said she didn't want to grow.

Suddenly, I want to be sick too, lying down under blankets, being stroked and watched. I'm okay, except for the tears that want to come out.

Hormones. That's what Dad would say right now if I cried. He'd roll his eyes at Marla and shake his head as if, being hor-mones, there was nothing to worry about. But he'd be worrying all the same though he'd think he wasn't.

I'm fine, I say. Dad nods his head as if in approval, as if he has faith that I'll never break down or collapse or malfunction.

Marla slides a thermometer past Ruby's lips. It bumps into her teeth. She asks Ruby to open her mouth, just a little, to let it in. There is no response.

Ruby, Dad says, the hovering hand grabbing her foot and shaking it. It flops like jelly. I try to find her chest with my eyes, but there is no movement.

Ruby, I shout, and slap my hands together. Marla and Dad jump. Ruby is as quiet as a stone but her teeth part and the ther-mometer slides in.

Ben comes into the bedroom carrying a glass of scotch for Dad. The ice tinkles like wind through leaves as he walks it across the room to Dad's outstretched hand.

How's Cerise? Ben asks.

Gone, is all Dad can manage, his grip on Ruby's foot not loosening, his eyes not coming up to meet Ben's.

Ben apologizes for not knowing.

It just happened, Dad says. It was a long time coming, though. The girls could attest to that. Ben and Marla nod but I can tell they have no idea. They have no idea how amazing the words are. I look over at Dad to make sure they are real but his eyes are glued to his scotch.

She was stupid, he says, into the stillness of his drink, but she sure was sexy.

I could faint from embarrassment, but then again, I could just as easily laugh and not stop.

No fever, Marla says, wiping the thermometer with the washcloth and placing it back in its case. I'm not sure if that's good or bad.

She's awfully thin. They both are, she whispers, as if she thought Dad didn't know. I turn my back to them and look across the rooftops. They are whispering over Ruby as if she were dead.

Perhaps the hospital, Marla continues whispering. But Dad shakes his head vigorously.

They have nothing to offer us but theories, he says, swallowing the rest of his scotch. She's young, he says, full of drama at this age, aren't they? Full of high feelings. It'll pass.

He smiles Marla an unconvincing smile which she doesn't return.

RUBY COMES TO after dinner but refuses to eat. I eat, a little, because Marla ran her hand across my back when she put the plate down and whispered in my ear, just try a bit, dear. So I did. Dad smiled at me from the other side of the table and tapped his fork against his glass like they do at weddings when they want the bride and groom to kiss.

It's good, I say. I say it for Dad. I say it like giving a present and with it comes a smile. It was true, I could taste it. Each thing tasted different, even felt different in my mouth. I had forgotten.

WE LEFT AFTER dinner without Ruby. Dad had tried to carry her to the car but she grabbed on to things and screamed that she wouldn't go. It was amazing how much strength she had. Ben pointed that out on the stairs when she had got hold of the banister and Dad couldn't budge her.

Let her be, Les, Marla said. Her bare arms wobbled as she reached out to pull Dad back. And when Dad released her, Ruby ran like an animal, on all fours, back to the guest room.

We got into our car and drove across the Macdonald Bridge to a bed and breakfast. The moon shone on the harbour showing everything clearly.

The submarine must be out on manoeuvres, Dad said. It's usually over there. There was nothing to see but the oily roll of water and the silvery moonlight upon it. I shivered thinking of such a huge thing sliding underwater in the dark. Something was under my skin, something secretive, trapped inside me like a dream. It felt as mysterious as the missing submarine.

I WOKE UP EARLY the next morning with my heart pounding. Dad was up early, too, drinking his tea, buttering his toast and talking in low tones to the bed-and-breakfast owner. His knife scraped across the bread, spitting out dark brown crumbs. There was a closeness to the air that stuck to the dining-room walls and tables and chairs. I knew the East Coast well enough now to know there was a storm on the way.

When will you call Ruby? I asked, pushing the chocolate milk away and passing him half of my toast. The ball of food Dad was chewing pushed against his cheek, bulging like a squirrel storing up for the cold. Then his Adam's apple bunched at the top of his neck and released.

I have, he said.

Ruby wouldn't come to the phone, he said. She hadn't left the bed, hadn't eaten, hadn't even gone to pee. Marla had wanted to know if she could call the doctor. Dad had said yes. She said she'd call us after the doctor had been.

Dad placed his knife on his plate carefully and brushed his hair back. Looks like we've got a problem on our hands, he said, staring at his fingers as he removed them from his hair and spread them out in front of him on the tabletop.

I couldn't think of anything cheery to say to make him lift his head or smile or even move. I could only think of that dark sliver of something inside me, something dreadful and wordless.

I'll make it up to you. Both of you, somehow, he said, raising his head and facing me. I had been sitting on my hands and they flew up in front of me, quite suddenly.

No, I heard myself saying, it's okay. It came out in a flash before I'd even heard the meaning of the words. Like lightning.

Stop! Dad said, flashing back at me just as quick. I'm old enough to look after myself and, though surely I've not been doing it, I'm old enough to look after the two of you, too.

This left both Dad and me stunned. We lowered our heads to think.

I'm not angry, Dad whispered, his hands over his eyes like bandages, I'm just terribly ashamed.

We sat for a long time, listening to his words repeating off the walls. Each repeat becoming more and more distorted until the phone rang.

It was Marla from the hospital. The doctor had insisted on admission. There were papers Dad needed to sign. Her heart rhythms had become irregular. She weighed no more than a six-year-old child.

Come on, Dad said, reaching for my hand.

thirty-two

R UBY IS ROLLING a smooth dark stone over and over in her hand. She's strapped to the bed at the wrists and ankles so the hand that rubs the stone lies palm up and tight to her body. It looks like a pile of moving bones.

Where did you get that? I ask, pointing to the stone.

I don't know, she says softly, I've always had it. I've just kept it hidden.

I knew where it came from. I remember it perfectly. The wet steps of the church and the wind, her hand reaching out for something, anything. And her sobs and calling out. I shrug it off, pretending it's not important, but something starts to howl just under the surface of my thoughts.

Would you itch my nose, she says, into the space between Dad and I. Neither of us says "scratch" which we would have said if she'd been normal. You scratch an itch. I grab a Kleenex and wipe her nose with it. Harder, she says, pinch it, it's killing me.

Tubes run into her left arm from a pole with bags. Wires are stuck to her chest from a machine that beeps.

My food, my heart, she says, when she sees me looking. It took me a moment to realize she meant the machines.

Why doesn't Mummy write, Missy? Her words are slurred. Her eyes move lazily in their sockets and her head stays pinned to the pillow, looking too heavy to lift. It's been almost two months, Missy, I can't wait much longer.

I don't know what to say.

Sixty pounds, she says when I don't answer, her eyes lie like puddles in her head. Like a six-year-old, she says. She's looking me up and down as tears run from the corners of her eyes. Do you want to die too, Missy?

Marla absorbs the question, walking into the room in soft pinks, even her cheeks glowing pink. Dad stumbles over his words and hugs Marla, who grabs his hands in hers and pulls him closer to Ruby's side. I stand back because there is only one side to reach her from. Leaning against the wall, with everyone's backs to me, I cry as big and as silent as Ruby. Tears run down my neck and catch in the hollows above my collarbones.

DAD CRIED WHEN we got back to the bed and breakfast. I sat with him, on the veranda in a swinging chair listening to his jarred breathing and the wind beginning to rise. We hadn't noticed Ruby shrinking, not that much. It seemed impossible that it had happened while we were watching. And me too. The bones at my wrists stuck out as if they were broken. My knee joints looked bionic, not at all human, no flesh. Hardly a person at all. Hardly someone you could count on, like Marla, to take care of you, to hold you up.

My stomach rumbled. And then the sky rumbled too, and the streets flooded with rain and the darkening sky with light. We let the rain blow at us, not thinking of the wet and cold.

What will we do? Dad asked, once the storm had quieted. I think he thought I was someone else, but I was just a shadow in the dark beside him.

thirty-three

OUR NEW APARTMENT hovers above the harbour. There's very little in it but sunlight. A few odd chairs that have lost their covers. The old gold chesterfield with the bottom falling out. Knives, forks, spoons: all bone-handled. Three beds. Ruby's, all made up, waiting for her to come home. Under the bed sits a big box of things neither of us has looked inside with "DO NOT OPEN" written on all sides.

There's a view of the submarine sitting squat and nasty, and the ferry creeping back and forth to Dartmouth. In the early morning we can see the sun rise from the balcony, at night it pinks up through my bedroom window. Dad says there are more people in these few buildings than in the whole town we were living in. A universe inside a universe, he says. The thought makes us both feel lonely.

Ruby is a walk away at the Halifax Infirmary. Down Brunswick Street with its houses and churches, along the bottom of Citadel Hill, windy and empty, past stores and cars and nobody knowing about Ruby. The little girl on the roof, on the cliff, on the edge. The little girl with bandaged feet, with weird prayers and chants, with mad ideas of her mummy returning.

It's as if we're invisible, Dad and I, and it makes us walk a little taller, it makes us look around clear-eyed and curious.

It was a quick move. Cerise had taken most everything anyway, and when the movers came, three of them, they joked about someone else getting to it first. It was dark when Dad paid them, thanked them, and shut the door of our new home. That included standing by the Causeway to look back at the island and the five-hour drive into the city.

Dad was quiet at the Causeway, walking to the edge of the lock and peering straight down where the water sat trapped and a long way off from the open sea. I stayed away from him, sitting on the hood of the car, afraid he was crying. The air was heavy with salt. Seagulls floated in circles overhead, peering down as if they'd lost something. I had just wanted to go and never stop. I wanted Ruby in the back seat, reading, and Dad whistling a stupid travelling song.

*D*AD HAD TO QUIT his job when we moved and when he's not at the hospital with Ruby he's standing on the balcony watching the harbour. Sometimes I take a sweater to him which he takes with a puzzled look, each time saying he hasn't noticed the cold. We eat boiled eggs for breakfast, sitting in silence in the perfectly white rooms with strangers on every side of us.

I haven't started school yet but I'll have to soon. I have begged for a year off, to be with Ruby, but it's illegal. Ruby trying to die is the illegal part, I say. Dad agrees but there's nothing we can do about it.

Stuck, he says, between a rock and a hard place. It's the kind of saying Ruby goes mental over.

Twice a day, before lunch and before dinner, we visit Ruby. I worry about what will happen when I go back to school, when there won't be much time for visiting, when I'll have to make new friends all over again.

You worry too much, Dad says, as he scoops some of Marla's homemade lasagna onto my plate. I eat it. Dad is referring to this as a miracle and hugs me when he passes me in the hall or in the narrow kitchen when we're fixing a meal. It's as if I've been gone a long time. I'm eating. No one, including me, is sure why.

Never question a miracle, he says, standing beside me on the balcony, our shoulders touching, as the pinks and reds spin off the office towers and the salt breezes chill the air.

Marla visits Ruby every day, too. We plan it so we overlap and can report to each other on her progress. We whisper in the hallways about how Ruby looks, what she said, what the nurses think, which doctor has come by. She brings food with her every time. Fresh baked things like chocolate-chip cookies, banana bread, cheese scones. She bakes for effect, she says, things that smell tempting. But Ruby is never tempted. She closes her eyes to us as we sit around her bed munching and staring at her bony hands lying above the sheets and the hollows where her eyes sit secretly under their lids like tiny new eggs.

We have told Ruby we love her. We have held her bony body and rocked her while she cries. We have talked to the doctors in the hallways. They shake their heads and shrug their shoulders and say, keep your fingers crossed. Dad says there must be something they can do. They say there are no known drugs to make a person swallow.

thirty-four

T HE PSYCHIATRIST WEARS black high-heel shoes. We can hear her coming down the hall like the huge dark front of an approaching train. Her suits fit tight and her glasses hide her eyes.

Now Ruby, she says, sit straight and look at me. Ruby's neck wobbles when it's not against the pillow, even her eyelids seem too heavy for her to lift open. I suggest to Dad that she's not soft enough, I suggest someone gentle, like Marla. He doesn't want to interfere, he says, folding his handkerchief carefully into smaller and smaller triangles.

Doctor Kline taps her pen against her clipboard. Her ankles are thick from sitting too long and waiting for people to talk. She is impatient. The end of her pen is chewed to a thin plastic point.

Missy, why did you stop eating? I am staring out the window into someone else's room, waiting for Ruby's response, when I realize the question is for me.

I am eating, I blurt out. She nods and explains that she knows but hopes to shed some light on Ruby's situation.

She wants to die, I say, hearing my voice come out quiet and matter-of-fact. Dad clears his throat.

Did you? the doctor asks. Or, do you? She is looking me up and down as if making sure I dressed properly, that my shoes are done up and my hair combed. Even though she wears no lipstick she reminds me of Cerise.

You remind me of my stepmother, I say. This gets Ruby's attention. One liquid blue eye opens to watch the doctor.

Cold, I hear myself say. Distant. The same hard mouth, the same hard . . .

My words start to rise above us.

Missy! Dad says, sounding alarmed. The doctor cuts him off.

This is good, she says, this has been stuck in her awhile. Her hand itches around her pen but she doesn't write.

What else? she asks, the light from the window bounces off her glasses and erases her eyes.

Nothing, I shout, I hate you.

I RUN ALL THE way home. The door to the apartment closes behind me pinching off the rest of the world. Ahead of me, through the living-room windows and past the balcony I see nothing but sky; a blue expanse, free of clouds.

Jump, I hear a voice say, jump, jump, jump. It's Ruby. Come with me, she says. Her eyes are lit from behind and not their usual colour.

Where? I ask, unable to stop the game.

She laughs, tossing her head back, rolling her eyes up into her head.

Stop it, I say, I'm not like you. Leave me alone.

And she does, as soon as the words are spoken. And I am left standing alone by the balcony door afraid to go farther.

DAD MUST HAVE called Marla and waited for her because I have time to cry before they arrive. It's Marla who sits beside me on the bed and rubs my back. I can feel her soft hips against mine. I wonder if fat has nerve endings and think that perhaps she doesn't know she is touching me. Her hands are hot, her breathing heavy.

How did you feel when Jason died? I ask. Her circular stroking catches for an instant and then continues.

Like I'd never be the same, like an alien, watching life from far away.

Her hands were burning, swirling round and round my back like the dark eye of a tornado.

That's how I've felt most of my life, I hear myself say.

My lips are loose on my face. My heart is calm, almost beatless, and I think of Ruby perched on the edge of the cliff. Ruby locked in. Ruby on the basement floor hatching Gandhi. Ruby on the roof. In every image she's alone, she's far away. In every image she wants to be.

Could she die if she wanted to? I whisper. Dad, standing with his back against the wall, coughs into his hands. Marla's hand stops swirling.

Yes, she says.

I can feel the building swaying, back and forth, like the slow ripple of wind through a huge tree.

Auntie Margaret, I say, spitting it out before my crying makes it impossible to speak. She should come. To speak to Ruby, before it's too late.

thirty-five

THE HALIFAX EXPLOSION, Dad is saying, pointing to the harbour and then up behind us, sent an anchor flying all the way over to the Northwest Arm.

I think of a huge body blown to pieces whenever I hear this story. A body so big you have to speak of it as north, south, east, and west. The northwest arm.

Auntie Margaret is gasping at the thought, holding her throat with one hand and a glass of sherry with the other.

A fascinating story, really, Dad continues. Such a normal day, blown apart. A whole city in ruins. I can't stop thinking about it. Auntie Margaret's gasping turns to "tut, tutting," the mole by her mouth quivering.

Not much left from your explosion, she says, a giddiness in her voice. The sherry. Dad snorts.

Got out alive, though, he says, looking down the fourteen floors below us as if he were considering dropping his glass on a passerby.

The sun has slipped to the other side of the building and we stand chilled in the shadows. Dad downs the rest of his sherry, goes inside for more and returns with the bottle, deck chairs and blankets. Here, he says, cuddle up.

We settle in. He has brought a glass for me too.

To your health, he says, as he passes it to me, almost full. His eyes are brimful of tears.

What does she look like? Auntie Margaret asks. The sherry numbs my tongue as I hold the first sip in my mouth. Dad is busy pouring more. I swallow and start to answer, my mouth parting to form the words, sure that Dad would rather not speak. But I'm wrong.

Small, he says, without hesitation. Odd. Attached to machines. Like a spirit, really. Not quite human.

We study the seagulls floating just beyond our reach as we think about this. It's as if Ruby were one of them. Not human. Their curious pin eyes and sharp beaks are full of rage. Some squeeze out a shrill protest.

Beautiful, Auntie Margaret whispers, beautiful.

What? I ask.

Your father. You, Les. Such beautiful words. You've never been one for words, have you? You surprise me.

Dad stretches his legs out before him, smiles, and then throws back his head to look at the sky.

Never had a chance, I suppose. Surrounded by women all my life. You're a complicated lot.

We laugh. It's been a long time since we laughed. Doing the dishes the week before Cerise left, probably. But the laughter now, like the laughter then, teeters on the edge of something dark.

Excuses, Auntie Margaret says, suddenly serious. I'm afraid to say there is nothing that excuses silence.

Dad stops staring at the sky. His smile sinks and his legs bend as if getting ready to spring.

Your mother wanted to kill me once, Auntie Margaret says to me, her voice echoing in the tiny hollow of her sherry glass. I should never have kept it a secret, nor you Les. Perhaps we would not be in this mess if we had spoken up. If she had received the help she needed the girls might have been spared.

Margaret! he chokes, don't.

A seagull twitches in surprise.

It's best we talk about it, Auntie Margaret continues.

I raise the blanket to cover my mouth. Its musty smell is a comfort.

Please! Dad begs, don't.

In fact there's more, Missy. A lot more to tell. There are reasons your mother never returned. Les, it would do you good, do you all good, to talk about it.

The seagulls are diving, swooping. I feel myself dropping with them. The sky comes down towards us. It's a ceiling. The shadows around us are walls pressing close from all sides.

There's a split second of something crumbling. Try not to be afraid, I say to myself. Try.

This is not a time for secrets, Les, Auntie Margaret says. She helps herself to more, the sherry bottle hitting the concrete floor like a judge's gavel. And I wouldn't have stopped her, you know. Back then I would have let her take my life.

I can tell she's curious, fascinated by the idea of it.

Margaret, please. Dad grips the sherry glass in his fist. He is breathless with effort. The effort of pushing away. It's as if a stranger were at the door trying to get in and there's the smallest of cracks. The stranger's got his hand in and Dad is pushing, all of him, to keep him out.

Did you ever ask her? Auntie Margaret says. She sits forward and stares at him as if the answer were written in the smallest of script on his face. You didn't did you? You still don't believe me, do you?

Dad shakes his head, pulls his blanket off his shoulders. No, he says, I didn't ask.

There's a hundred miles between us and the ground; a helium feeling, a lifting off. Dad is gathering his things. Bottle clangs against glass. Auntie Margaret leaps to her feet to help.

I think it's over, the discussion, the leaking secrets, until she speaks to me. Missy, do you want to know? The question stings the air. All I see is her half-turned face, her quizzical left side turning, twisting towards me.

My head falls forward, tumbling into my hands. A coward's posture, I know.

Oh . . . I hear her whisper. How utterly insensitive of me, at a time like this. I thought . . .

Maybe later, I say, pulling my head up and then the blanket off.

A boat horn sounds. A faintly salty breeze blows between us. Auntie Margaret's hands are one knitted knot until she holds one out and helps me up.

Let's go, Dad says, stepping through the balcony door, bottle and glasses in hand. Ruby's waiting.

thirty-six

HAIR SO THIN IT looks like the first sprouts of new grass. Fingers like spiders. Voice so quiet we have to lean forward to hear her speak. Every day she is different. Smaller, older. Every day I am surprised when I enter her room. Every day I hold my breath until the newness sinks in.

She isn't human. Dad is right. The flesh has disappeared from her cheeks, making her eyes look huge. Even her chin has shrunk. Why had we not seen this before? "How could you? How could you? How could you?" That's what Auntie Margaret must be thinking. But if she were to ask neither of us would have an answer.

I hold Ruby's cool dry hand and squeeze. She squeezes back. There it is again. I can feel her wanting to take me with her, like on the balcony last week. My will feels nothing against hers.

Auntie Margaret's here, I say. A stupid thing to say with her just inches away. She nods and lets go of my hand.

I'm not blind, she says, her words coming out bullet-sharp.

A weak light seeps in through the window and sits cat-like over her feet. Dad and I watch as Auntie Margaret moves towards Ruby, sits down and takes her hand. Surely Auntie Margaret can convince her to live.

How are you, love? Auntie Margaret asks, rubbing Ruby's

hand in both of hers, then bending and giving it a kiss. So cold, she whispers and blows on it as if breathing it back to life. Ruby shrugs and pulls back her hand.

Did you send the letter?

Auntie Margaret nods, studies her fingernails. Did she not reply?

Ruby shakes her head, no, and seals her mouth shut to stop it from quivering.

Mummy keeps coming to me in my dreams with her wild eyes, Ruby whispers once the quivering has stopped. It's a small voice.

She's doing it with her mind, like she used to, digging in here and wanting to know. She presses her head back and forth against her pillow, every muscle in her neck straining.

Auntie Margaret nods.

Why did she go? Please, where is she?

Auntie Margaret pulls herself back from Ruby. But Ruby follows her, pulling forward and staring at her as if she will say the one perfect thing. Auntie Margaret glances at Dad. He shakes his head, no.

No, Ruby, Auntie Margaret says, holding both hands up, palms towards her as if warding off evil. It's your mother's story, only she can tell it.

Ruby falls back on her pillows and closes her eyes. You said you hated secrets. This summer you said that. Only her lips move. There is nothing else moving on her face, no way of telling anything about her.

I did, Auntie Margaret says, but this is not my secret to tell. Perhaps your father . . .

But when we turn to face him he has left the room.

thirty-seven

MUM, IS ALL I SAY, when I open the door. I recognize her from pictures. I remember her eyes from when I was seven. Or was it eight? I remember them clearly, in that fleshy way you do that a picture can't catch. Mum. I could be saying, numb. That's how I feel.

Your eyes are still blue, I say, stupidly, because I have nothing else to say.

Can I come in?

I watch her pull her suitcases in, one at a time, before I can answer. Calves, straining in her high heels, bulge like fists. She walks in and onto the carpet in her shoes, wobbling a little in the deep plush.

No shoes in the house, I say, but she pays no attention.

There are cigarillos in her open purse.

No smoking in the house either, I say, pulling out a dining-room chair to sit on and leaving her the couch.

Dad is out, Auntie Margaret is at the hospital and I know I can't reach them. My ears are ringing. I can't call them to warn them. Help, I want to say, come quickly. Help. She's walked right in. Her suitcases are there in the hall. She's here with her legs crossed, playing with the strap of her purse, bending it where the leather is cracked. And staring at me.

I've been visiting with Vivian, next door, she says, drawing her tongue across her lips.

Who? I ask.

Your neighbour, lovely woman, I met her while I was waiting, she showed me the view from her balcony. Nice to be so near the sea. So high up.

We sit across from each other. I pull my legs to my chest, feeling suddenly exposed with her knowing the neighbours when I don't.

You never wrote back to Ruby, I say. She's been waiting for months now.

Mum offers nothing but an irritated shrug.

Her purse leans against her thigh. Perspiration jiggles on her upper lip. She's wearing nylons and a knit wool skirt and jacket.

Well, I'm here, aren't I? She takes a handkerchief from her purse and wipes her lip.

I suppose, I say, feeling uncomfortable, as though it were me who was in the wrong.

You suppose? she asks. Do you think I'm a ghost? A figment of your imagination? She reaches into her purse for her cigarillos, rolls one between her fingers but doesn't light it.

I try to imitate her irritated shrug.

It is unreal, I suppose, she says finally, putting the unlit cigarillo in her mouth and giving me a good look over.

You've grown, she says in an uninterested way. How long has it been?

She speaks carelessly, leaning back on the couch, resting her head against the wall, removing the cigarillo from her mouth and brushing it back and forth across her lips, and continues to stare.

I would have guessed six or seven years ago, but looking at you now it could even be ten. What's your guess?

I shrug, embarrassed that I don't know myself. Ruby would know.

*T*EA? I ASK, WHEN it's obvious we have nothing else to say.

Please, she says. There's a snag of pale lipstick on her teeth when she smiles. It's not a polite smile.

The kettle starts screaming while I'm in the bathroom washing my face. I dash through to get it, thinking that, well, she was a guest and she would sit there like a guest and I would serve her. But she is in the kitchen making sandwiches, cutting the bread into the thinnest slices I've ever seen, and buttering them.

I make the tea, trying to avoid touching her as I pass back and forth. She finds the plates by herself and sets the table with knives and spoons, slabs of cheese, slices of buttered bread and teacups with milk already sitting in the bottom.

I thought you were useless in the kitchen, I say. She shrugs and pours herself tea.

I see my reputation precedes me, she says and laughs.

What do you want? I ask. She watches me over the edge of her teacup. She is all eyes, but there is nothing in those eyes that wants anything. A familiar feeling comes over me. A feeling that my words make no difference, that words are silly, unimportant.

You're staring at me, I say.

Again, she has no reply. She eats every slice of bread, twice offering some to me, which I refuse.

You're awfully thin, she says, you should eat. Gobble up all that life presents you. That's my motto.

She laughs as if she's making fun of me and I can feel my face pink up with embarrassment.

These were a wedding present, she says, holding the

bone-handled knife in her hand and stroking its silver surface. Still, her eyes are on me.

Your father took everything, she says, scratching at a raw piece of skin under her eye. I lost everything to him.

I feel I could slap her in the face and ask her what she thought had happened to Ruby and me, especially Ruby, if she wanted to talk about loss. But I don't. I rock a bone-handled tea-spoon between my fingers until it tips off balance and falls to the floor. And I let it stay there. Neither of us moves to pick it up.

Stop staring, I say.

She looks away from me and at her watch. Six o'clock, she says absently, but I can tell that the time means nothing to her.

I've been locked away, she says. Her voice is blank. I nod, pretending that I know, hoping that she will not go on. I've been shut in rooms without windows. I've been chased by lesbians.

That word "lesbian" is thrilling, it makes her seem dangerous.

Lesbians would sit beside me, stroke my forearm, and stare, she says. Her eyes are fixed on a bare spot of wall. She twirls a teaspoon inside her empty cup.

I was lonely beyond words so I decided to take my own life. She pulls her bracelets up the strong flesh of her forearm, revealing uncountable scars on both wrists. But they found me. They bound me up. Electric shock. Bottles of pills. Until you change your mind about living, they said, you will not be released. Living is never a choice I've made, I said. But they were stupid people, they didn't understand.

Why did you come? I ask. Why didn't you just write? She smiles an odd smile, biting her bottom lip gently and folding her fingers together to form an almost prayer-like fist. Her bracelets fall together in a tinny pile by her elbows.

I wanted to see you. I felt dragged here by Ruby's letter.

Curious, I suppose, wondering what young ladies you've turned into.

The evening sun slants across the room, colouring her face and hands a hot orange. Outside seagulls glide past the window.

You have my lips, she says, and stands to pace the space between table and couch. My lips and those hooded eyes.

*T*HE ROAR OF the day, the surprise of it, seems to gather in my head and starts to swell. This is my mother, a voice says, tucked away at the back of me. But they are only words, printed in a long line, black on white. There are no pictures. There is no softness, no familiar feeling. Another seagull, this one not gliding but slapping its wings in a hurry, passes by the window. The smallest trace of lace shows behind her silk blouse lying against her skin. Her breasts, rounded under there, so unlike the flat Cerise. Like me. Like I used to be, before.

What are you looking at? she asks, one out-of-place hair smoothed back, one knee happily lounging over the other as she comes to sit down again. She pours more tea, holding her teacup like a movie star, pinky out.

Go on, she says, what? There is a smile on her face; a slight turning up at the corner, a crinkle around the eyes.

I don't know.

What are you looking at?

I have no answer. As I stare all I see are bits and pieces. The top leg floating all alone. The high-heel shoe tipping on the toes with its heel come loose. The hand resting on the purse. The fingers bound around the leather strap. The fingers coming separate from the hand, drumming impatiently, running like mice. The rounded belly under the tweed skirt, the silk blouse, the breasts.

What are you looking at? she asks, one last time.

Nothing, I say, trying to practise the same look she has on her face, the same odd smile. Absolutely nothing at all.

GILLIAN! DAD SAYS, dropping a bag of groceries and squinting at her in the dark hallway. They shake hands and hold them there until she lets go and turns towards the living room. Dad follows her in as if he were the guest.

Auntie Margaret's reaction is more rewarding. She has brought fresh-cut flowers for the supper table which fall from her hands and scatter like an offering at Mum's feet. Her mouth falls open.

Oh! she says, how nice to see you.

I can tell it is a lie.

They seem giddy, as if they are preparing for a party. I stay in the kitchen, chopping vegetables for salad. Dad comes in several times pouring drinks on ice and waltzing them back to the living room, weaving a little on the sides of his sock feet. Mum smokes on the balcony. The sunset and the silhouette of her body making her a giant, a ghost and a mystery.

Aren't you curious about Ruby? I ask, as we sit down to dinner. I want to throw the fork I have in my hand. I want it to land in her chest, between her breasts where she is fleshy and full. It would stay in nicely. Dad butters his bread thickly.

She's not well, Mum says, I can feel it. Where is she? Auntie Margaret nods as if she had been expecting this.

How did you hear, Gillian? Dad asks. She smiles oddly, reminding me of Ruby.

She's in the hospital, I say, she wants to die.

Mum nods calmly. It seems there's nothing I can do or say to hurt or shock her. I want to see her cry, collapse, beg forgiveness.

Don't you have any questions? I ask, thinking surely she must be curious. But she just shakes her head.

It's your fault, I say, not caring about the consequences of my words, you should have written, you shouldn't have kept her waiting.

There is no response from anyone.

The sun sets, throwing us pinks, then greys, then emptiness. We let the room darken around us until there is very little to see.

She is all in shadows, her strong shoulders holding up her head so easily, her confident mouth chewing, her throat swallowing. Perhaps she's just a person, I catch myself thinking. Perhaps she cares. Perhaps if she told us her story, why she left, all the things Ruby wanted to know. Perhaps it would make a difference. Perhaps she could save Ruby.

She'll sleep in your room, Missy, Dad says, folding his dinner napkin in even triangles. When I protest he stands up, sliding his chair neatly under the table. I will not have your mother sleep in a hotel.

thirty-eight

WHO WILL TELL RUBY? I ask Dad the next morning.

I will, he says, and I'll speak to the doctor. Stay with your mother, take her for a walk, I'll go down to the hospital and see what I can arrange.

IT IS SATURDAY and I walk out into the early morning with my mother on one side and my aunt on the other. Our feet strike the ground together, our arms swing out and back in unison. This is crazy, I think, but it's hard not to enjoy. I tour them around as if I'd lived here all my life. Down Brunswick Street, with the wind coming up off the harbour and a hint of salt coming with it.

Oh, look, Mum says, disappearing through a doorway, art supplies!

She buys a sketchbook and charcoal.

I shall do your portrait and Ruby's too, if you'll let me.

I can't imagine Ruby on a sheet of paper; there'd be nothing there except, perhaps, the black stone that never leaves her hand.

We'll see, I say.

*C*AN WE GET down to the water? Mum asks.

Oooo, yes, Auntie Margaret says, clasping her hands to her chest.

It's just old boat docks, I say, it's a creepy place.

But they insist.

The air was almost metallic it was so thick with salt. Dead fish, caught in seaweed, bumped up against the docks, rocking with the suck and pull of the water. Seagull feathers, pop cans, a baby's shoe all pulled and pushed together.

Oh look! Auntie Margaret says, a baby's shoe just like you and Ruby used to wear. She gets down on her hands and knees and tries to reach for it.

Shall I push you in, Margaret? Mum says, lurching towards her.

Perhaps because I'm nervous, perhaps because so much seemed to be happening so quickly, I thought she was serious.

No! I scream and grab the back of Mum's coat and hold her back. She spins around in surprise and stares at me, saying nothing. Auntie Margaret slowly rights herself, brushes off her knees and takes my hand.

One day, she says, you must let me tell you how your mother tried to kill me. I can see it is haunting you.

Are you still on about that, Margaret? Mum says and laughs.

*W*E HAVE LUNCH in a crowded place. The noise makes us close, makes it possible to speak without my voice sounding strange.

Okay, I say, tell me why you tried to kill Auntie Margaret.

I ask recklessly. It seems, suddenly, there is nothing I can't say, nothing I don't want to know.

I look at my mother. She is looking straight back. And I have a sick yet enticing feeling that I am looking right into myself.

Missy, she says. I gave you that nickname, do you remember? I nod my head. Because you were sensible, straightforward. You never took your eyes off me. Not because you were wanting to learn from me but because you were suspicious.

I am nothing but a balloon full of cool breeze, and I'm staring into my mother's blue eyes. She's just a person, there is no mystery, there are no secrets.

Tell her, Auntie Margaret says, she has squashed all her mashed potatoes into a white pool on her plate and is looking out the window peacefully.

All right, she says. Her bracelets seem to bind her wrists to the table.

It was both of us. She wanted it, but I was the one with the will. Margaret couldn't do it, couldn't take her own life.

Auntie Margaret is saying nothing, she is watching the heads as they pass by the window: animated faces without voices, without bodies. Some we can only see the tops of, some, I suspect, we can't see at all.

Is that true? I ask.

She hesitates to answer. Truthfully, I'd never thought about living or dying, she says with a smile. Perhaps I never had the courage to think about it. I didn't want to die, no. But in that moment I couldn't think of a good argument for living either.

But now you're glad you lived? She nods again. What happened? Why didn't you die? They look at each other and start to laugh.

Well, you would think with me being the eldest I'd be in charge, wouldn't you? You'd think being an adult would give me some control over my life. Auntie Margaret stares at her potatoes as she speaks. Well, I'm afraid that's never been the case. Your mother has always had the edge, the daring, haven't you Gillian?

Mum lights a cigarillo and motions for her to continue.

Really Gillian, you know we both hate the smoke. Mum shrugs, picks herself up and plants herself at the next table.

Carry on, she says, I'm listening. Auntie Margaret doesn't seem to mind and raises her voice above the general noise to be heard.

We were neither of us in our right minds. Gosh, I remember those days so clearly. Grief was everywhere. I saw it in the stones. The trees wept. Terrible time. I came down to visit you. Gillian, you'd lost the baby. You were in a terrible way. I came down to help out. Some help I was!

Mum is staring at us through the smoke of her cigarillo. Staring as if she can't quite see us.

You two are very much alike, she says and laughs. Look at you there, a pair of goody two-shoes. Always doing the right thing, aren't you?

Could you continue with the story? I ask.

Yes, of course, Auntie Margaret says, patting me on the hand. Your mother took me into the woods. There was a clearing, she said, and I must see it. I remember walking just behind her, my head teetering atop my neck like the pea head of a giraffe so far away from its body. Awful feeling. As we stepped into the woods they lost their colour. The floor, the wall, the ceiling of the woods, all grey. All grey and tight and closing in.

Get on with it, Mum says, all this fluffy talk is not what Missy needs. She throws a serviette at Auntie Margaret.

Yes, yes, Auntie Margaret says, taking the serviette and straightening it. Kneel down and pray for yourself, she said when we reached the clearing. I knelt, keeping my back rigid and my head bowed. Between my shoulder blades I could feel a burning. Could feel her there behind me, arms raised.

People around us were listening. They weren't looking at us

directly but their conversations had stopped and they were bent ever so slightly towards us.

Keep your voice down, I whisper. Auntie Margaret nods but when she starts up again it's with the same strength.

Three old leaves from the fall, wrinkled and brown. A gnarled twig like a broken finger, twisted and wrenched at its sockets. Green shoots. Bluebells. A white button with four dirt-filled holes. Moss carpets over stones. Seven stones, naked and smooth. Odd isn't it, I remember each one of them as if it were yesterday. She was behind me, her huge body swaying, her arms raised over her head, her glare focused at the root of my neck. I could feel it there, I knew. Roots severed from trees, heaved up from below. Beetles with shiny backs, in a hurry. Grasses. A purple thread. A boot print. Perhaps it is best that I die, that's what I thought up against her violent will. I was ready to collapse, to give in if it was her wish.

Fool, Mum says, extinguishing the last of her cigarillo and standing abruptly. A few people's heads turn involuntarily when she moves. She starts pacing around our table, arms crossed.

You always were sentimental, Margaret. Even in the face of your own death you make it poetry. You're talking about a gentleness, a beauty that just wasn't there.

Gillian, I thought it was the end of my life. Those moments are precious to me. Stay quiet while I finish this for Missy. It was a dog, Missy, that saved my life.

They both begin to laugh. Mum stops pacing and laughs, holding her hands to her chest. The other people listening in relax, smile to each other, rearrange their cutlery.

A dog, I say, giggling myself.

Yes, he came waddling out of the woods, his tail straight as a stick in amazement when he saw us. I heard your mother's arm swish to her sides and that was it, the spell was broken. Come here then, I called to the dog. He trotted forward, his curious head cocked sideways. Then we heard the owners. Wil-li-am, they called.

William! I said, William the Conqueror! And with his name he jumped towards me and began licking my hands and face. His tongue was hot and rough. He jumped into my lap and covered my face with his kisses. I tumbled to the ground and, lying on my back, let him run the length of me, up and down. The sky was swirling, the tips of the trees bowed and bent as if peering down to speak to me. His breath was sweet. Sweet, sweet William, I whispered to him. And the sky managed to crack open with sun and the world rocked and tilted as if, like an egg, it were about to crack open too.

There are nods of approval from the patrons. Mum begins her pacing again. Everyone likes a happy ending, she says, letting her eyes glance over the secret observers and embarrassing them.

Carry on Margaret.

William was retrieved by fretful owners. They lent me a hand, pulling me up as I laughed and stumbled, a little giddy, insisting I was fine. They tried to brush the mud from my skirt. They tried to untangle the twigs from my hair. And all the while I kept saying, I'm fine, it's all right, just fine. And strangely I was.

There is a pause and then Mum begins to clap. She claps and claps.

Congratulations Margaret Hurst, she says, Margaret Goody Two-Shoes. Queen Sweet. If actions are what we believe then you're an angel, a good girl, a darling. And, oh, how they love you!

My face is hot, burning. Auntie Margaret stands to speak to Mum but Mum turns and marches towards the door.

You, she shouts, turning towards both of us, have never taken a stand on anything. Never a risk. Never a wild dream.

Never stepped on anyone's toes to get what you want.

She starts walking back towards us, staring at the odd person who's watching. But someone from the restaurant grabs her elbow before she can get too far. She yanks herself free and raises her liberated arm and points at me. Her mouth opens to speak but she is pushed out the front doors and is gone.

She's always been troubled, Missy, Auntie Margaret says, almost whispering as she pulls on her jacket and motions for me to do the same. She was born troubled. It's no one's fault, not even hers.

thirty-nine

A LL DAY, EACH DAY, I walk around with the knowledge that my mother is close by. I avoid her, leaving the apartment without saying goodbye, closing the door silently, especially when I go to visit Ruby.

She tries to encourage me to spend time with her. Come shopping for makeup, she says. We could buy the whole store.

She waves a credit card above her head, tipping precariously on her high heels which she still refuses to take off inside the house.

I've never worn makeup, I say.

You've never had me around to show you. She waffles about looking coy.

I never needed you, I say, trying to make it sting. Sometimes I am desperate to hurt her. Sometimes I just like to try out this new, direct me.

Some days she comes home with a new outfit or new makeup and a new face all done up in a vulgar way by someone down at Eaton's. Her eyebrows tweezed to a thin line, her eyelids heavy and purple. She looks like a woman punched in the face, and I tell her so. If Dad hears me saying these kinds of things he raises his voice.

Apologize for that remark, young lady, he says, and I just turn from them and walk away with nowhere to go but Dad's room, where nothing belongs to me except for a pile of my things stuffed in the corner by the window.

*H*OW LONG IS she staying? I ask Dad, after a week. He shrugs and won't look at me. Ask her, I demand. But he won't.

The problem is that Doctor Kline won't allow Mum to see Ruby. She wants to speak to Mum first, but Mum won't go.

I've had enough of those crackpots, she said, pulling a cigarillo from her purse and sucking on it.

Don't you want to see Ruby? Don't you care? I ask. She doesn't answer for a while and I sit across from her watching her dismember the cigarillo, pulling off the brown skin and separating each tobacco layer, one from the other. The longer pieces she puts in her mouth and chews.

Well? I say, when she seems to have forgotten I'm there, waiting for an answer.

Stop asking questions you don't want answers to, she says, a tiny brown flake sticking to her teeth.

*O*NE EVENING AFTER dinner, as I am doing the dishes and they sit in the living room with a drink, I hear her say, Now, Les, why did you have me locked away for all those years?

I stop the running water. I hear Auntie Margaret get up and leave the room. The windows are open and far-off sounds seep in at us.

Why? she asks, again. And again there is no answer. She stands up with her cigarillos and walks out to the balcony. She leans against the railing, her back to the fourteen-storey drop. Why did you leave me in there all those years? All alone? She shouts it at us through the balcony door so the whole world can hear.

Hot oranges in the sky. Mad lines of reds and purples. I watch her from where I stand by the sink. She lets the smoke out her nose and squeezes it through her tightened lips. Against the sunset, with her face gone dark in shadows, she is everything awful I've always believed her to be.

Missy, she says, suddenly looking in at me. I want you to know, I have been betrayed.

Shut up, I scream, dropping a handful of wet knives and forks on the floor. The thought of her raised arms above Auntie Margaret's small neck suddenly terrifies me.

Shut up, I scream, running through the living room where Dad sits on the couch, a drink resting on his knee. Never a risk. Never a wild dream.

Shut up, I scream, flying past my own room that isn't my room any more. My room that's been poisoned by some crazy, stinking it up with her smells.

Shut up, shut up, shut up, I scream, trying to erase the picture of her towering over Auntie Margaret. Trying to shut out the words that come so easily from her mouth. Something keeps opening and opening inside my head; a cavernous mouth full of secrets and evil.

Auntie Margaret sits on the edge of our bed with her hands in her lap looking through the window. The sunset, burning through the glass, lights the room in crazy colours. It's unreal.

Try not to fear the truth, Missy, she says, calmly. It will only make it harder. Her hands rest like cups, one fitting perfectly into the other, waiting to be filled.

I'm trying, I say.

I'm sick of trying. Of trying harder. Of being good. Of being better.

Why weren't we taken away sooner? I ask. We were so small. We were so alone out there. Left in that place. Why did no one come?

Auntie Margaret shakes her head. Her face is lit up in devilish reds, streaks of oranges. Yet it's a smooth, lineless face. Angelic.

And she talks about being betrayed! I can't keep my voice steady or quiet.

Auntie Margaret nods, holds out a hand to me but I shake her off.

Why did she take us with her if she didn't want us?

She did what was expected, didn't she? Auntie Margaret shakes her head again and again as if she finds it hard to believe her own words. Children belong with their mother. That's what everyone believes, isn't it? The soft open palms of her hands wait, wishing for an answer that doesn't seem to be there.

*I*T IS SHORTLY after all that that Mum announces her departure. She places her ticket in the middle of the table during dinner. Here it is, she says. Soon I shall not be in the way.

Dad shifts uncomfortably in his chair. I grab the ticket folder.

Next Monday. Eight thirty-five, I announce, closing it up and putting it back in its place. Everyone is looking at me.

Good, I say, this has been difficult. Dad puts down his fork and wipes his mouth.

Well, she says, taking the ticket and tucking it into her purse, I suppose that is true.

My legs are stuck to the seat of the chair. I sweat as if it were mid-July. There are candles, unlit, in the middle of the table, waiting for the dark. There's some English dessert in the fridge, creamy and too sweet.

I wonder what you want, Missy, from me? She is flattening her napkin full out with the edge of her hand, the wrinkles won't come out so she presses harder. It spreads onto Auntie Margaret's part of the table.

Me? I ask. She nods quite comfortably.

Nothing any more, I guess.

She strikes a match, the candlelight flickers across our faces.

You never wanted us, I say.

True and not true, she says, lighting another match, then a cigarillo. She knew no one would stop her.

forty

DOCTOR KLINE SAYS YES. She says Mum can go and see Ruby before she goes. Before who goes? I ask. Dad says that's not funny. He says don't joke about things like that. I'm not joking, I say, standing outside on the balcony in just a T-shirt, shivering. I can feel the long drop down when I look over, a familiar dread, a sort of fear that I might just do it, might just jump or rather tip over without much of a thought, and be gone.

WE ALL GO. I try walking there with my eyes closed, holding on to the back of Auntie Margaret's jacket for direction. The curbs jar me every time and my teeth jam together. A cold wind drags leaves from their branches, pulls them along the ground and piles them in useless places where I feel them bunching underfoot as if it were not concrete we walked upon but a forest floor.

The hospital doors are hard to push open. The hallways are long and empty. It feels like we're not supposed to be here, I whisper to Auntie Margaret. She doesn't seem to hear. Then Ruby's door. We hesitate like a clot around it. All of us but Mum, that is. She holds one arm out in front and ploughs through looking like a figurehead on the bow of a ship.

Mum is sitting down with her sketchbook resting on her knees before the rest of us have settled. The charcoal rocks between her fingers like a cigarillo. Her wool skirt grabs tightly around her thighs. She sits like she's perched on the smallest of islands and I think, just for a second, how brave she has been to return even for so brief a time.

They look at each other, Ruby and Mum, like they're looking across a great distance, squinting a little, not sure what they see.

Hello, Mum says. Her back is straight, almost regal.

We have all been bending towards Ruby. Not Mum. Ruby nods, once, opening her eyes wide so we see them whole: the whites, the blues, the black centre. They are huge, like bug's eyes, in her tiny shrunken head.

You look different, Ruby says. Her voice is raspy and foreign.

Mum gives her one of those indifferent shrugs that she's been giving me and draws the first dark line across the paper.

Ruby starts to shake. Her eyes dart back and forth like tropical fish, hungrily nibbling at Mum. So I look closely at Mum, too. This is your mother, I tell myself. I say it strictly like you would if you were speaking to a child that was having trouble listening. I try again. It's my last chance, the last day. I try to feel it, the feeling of having a mother. There are wrinkles at her wrists, freckles on her hands. There's a softness at her hips, it pushes against the wool weave of her skirt. This is my mother, I tell myself. But, like on that first day, there is nothing there. Her cheekbones push out from her face. Her jaw is set in concentration. Her hair is blonde, today. She's changed it twice since she arrived. Red, chestnut brown, blonde, take your pick. I suspect it's rather like mine underneath, a dull, unremarkable brown.

Bit by bit Ruby's eyes start to narrow. Bit by bit her face collapses. And then she's shut herself out, again.

Mum begins to draw, unaware that Ruby came and then left. Her hand, moving across the paper, is the only thing we hear. She notices the stone, she makes it big and juicy. She makes Ruby's thin hands, still bound to the bed, look like claws. She looks to be grabbing the stone like you would if you were slipping; it's that last piece of earth left before you fall.

A black scrawl of charcoal for her arm. It lies along the blanket like a child lying in the grass by a stream. Like it's summer and there's nowhere you have to be. As if the wind blew lazily across her, just a whisper, and she was floating off to the sound of it and the trickling water.

I wonder how she can draw it like that, panic next to peace. And all in a few strokes, one melted into the other.

The hospital gown hides Ruby's shoulder like Christmas wrapping. Such surprises. Such unknown. What's in there? Something wriggling? A puppy? A pair of socks? Something you've always dreamed of? Mum holds the charcoal tightly, its black rubbing off on her fingers. When she pushes her hair back a black smudge is left on her forehead.

Ruby's head peeled away to bone; to rough surfaces like driftwood and dried fruit, like stone that has been tortured by drops of water for millions of years. Her eyes are hollows, sunken in and not wanting to come out. Each stroke on the paper is sharp and short.

Why are you so sick? Mum asks, splitting the silence with her words, though they are spoken softly. She's tracing the last lines around the mouth over and over until they become darker and thicker than the rest of the face.

I want to die, Ruby says. A twitch starts at the corner of her mouth and pulses into her shoulder.

Yes, Mum says, as if it were a simple request like wanting candy, you do. She hasn't looked up at Ruby. She hasn't seen the twitching or the one, small tear that has bulged out of the corner of one of Ruby's eyes and stayed there. Mum keeps the line going around the mouth. Sometimes it looks like it's sinking farther and farther into the face. Then suddenly it shifts and appears to be swelling, reaching out towards you looking for a kiss. Almost like fish lips but not funny or playful at all. There's a desperateness about them that makes me want to pull away.

Will you stay? Ruby's eyelids flutter. Her eyes roll under her lids. Her mouth twitches. Her shoulder jerks.

Auntie Margaret begins to cry.

Dad sits on the bed and takes one of Ruby's feet. I sit next to him. He lets me lean, light at first, then all of me. His body is so still it feels like a wall I'm pressed against. Auntie Margaret's cry is as rhythmical as waves, washing and washing over all of us.

Mum stares hard at Ruby as if she is trying to remember something. She rolls the charcoal between her fingers then places it in its case.

No, she says. In the silence of the room the tinny snap of the case closing sounds like gunshot.

Mum walks over, disconnects the drip and the wires, releases Ruby's arms and legs and picks her up and rocks her. We watch her like a movie, it's as if we can't touch her or stop her. Nothing in her has to strain. She holds Ruby in her arms, draped like a blanket. Look, she says, tiny hairs, like a newborn's, all over her. She strokes one of Ruby's fuzzy arms with amazement.

Has it always been like this? she asks. None of us answer, we have all been afraid of what has been growing there, like moss or fungus. It reminds me of Gandhi's little body, too young to have feathers.

When you were born I didn't want you. Of course, you must know that by now, she begins, speaking across Ruby's body and over our heads and through the walls as if it were God himself she were addressing. There's nothing much I ever wanted but to be free. To paint. To follow God. She pauses, brushing an absent finger along Ruby's arm. If I've learned anything at all in this life it's this: at all costs, if you're going to live, then live your life, really live it.

I'm soaring. I'm light. I could be tossed, I could be thrown from great heights and not get hurt.

I said that, Les. I said it again and again but you wouldn't listen, no one would listen. Isn't that true? That's all I ever wanted. To be free.

Dad is nodding. He has removed his shoes, his sock feet squirm against each other like small animals.

Auntie Margaret is mesmerized, she's holding her two hands together in front of herself as if in church. She's nodding too, like a tree branch in the wind.

But I loved you and love you now, she says. They are flat, meaningless words sounding more like a memorized poem or a series of numbers than a mother speaking to her daughters.

Liar, I say. It springs out of me like a jack-in-the-box. Nobody shuts me up. They all turn towards me. Perhaps they want to hear more.

I'm high up, hovering. It's like I'm waiting for something. God, perhaps, though I don't believe in him.

It's too late for Ruby, I say, feeling a bit wise with everyone watching so curiously. Mum is nodding now. And you did it, I say, you and you. I point with my head at the two of them. My mother and father. I can't stand to use my fingers, a nod of my head is all I can bear.

I think perhaps it will kill him. I wait for my words to make it happen. I wait for the cracking open of his head and something spilling out that we cannot stop. Something violent. But there is nothing. Just air pressing in through the vents. Just the usual clatter in the halls and Auntie Margaret smiling at me, almost laughing, with her hands cupped over her chest and her mole, Ruby's favourite mole, twitching.

And, I say, feeling words rush in behind my eyes, me too, it's my fault too. Saying it makes me feel the truth of it, how I betrayed her. Tiny, shrinking Ruby. A doll, really. My baby sister.

I'm sorry, Ruby, I say. My head is packed full of a million sorrys.

Someone's hand lands on my leg. I push it off.

Don't, I say, it's the truth. There's strength in the confession. I feel my lungs expand and then my hands. I feel my heart beating as if it were squishing through my ribs. Then my legs and feet expanding, spreading out like the roots and branches of trees until I'm feeling a hundred times my size. It feels like the roof has lifted from above us and the sky is pouring in.

When Ruby speaks her voice rattles like a dried pod, like a gourd, a primitive instrument. She lifts her head from the crook of Mum's arm and her neck pops alive with sinews: taut, inhuman ropes.

Why did you go? she asks. She looks straight at Mum, their faces are just inches apart. Before Mum can answer she speaks again.

And, why didn't you come back? Her face cracks open with a grimace. It's cracked open with wickedness as if she's caught Mum stealing something, doing something wrong.

Ruby, weren't you listening? I say. She doesn't want us, she never did.

Ruby shakes her head. There's something more, she says, so certain. Then she lets her head down, all the ropes relaxing, and closes her eyes. Her eyelids seem transparent. Her eyes move back and forth underneath as if she's watching everything. And of course, she is.

forty-one

PERHAPS YOU REMEMBER the little cottage? Mum says, placing Ruby back on her bed. The one by the cliffs? That's where I went. Johnson and I lived there for a few glorious weeks. Alone with the sea. I needed to think things out in a way I couldn't with the two of you around.

Pay attention, Ruby, this is for you. Open your eyes so I know you're listening. Life's too short for me to be repeating myself.

Ruby does, just one. It slips a little, slides around until it finds Mum.

Good, Mum says and pulls a cigarillo from her purse.

Not here, Dad says, springing to his feet. Absolutely not here! Mum holds her cigarillo hand up.

I'll suck on it, relax, she says.

I had to get away. The two of you were at me day and night. You Ruby, curled into your ball, crying constantly. And Missy watching me, like I said before, because you were suspicious. Do you know how many times I've been looked at that way? Do you know how it feels?

She's pacing now. Running her fingers along the window glass as she passes. Each time her heel hits the ground I think she'll continue, but we wait. And wait. And Ruby's eyes slide shut.

Johnson was a peculiar man. Simple. Stupid, really. He looked odd in that little house, what with the size of him. I laughed at his hands around teacups or teaspoons. His shout, his anger. Quite refreshing, I suppose.

She turned and glared at Dad.

I had never been so happy as in those weeks by the sea. Every morning I beat the rugs out into the wind and sang from the *Messiah*. The small bits of washing we had dried quickly on the line, flapping like gull's wings. Then, every afternoon I painted. All that height and space, all that blue and white and wind. It was the life I was meant to have. This is it, I told Johnson one afternoon, this is where I'll die.

But, the day of my birthday, the weather turned.

It was while we were having our morning tea, with the wildflowers Johnson had picked for me rustling on the kitchen table, that I spied the clouds, far off but black.

Things always turn on my birthday, I said, feeling fear come over me like a cold fever.

Johnson laughed, snapping off a piece of biscuit in his mouth and spraying its crumbs towards me. "Well, well," he said, "the adventurer is having doubts. The game is turning nasty."

I spat at him.

He grabbed my neck from across the table and squeezed till he heard me choking. "You're a stupid woman," he hissed, his eyes a devilish red. "You're an idiot to think you can just walk away from them. You're their mother for Chrissake." He released me sharply and I sprang back from him as if I'd been pitched, like a small child, against a wall.

You think he was right, don't you, Missy? I can see it on your face.

She stood in front of me and stared. I could feel her taking in the whole of me, looking me up and down. Her cigarillo rolled impatiently between finger and thumb.

Perhaps, I say.

But mostly I don't know anything any more. Ruby was right all along. She was there at the little cottage. We could have gone to get her. Everything would have been different.

It is at that moment, imagining going back to get her, that I realize it had been a great relief for me, her disappearance.

No, I'm glad you went, I hear myself saying.

Mum gives an awkward laugh and turns away from me.

Anyway, she says, I felt the world was against me. I felt I'd made my bed and now I had to sleep in it, as they say. Vulgar saying. So, the next morning I went back to the bed and breakfast to get the two of you. It was what a mother was supposed to do, wasn't it?

She directs her glare at Dad. But he doesn't see it. He has his head in his hands and is staring at the floor.

Johnson slept as I dressed, as I opened the door, started the lorry and left. I kept thinking he'd wake and pull me back. Tell me to stay. But he slept on.

Dark clouds lay just above the roof, pressing down hard like a huge black boot. No one, nothing stopped me. Children are a mother's, I kept saying to myself, over and over, so I wouldn't turn back. I could feel the earth spinning beneath me.

I pulled a few flowers from the garden and walked through the front door. Your shoes were not there, your coats were not hanging on the pegs in the hall. What had it been, then, two or three weeks since I'd left you?

I walked through to the kitchen, where she stood at the sink. Flowers in my hand, a peace offering.

What have you done with them, I wanted to ask. But there was something in her eyes when she turned to look at me, an accusation, a glint of enjoyment. Something like the smiling egg on the sign outside her house that mocked me. She looked, then turned away. She had a back thick and fleshy, and ankles puffed and swollen.

I picked up a knife. It lay on the kitchen table. And I raised it, slowly, above my head. Like in the woods with Margaret. A turned back, a head bowed. I felt my arms tremble above me. And then, I pulled it down and in.

She was stirring something. It fell to the floor. She was singing something. It came from her mouth in a dull rush of air, a deep groan. I dug with the knife, again and again, cracking and splitting into her. She turned to me, her thick neck straining, fleshy folds of it, layer upon layer, twisting backwards over her shoulder, her mouth wide open and wet. Pale blue eyes like yours Ruby, though her face was huge and swollen. Silent like you are Ruby, no words, just a low wheeze, a rumble.

But, like Margaret in the woods, she was spared. A rushing on the stairs, the sounds of fabric and air. The yell of an inhuman voice. Something pushing. The crack of my head against a cupboard as I fell. The Devil: his feet in the small of my back. My face jammed against a wall, my cheeks resting in egg yokes and blood. Eggs: the godly colours of gold and white. The blood of Christ. I began to laugh. Good and Evil; we battle them to the end. Evil: its hard heel in me like a knife.

And there she was on the floor beside me, gasping and gurgling like a snagged fish. Where are the children, I asked. Her eyes sliding until they found me. She was the palest of colours, like bread dough before it's punched down. The corners of her mouth turned then sagged again. The children, I shouted. She lay limp, wordless.

The Devil dug his heels in deeper. I tried kicking back, I tried swatting with my hands. I couldn't find him, though he was there; a pinpoint of pain, a skewer, a nail, holding me to the ground. Nails to a cross. Judas, I shouted, betrayer.

Give them back, I screamed, though I knew I couldn't keep you. Though you didn't want me. Give them back, I screamed, over and over until I forgot what it was I wanted.

*W*E ARE ALL SILENT. Mum has rolled her cigarillo between her fingers so vigorously that it is breaking apart.

I was put away, she whispers, dropping the mangled cigarillo on the floor. There was a trial. It was in all the papers. Wife of a scientist! Mother of two! There was a picture of me walking from the courtroom, handcuffed, looking straight at the camera. And what do you think it said underneath? "How dare she!" That's right. "How dare she!"

Mum squashes the crumbled cigarillo with her foot and laughs. There, Ruby, she says, there's your story. Not the mother you imagined, I suppose.

Ruby, I blurt out, are you okay? I shake the leg closest to me but she pulls it away. And then both her legs start kicking and her head flailing and the strangest sounds gurgle up from deep in her chest. Her lips don't move.

Ruby! Everyone startles at once but Mum gets to her first, heaves her up into her arms again and shakes her.

Stop! Ruby, stop and take a breath! Now, what's the matter? The rest of us are just inches away with our arms straight out and open. Stand back, Mum says, motioning with her chin. Give her some room to speak.

Now Ruby, speak up. You've been quiet for too long.

It all seems so simple when Mum talks. So straightforward.

I knew you were there, Ruby whispers. Her chest labours as she speaks. I told them but they wouldn't let me go. I would have come to get you. I would have stayed there with you, on the cliffs. Her breath sounds like sawing, it grinds under her ribs and flings itself out past her tiny crusty lips.

It was Missy that caused the trouble, not me. She kept you away.

She heaves this into the room like it's a weight she's carried for years. Like a bomb flung through an open door.

Ruby! Dad shouts. He grabs my head, planting both hands over my ears as if he could protect me from the words, as if I hadn't heard them yet. But nothing can protect me, nothing can make it go away, the feeling that I have just been sacrificed by my own sister who lies there in my mother's arms trembling.

forty-two

*G*ILLIAN, PUT HER DOWN. Dad leans slowly forward, pointing to Ruby as if there might be some confusion as to who he's talking about. Mum is holding her as if it were a pile of laundry in her arms, not her daughter. She shifts her feet impatiently. They are stuffed into high heels and puff out the sides.

Gillian, put her back. Dad is on his feet and walking towards Mum. His shoulders are rounded and the sleeves of his cardigan are too short. When he holds his hands out for Ruby the sleeves slide farther up showing his pale wrists.

You tried to come back, I say, my voice tunnelling through the room, not sounding like mine at all.

I guess that's something.

I'm saying it for Ruby, to Ruby, in case she didn't hear. Or perhaps I'm saying it for myself. A sort of screen, a diversion from the truth.

Ruby, I say loudly, she tried to come back. I pretend this fact will change everything.

No one speaks. We are all listening to a lie. Not the words but the meaning underneath them. Me, trying to save Ruby. That's another lie. Pretending I have the power to. Pretending she cares what I say. Pretending she has not just betrayed me.

There is silence for a long while. Ruby lies limply in Mum's arms, her bare feet resting one on top of the other. Mum is bored. She moves towards the window and sandwiches Ruby against the glass.

Give her back, Gillian, Dad says, as if Ruby were a ball. A red ball that everyone in the playground wants to have, to kick around, to toss in the air.

You have no rights, Gillian. You gave them away.

Either Mum is thinking about this or she's not listening. There's an almost child-like look on her face. A look that smoothes out slowly across her face like a rising sun.

You tried to kill someone, I say. The outrageous look on her face makes me forget about Ruby. All I want to do is hurt her. Yet this outright statement has no effect on her. No head bowed in shame, not even a shrug or an uncomfortable laugh.

Don't you feel bad about that?

Mum stares right through me as if she doesn't understand the question.

Why didn't you tell us? My voice sounds small. That's partly because the question is for Dad but I can't bear to look at him when I ask it. I speak to the only part of the room that isn't populated, a spot where floor meets wall. There's an electrical socket there jammed full of plugs. I imagine forcing myself through one of those holes and disappearing.

Dad shakes his head at my question so I have to read his mind. I'm sorry, I imagine him saying. I imagine him saying it in the same way he said it before Cerise left. I imagine him holding Ruby and saying it over and over to her, whispering it, shouting it until she fills up with his sorrys and decides to live. Perhaps he doesn't know why he never told us but he knows now that he should have. He knows now that Ruby might not be here dying if he had spoken.

Suddenly, without words or warning, he lurches towards Ruby and Mum. His hands are drawn in tight to his side as if his wrists were tied down. Then he springs them loose. He grabs Mum's shoulder and spins her around to face him.

Stop this nonsense this minute, he shouts. Ruby dangles between them.

You are a foolish woman, you always have been.

It's a strange, tame thing to say to an almost killer. It's embarrassing.

All her life, every day, she waited for you! I'm shouting too, I think. Either that or it's a hissing whisper coming out under pressure. It's the pressure of too many words piled up, stuffed under. So much pressure it's almost blinding.

And this is it? You'd just let her go?

Mum has turned full circle to face me. There is a knowing smile on her face. It says I'm a fool. I can feel my brain shutting down, bit by bit, like a huge machine would. Not all at once but grindingly slow.

Missy, most of my life I've been kept from what I wanted. It's a death, it really is. If this is what she wants then let her have it.

Dad grabs Ruby around the belly. His fingers flex like vulture's claws. If only Cerise could see him now. If only Ruby would pay attention and see how Dad could fight. For her.

All she ever wanted was a mother, I shout. This time I know I'm shouting. I can feel my voice chewing at the back of my throat.

Precisely, Mum says. It's a clipped, certain word and she delivers it as if she were saying "checkmate."

Tell me, Mum continues, do you believe I am a mother or could be a mother, the way Ruby wants a mother? She manages a smile that is at once both grim and satisfied.

I am cornered. We all are. There's no escape now, not for Ruby.

A nurse's head appears and then another, in the doorway.

Mum is still holding Ruby against the glass. Dad's arm is wrapped around her, still attached to Ruby. All I can see is Ruby's almost bald head, flopped back. The nurses circle.

I am her mother, Mum says, unaware of Ruby's falling head. Unaware of the ridiculousness of the statement after what she has just said. One nurse reaches out at Mum. Another cups Ruby's head in her hand. They ask Dad to step back.

She has all this baby hair on her skin, Mum says. She's staring at Ruby like she's a newborn or an exotic butterfly that's just landed on the inside of her arm.

That's normal, the nurses say, for this situation. "Normal" is not a word I would have expected at this moment. Normal.

Suddenly, Ruby's head jerks. The nurse grabs it with both hands.

Let this child go, immediately! One nurse grabs both Mum's arms from behind, the other takes Ruby, and Mum is pushed aside.

MUM FALLS AWAY like a starfish loosened from its place on a rock. Like a gull dropping from its perch with the whole sky between it and the ground. She floats away. It's the most natural thing for her to do. Her arms fall to her side, a foot steps backwards to catch her balance. She teeters on her high heels and looks up as if catching a glimpse of someone who'd just played a trick on her; someone high in a tree who was up there, laughing.

All of her is balanced on those tiny spiked heels. Her calves are bunched up under her like animals ready to spring. At first she staggers; feet planted apart, working to keep her upright. But you can see her strength at work, you can see her looking straight ahead as if she were on that cliff in Dover and you can see that she's already gone.

forty-three

ALL I COULD DO was get the camera, focus and press the button. I had no choice but to take it, snap it quick, before everyone's head turned. Before they noticed themselves; their knotted bodies, their neck aches and tired eyes. Before they saw themselves separate from each other. And from Ruby. Before they started to forget.

Ruby lay all week like a string strung across a canyon, narrow and taut. It had been that way since Mum left. Our hands clasped on our laps, our heads turned towards the bed. Averted from the windows and doors. Averted from ourselves.

Ruby was building for her final push away. I waited for that moment with the camera. I held it on my lap and watched the light change across our faces. Morning to afternoon. Afternoon to evening. Evening to dark. Those last days, after Mum's grand exit, were just a series of shades of light, bleeding one into the other. We took turns sleeping on the floor, coats tucked under our heads.

I listened to our breathing, each in and out identical with Ruby. The odd heavy sigh or sudden intake that I felt like a shiver in the room. We would cross and uncross our legs together. Or sniff. Or clear our throats. We began to move as one being. A sea creature without edges, Auntie Margaret said. She said she had dreamed of this long ago. And now it was here.

*T*HE LAST DAY. I woke as it was getting light. I could see between the buildings, the cool breath of clouds sitting heavy on their tops. A bit of pink ocean. A tiny green corner of George's Island. She's still breathing, I thought, the clouds reminding me. Auntie Margaret sat beside her, one hand around her wrist, the other held upright, cupped, as if ready to catch anything that might fall.

Come, Auntie Margaret whispered, seeing me awake. I pull up a chair and sit, shoulder to shoulder, beside her.

You know, she says, letting her lips brush across my ear with her secrets. You know, I hate my sister for what she's done to you two. Her selfishness, her brutal selfishness. This is none of your doing, none of it. Do you hear me? I nod, but I'm not sure the nod is true.

I've been sitting here all night, contemplating. This is really it, Missy. Her eyes are brimful of tears, but they don't fall down her cheeks. This is Ruby's decision. So many years of having no control over getting what she wants and it comes to this.

The pool of tears swells some more, wobbling as she speaks. There's something about absolute resolve, don't you think? Gillian and Ruby both have it. That absolute attention to getting what they want. Should we admire it, I wonder? Or despise it?

Suddenly, Ruby's breathing separates from ours. Becomes slower. Her chest is working harder. We can't match it. We have to breathe above her. Faster and fuller and quiet. Her own breath becomes louder and louder so that we become the silent ones, sitting as if we were on the crest of a wave waiting for the next in-breath, the next whoosh of air reaching in to feed her. We don't know if it will happen again. They warned us the last breath was coming. And now we wait for it.

Wake up, Auntie Margaret whispers to Dad and Marla. I think it's time.

I'M HUNGRY, RUBY would whisper, a long, long time ago.

Hold on darling, Mummy would say, I'll just finish my ciggie. Or book. Or painting. And then she'd forget. And the dust and the dark would gather around us as we waited. For food, for bed, for Daddy. Everything took forever to happen.

And when she was gone, we waited for her.

Stupid, I'd say to myself if I caught myself waiting. Stupid. Stupid. Stupid.

But Ruby revelled in it. She waited like she was sucking on candy, like she was turning it around and around in her mouth, tasting it as if she'd never have another.

*B*EFORE THE HEART stopped it was the breathing. We sat on the crest, on the top of the rhythm where it was supposed to happen again, another breath, and waited.

Nothing.

Everyone leaned forward. I pulled the camera to my eye and focused. Ruby in the centre, so clear. The jewel, the red centre, the wound.

I snapped. I held the camera steady on Ruby, on the sides of all their faces as they bent towards her. On the clenched fists and awkward postures. Snap. On the partly opened mouths. On the frantic beeping of the heart machine. Snap. On the morning light as it seeped into the room. It was the only chance to get it, just that once, because after the snap I knew they would shake awake. I knew that we would rush to feel for a beat or a breath and when there was none everything would end, and then start again. A blip, a tug, a catch, something so strangely quiet and still that would change everything. Forever.

Dad began trembling. His hands shook as he smoothed the blankets over her still legs. They were sticks. She lay like the odd bits of wood you gather before you pile them like a teepee and burn them. We stood around Ruby as if she were a campfire, Dad, Marla, Auntie Margaret and I. We stared into her, mesmerized, as if she flickered and twisted like a flame.

Dad closed her eyes, pulling the lids down gently as if they were butterfly wings. When he pushed her jaws together her teeth clicked. It was the last human sound she ever made.

And as he closed her eyes I remembered something. It was after Mum disappeared but before Cerise, somewhere in that mostly forgotten time. I don't know where we were but we had just walked out into the light of a summer day. We had hesitated like a cough, a throat tickle, and then carried on.

Ruby had stood beside me small and trembling. I had tried to take her hand but she pulled it away. And I remember the thought in my head exactly. It's just us, I thought. It's just Ruby and me at the door, waiting. That thought felt massive as we stood there, the weight of it almost impossible to bear.

Paint peeled like curling tongues on the door frame. As if something were too hot, something singeing, untouchable. Ruby took her tiny, translucent finger and pushed a paint peel loose and the sunlight grabbed it. It was a strange white, a foreign yellowing white. There was something about the feeling of that moment and the intensity of the light that confused me and I wanted to ask, what is it? I want to ask Ruby except I couldn't because I was the one, the oldest, who was supposed to know.

We walked out into the light. It stung. It was a hard light, and my eyes started to tear. I looked at Ruby. Not hers. Hers were like deer's eyes, wide and huge and full. Not startled by the light at all.

Mummy's coming, she whispered.

I remember the suddenness, the surprise of those words. I had wanted to scream no, no, no, over and over until I'd squashed her into the ground, until she was all flat with my screaming, until she had become a piece of flatness you step across without thinking. But I didn't. I was silent and still, my eyes squeezing shut against the stinging light.

And she had just nodded and smiled to herself, there in the doorway, unaware of my hatred.

Sorry Ruby, I whisper, as Dad slips his fingers from her face.

Whatever you're sorry about Missy . . . Dad starts to say.

He can't stop looking at Ruby, but he reaches out to hold my hand.

Whatever you're sorry about Missy I can guarantee it did not cause this. This is my responsibility and your mother's and no one else's. His words are sweet and gentle.

Isn't she beautiful, Auntie Margaret whispers, she's an angel. I feel her arms sweep around me and lock across my chest. Touch her face, Missy, and say goodbye.

I touch her cool face. Auntie Margaret keeps herself locked around me. She's comforting, she's something to breathe into.

forty-four

 HE BLACK STONE was hard to take from her. I suggested we leave it be but Marla said no, we were the living, we were the ones who needed it now and she insisted I help.

Ruby was as strong in death as she was in life. We had to move slowly so as not to snap anything. Each finger we had to pull off and hold back or it would spring shut. Marla pulled them off and I held them back. This little piggy . . . I started in my head, as I held the first one. It cramped around my own warm finger, cool and mechanical. Marla worked slow and delicate.

It feels like stealing, I say. Marla shakes her head without looking up from her work.

She has left everything for you, Missy. She was silent awhile. And you've been left with a lot. Having this stone might help. It's odd how the smallest things can make a difference. There was something in Marla's voice that wasn't sweet or soft.

Auntie Margaret started singing weakly, reaching high with her voice so that it trembled like a hovering angel. Dad stood at the window, rocking back and forth from heel to toe. His leather shoes creaking like an opening and closing door. Sky, that's what he saw, his head tilted up to it, his hands locked behind his back, rocking.

You must give her something of yours, Marla whispered. We were close enough that I could feel her words creep across my face. Something she can take with her. Something you cherish.

When we got the stone out I slipped my hand into hers. Her fingers clawed around me as if she had changed her mind and wanted to come back. It had been a long time since Ruby had taken my hand. When she was four or five years old, perhaps. When Mum disappeared. I remembered the stones we collected the night she didn't come back. I remembered the heat of the setting sun pushing me into the ground as if I'd never be able to move from that spot again.

I still had the Mummy Stone, tucked underneath my sweaters in a bottom drawer.

There's another stone, one that she always wanted, I say, I found it but Ruby named it. I used to keep it on my dresser, wherever we were. But then when Gandhi died, that was a bird we used to have, I started hiding it. I knew I was being selfish but I couldn't help it. She called it the Mummy Stone. I'll give her that. She's waited for it long enough.

1975

forty-five

T HEY DIED, RUBY and Mum, on different continents. Mum in England, near Dover, by the small cottage on the cliffs. At the bottom of those cliffs, in fact, rocking back and forth in the sea.

There was a note waiting on the kitchen table. Auntie Margaret said the damp and the salt air had tortured it, had made the paper edges cringe and the ink weep. That's Auntie Margaret for you, everything has feelings, even the stones.

"You shall find me in the sea," it said. Those were Mum's last words. They sat on that piece of paper, innocent and peaceful.

She had a few last words for me too. There was a little brown package with my name on it. It sat beside the note, Auntie Margaret said, just waiting. My name was scrawled across its bumpy surface, written in a hurry. I stuffed it, unopened, into my chest of drawers where I didn't have to see it.

Ruby left more for us. We opened the box that she had always kept under her bed. Things hidden and layered like fossils. Library books never returned, and the Bible. A small plastic bag of crushed eggshells. Stones and twigs. Serviettes from restaurants and their matching neon swizzle sticks. Photos.

Money. In one bag, a curl of hair, blonde and brittle. A bright silk scarf, a ripped silk slip, a pale tube of lipstick. A tiny notebook full of symbols she'd drawn. Everything, every shape you could imagine, tucked away inside a circle or an egg. Auntie Margaret said it was the womb, that circle, that egg. She said they are the symbols of completion. Ruby drew what she yearned for, according to Auntie Margaret.

I'm not sure what I yearn for. Food perhaps. Now I'm hungry all the time. One look at that photo of Ruby, just dead, and I have to eat. The thought of her not taking that next breath, the thought of her not here, ever. It all makes me eat. Auntie Margaret says it's my life force, my appetite. She says one day I'll learn to enjoy it.

Everyone's got something to say, some piece of advice that they think will fix my life. It's weird. After all those years of being left alone, of being an invisible pair of eyes, now here I am at the centre of it all.

There's Doctor Julius, with his tiny hands almost as translucent as Ruby's. He's written a book on me already. From the time we met, just over a year ago, he's been writing. Everything I say is recorded as if it mattered.

So, he said the first time we met, what have you got to say for yourself?

I sat there like an idiot and shrugged.

Sad? Mad? Glad? Think about it, he said, it's important.

Auntie Margaret says I have everything to say. She agrees with Marla. Marla says I've been left with stories to tell. It's like holding a life in your hands, a small chick, a beating heart. Thinking about it makes me want to cry. But I can't. You will, Missy, Doctor Julius says. You will.

I'm the keeper of both of their stories, I guess, though I don't have much to say about Mum's. Auntie Margaret says wait. She says understanding Mum and Ruby, by telling their stories, will free me.

Dad needs freeing, too. He hardly gets off the couch. If he could he'd go to bed and never get up. I know because that's how I feel, sometimes. He's hardly spoken since Ruby died though when we got the news about Mum he grabbed his head, as if it were a watermelon teetering on a stick, and screamed. Screamed so loud that Viv, from next door, came running. He's "borrowed" her Valium ever since. She brings it for him every Friday wrapped in a newspaper. Small white pills folded into Kleenex that he tucks into his shirt pocket and buttons down.

I've never told Doctor Julius about the Valium, not even when both of us are in a session together and Doctor Julius asks Dad why he seems to be on another planet.

Will you join us today, Les? he asks, flattening out his pant legs with the palms of his hands. Dad nods or smiles or frowns but he doesn't speak, hardly makes a sound. Sometimes he'll reach out and hold my hand and give it a squeeze. Sometimes he holds on for the whole hour like he's in a crowd and afraid of getting lost. I talk in fits and starts, trying my best to fill in the silence. But there's a lot of silence no matter how hard I try and Doctor Julius sits calmly through it like he's just another piece of the furniture.

I have resources, Doctor Julius says: my memories when they come, for instance, and my courage. He doesn't know me well if he thinks I've got courage.

The only thing I have, I tell him, is my fat. And I grab at it around my middle and pull a chunk of it out like it's a dresser drawer. He's not amused, he has said over and over, by my hatred of my body. It's the only one you've got, he says, so take care.

*I*F WE DON'T jiggle you free, Missy, Doctor Julius said just yesterday, we may find you six feet under, too. Dad had grabbed my hand and started to cry.

That's it, Doctor Julius whispered, putting a box of Kleenex on Dad's lap and pulling his hand out of mine. Then he reached behind his chair and handed me a hardcover book. It had no title and no words. He passed me a fountain pen. Go on, he said. Just one sentence.

I could feel something moving in my chest, something achy and old. The pen was cool and smooth and when I moved it across the paper it scratched and tugged at the fibres. Then it ripped itself a hole through to the next sheet. Not so hard, Doctor Julius said. Easy does it. He straightened his already straight hair with his baby finger and smiled his soft smile.

Dad cried and cried, holding his head in his hands, his thin shoulders shaking.

"All I know . . ." I begin to write.

And suddenly there's Mum, her flashing blue eyes, her wild blonde hair, her strong nose, the lines around her mouth and something fierce, something determined about her. I remember her as she was holding Ruby in the hospital. I remember how strong she looked, how sure. How clear she had been when she said she wouldn't stay.

I lifted the pen from the paper and looked at Doctor Julius.

I just wanted her to be good, I said.

He nodded, pointed to the book where my pen hovered, encouraging me to go on.

A good mother, a real one, strong and sure and . . .

She wasn't, he said.

Dad stopped crying and raised his head to watch me.

Just try to write it down, Doctor Julius said, giving me a weak smile.

But I don't want to begin with her, I said, putting the tip of the pen on the paper and watching the ink seep into it.

Don't, he said.

"All I know," I began again, scratching it into the page, "is that I want to live." *That* was the place to begin. I knew it was as the words were forming.

*T*HAT NIGHT I DREAM. In my dream I lie over the ends of Mum's lap. I see the long drop of her legs. Her feet: stumps on the floor. Her huge toes: roots. I lie still and full of wonder, every bit of me waiting like an exclamation point, a series of surprised lines, dark and abrupt. What will she do? Hold on to me? Push me away?

Missy, she whispers, JoJo, Joanne. I hear my names like birds, something free that has lifted off. Which name? she asks. Which one will you have? She tells me I must choose. She shakes me to make me hurry and I feel myself rock back and forth across the top of her lap as if I were as tiny and insignificant as a sailboat on the sea.

The whispered names line up. Black words with wings. Crows calling, curling in the sky. Which one? Which? But each one, as I try to choose, flies away and disappears.

I'll make up my own, I say.

She doesn't reply.

I'll make up my own, I say again, this time louder, feeling desperate that she must hear me.

Her legs stretch out suddenly in front of her becoming a slope instead of a cliff. I start to roll. I tumble and toss. Her legs seem endless as I reel like a child down a grassy slope. She starts to laugh and I laugh with her, my laughter pulled out of me from so far down that it aches.

Yes, she says, once we've stopped our laughter and I've come to rest at the bottom facing the sky. Very good, she says, her eyes a brilliant spring blue, perhaps you are a daughter of mine after all.

*I*N THE MORNING, with my bedroom door closed, I take the package from Mum out of my chest of drawers. I open it, tearing through my name, scrunching the brown paper into a ball, almost missing the note. "From Bruised Fell," it says. And inside sits a small polished stone.